# The Mammoth Murders

Minokee Mysteries,
Book Two

IRIS CHACON

ISBN: 9781698831008

In Memory of

JOSHUA BENNINGTON

1980 - 2018

Award-winning voice artist, ardent mariner,
courageous inspirer, constant encourager,
animal lover, and extraordinary, gentle man,
he will be greatly missed.

Gifts in Joshua Bennington's memory
may be made to his hometown SPCA,
online at
**https://donatenow.networkforgood.org/AACSPCA,**
by mail to
**SPCA of Anne Arundel County**
**P.O. Box 3471**
**Annapolis, MD 21403**,
or by telephoning
(410) 268-4388, ext. 120..

# CONTENTS

## Special Offer

Get the inside scoop on new releases, giveaways, and special events — AND download the award-winning, humorous family novel, *Schifflebein's Folly,* for FREE when you join the Iris Chacon In Crowd.

Go to
**https://www.instafreebie.com/free/zfcm1**
to sign up for the Iris Chacon Newsletter,
and get your FREE ebook copy of *Schifflebein's Folly.*

Watch the video trailer for *Schifflebein's Folly* at https://youtu.be/SbTATV2uquY.

# PROLOGUE

This was not the time or place to capsize a canoe. In fact, the blind man called Shepard did not want to be canoeing at all in the middle of the night, especially on this remote stretch of wilderness river.

Nevertheless, Shepard kept paddling, shoulders and back muscles cramping from hours of abuse, because the criminal in the bow of the canoe would not permit Shep to stop.

The criminal had a gun.

The gun was pointed at Shep's passenger, Miranda. Shep usually called her "Bean," a nickname based on a private joke the couple shared.

The river was full of alligators, their red eyes shining out of the dark water toward the passing canoe, and the woods along the shore were full of four-legged night hunters with notoriously big teeth and bad dispositions.

No lights shone from the shore because no people lived anywhere near this stretch of river. Yes, this was a horrible time and place to capsize a canoe.

So, of course, that is exactly what Shepard did.

Providence was smiling on Shep and Miranda: the gun was the only thing from their canoe that did not go underwater. Shep found shore first, after dealing their captor a hard blow with a heavy oar. He heard the man crawl out of the water moments later and collapse on the sand.

Miranda had surfaced in chest-deep water and, with her eyes adjusting to the moon- and starlight, recognized the outline of Shep scouring the ground on hands and knees. In a moment, he found the pistol that the man had thrown when Shep (navigating totally by sounds) smashed his wooden paddle into the criminal's torso.

Miranda was slogging her way onto dry land when she saw Shepard lift the gun and cock it.

"No! Shepard don't!" she yelled and ran to grab his left arm. "It's not worth you going to prison!"

"Don't move!" Shep said.

"What— ?"

"Shhh!" He tilted his head, listening. The jungle had gone silent.

Even their erstwhile kidnapper stopped moaning in the dirt and listened.

The moon slipped behind a cloud, burying them in utter blackness.

"Be still!" Shep hissed. He eased Miranda behind him with his left hand, gripping the gun with his right.

Something agitated the plants at the jungle's edge, only a few paces away. Shep focused on the sound, tensed for action.

A twig snapped.

A bear-sized creature charged from the bushes, grunting its war cry. Heavy feet shook the ground as it pounded forward.

Shep fired the pistol at the animal's sounds, three times in rapid succession.

In the strobe light of each muzzle flash, Miranda glimpsed the attacker, closing fast.

She braced for impact.

The beast sideswiped the couple with its curved tusk. Miranda inhaled sharply and staggered.

Keeping her behind him, Shep swung left, still following the noise of the animal. His gun flashed a fourth shot.

The bestial war cry ceased.

With a thud, the attacker fell.

It slid forward across several feet of sandy soil, plowing the mud of the water's edge with its head.

There it stopped.

Dead.

Then Shep heard Miranda fall.

# Chapter 1 - The Daredevil

*Three and a half weeks earlier*

Had Miranda Ogilvy known of the danger at home, she might have driven faster that afternoon when she left her job in Live Oak, headed for the settlement called Minokee.

Live Oak, Florida, was a small town by almost anyone's definition. It was a bit smaller than Lake City or Gainesville or Ocala, and much, much smaller than Jacksonville, to the east, or Tallahassee, to the west.

Live Oak had a town square, with an old, red brick, cube-shaped courthouse, white-columned like Tara in *Gone with the Wind.* Live Oak had traffic lights, sidewalks, grocery stores, and even a public library.

Minokee had none of those things.

Minokee was even smaller than Live Oak.

In the local vernacular, Minokee was "not big as a minute."

Minokee had cypress and live oak trees, spiky palmetto clusters, and ferns. It had snowy egrets, arc-billed ibis, pink spoonbills, blue herons, redheaded woodpeckers, sandhill cranes, ospreys and bald eagles.

Instead of sidewalks beside its only two streets, Minokee boasted deer paths and pig trails through the surrounding cypress wetlands, oak tree hammocks, palmetto scrub, and pine barrens.

Minokee owned no public building, such as a courthouse, a post office, or a library. The community boasted only a dozen ancient, wood-shingled houses, each squatting behind wide, shady verandas.

Miranda Ogilvy worked in the Live Oak public library. Minokee lay sixty miles southeast, geographically, and seventy years earlier, culturally.

Every person (and many animals) in Minokee knew Miranda, even though she was the newest resident.

New neighbors were rare. Nobody moved to Minokee unless somebody old (usually *very* old) died. Miranda had relocated from busy, cosmopolitan Miami to her deceased aunt's creaky, sun-bleached cottage in quiet, isolated, ultra-rural Minokee.

It was part of the magic of Minokee that everyone loved the shy librarian and treated her as family. Back in Miami, Miranda had been virtually invisible.

Even at the small public library in Live Oak, Miranda's primary co-worker would seldom remember Miranda's name or notice her presence.

However, one Minokee resident had taken exceptional notice of Miranda, ever since the first time he jogged by her house and discovered its new owner hiding under a leafy castor bean bush.

That day, Shepard Krausse and his dog, Dave, had learned that someone very special now lived in the house just across Shepard's back hedge. On the same day, Miranda had learned not to try to sneak out for the morning paper wearing only her Sponge Bob Squarepants tee shirt.

Ironically, Shepard was totally blind, but he was the person who spotted her first and tracked her down most often. He saw her better than anyone did, or ever had.

Beginning with their first meeting, Shep had casually proposed to Miranda every day for months.

She always said something equivalent to "Not today. But thanks for asking."

He called her "Castor Bean," after the plant she hid under the day they met — the day he caught her on her front lawn in her nightie.

She called him Shepard.

Every day after work, Miranda crossed her backyard hedge into Shepard's backyard, crossed Shepard's backyard to his kitchen door, entered Shepard's kitchen (it was never locked), and kissed the muscular man with the long blond hair.

Unless he was out, then she kissed Shepard instead.

Just kidding. Shepard was the only big, blond, blind hombre in Minokee.

Most days, he looked forward to greeting Miranda when she returned from work, but something was wrong this particular day. Shep's kitchen was deserted.

When she called his name, only the softly humming refrigerator answered.

She plucked a cellphone from her pocket and tapped Shepard's number. A ringtone of "I'm Getting Married in the Morning" chimed from the bedroom down the hall.

The new ringtone was Shep's private joke: Nobody knew it yet, but Miranda had finally said, "Yes."

She hurried down the hall and peeked in, but except for the singing cellphone on the dresser, his bedroom was vacant.

Curious, but not yet alarmed, Miranda left Shepard's house and walked past her own cottage, across the street to the front garden and shady porch of neighbor Martha Cleary.

Seventy-five-year-old Martha spent many hours in her front porch rocking chair, overseeing her garden, with her rifle on her lap.

Two benefits accrued from Mrs. Cleary's habit: (1) Martha knew everything about anybody on Magnolia Street, and (2) any veggie-chomping rodent that entered her garden faced serious consequences.

Mrs. Cleary would know where to find Shepard Krausse.

All the ladies on Magnolia Street (average age 73 years 8 months) kept careful tabs on Shepard. They even scheduled their morning coffee so they would be sure to see (and greet; but mostly see) Shep on his morning jog.

Their handsome, well-built neighbor jogged in shorts and, sometimes (oh joy!), with no shirt. Yes, Martha Cleary was an infallible source of data on Shepard's whereabouts.

"Good evening, Mrs. Cleary," said Miranda, approaching the lady's garden gate. "You haven't seen Shepard this afternoon, have you? He's not at home."

"Hmmm." Mrs. Cleary stroked her chin and looked upward as if searching her mind. "Would he be a feller with yeller hair and a big smile? Always wears them sunglasses with the mirrors on 'em?"

"That's him. Have you seen him?"

The old lady pointed toward the sky.

Miranda's eyes followed the finger upward, to the top of a streetlamp pole nearby. Forty feet in the air, supported only by his bare feet and knees grasping the pole, Shepard Krausse had his hands full installing a football-size bulb in one of the neighborhood's six security lights.

All good cheer fled Miranda's face, replaced by numb terror. She drew breath to shout something, she wasn't sure what.

Mrs. Cleary murmured, "Prolly not a good time to startle him."

Miranda blew out her unused air supply. Staring at the top of the pole, she stage-whispered toward the old lady on the porch, "What is he doing up there!"

"Changin' a light bulb," said Mrs. Cleary. "Ain't it obvious?"

"I can see he's changing a light bulb. I meant, why is *he* changing the bulb? Don't these poles belong to Montgomery Power and Light?"

"Sure, they do, but MPL ain't gonna waste money sendin' a truck all the way to Minokee to change one bulb. They gimme a few spares ever' now an' then. I keep 'em in my closet, and we change 'em ourselves when we need to."

"And by 'we,' of course, you mean Shepard."

"O' course. No need to fret yerself, honey. Shep's been

climbing everything around here since he was knee high to a grasshopper. Trees, vines, drain pipes, light poles, ever'thin'. He'd be plum insulted if we asked somebody else to do it. He loves it."

Miranda cast her gaze at the ground and shook her head. "I'm sure he does," she admitted. She had seen Shepard Krausse blithely take on situations much more dangerous than a burned-out streetlamp. Unfortunately for Miranda's peace of mind, Shep seemed to be fearless.

At that moment, Shep called from four stories above the ladies, "All done, Miz Martha! Any others today?"

"That'll do 'er," Martha shouted. "Come on down, now. Yer scarin' Miss Ogilvy."

A wide grin lit his face. "Castor Bean!"

"Could you just come down, please?" Miranda *almost* stifled the quake in her voice.

"Sure thing!" he called and whooshed down the pole like a firefighter answering an alarm.

An involuntary squeak burst from Miranda. She stepped forward as if to catch him before he hit the ground. He reached the base of the pole ahead of her, or she could have been flattened.

As soon as his feet hit the ground, she leaped upon him, wrapped her arms tightly around his neck and clung there.

"Whoa, Bean!" He chuckled and enveloped her in a bear hug. "What's this for?"

Her face was pressed against his clavicle. "Mmf cm hv bn kmm!" she said into his pectoral muscle.

"What?"

She jerked back a few inches to speak at his face, "You could have been killed!"

He laughed and hugged her until she loosened her chokehold and relaxed against his chest. "Don't worry, Bean. I do this all the time. The secret is not to look down."

She backed away and punched his bicep with a fist strengthened by shelving lots and lots of heavy library books. "Not funny!"

"You just don't get blind humor," he said, rubbing his arm. "And, ouch, by the way."

"Come home now. It's time to make dinner."

"Yes, ma'am."

"Say goodnight to Miz Martha."

"Goodnight to Miz Martha," he parroted.

"And a good evenin' to both of y'all," said Mrs. Cleary. "See ya in the mornin', Shep." She continued rocking on the porch, rifle always to hand.

Shep and Miranda held hands as they walked toward her house, then past it toward his.

"I have a surprise for you," Shepard said.

"No!"

"I promise not to leave the ground for this one."

"I'll think about it.

## Chapter 2 - The Archaeologists

Everything on Tom Rigby's old pickup truck was round, instead of sleek and straight. The roof's corners and the hood were rounded. The frog-eye headlights were practically spherical. The quarter panels and the fenders surrounding the tires were as rounded as balloon animals.

The rear window of the narrow cab was not round. It was oval.

In the 1930's and '40's, such a truck would have been the cutting edge of automotive design in the same way Miami Beach hotels epitomized Art Deco.

Farmers had fallen in love with the Ford pickups, not out of any brand loyalty, but because the trucks were dependable. Not beautiful, not stylish, not painted with jazzy stripes or gilded with yards of chrome, they were not even especially fast. But the trucks were solid work horses. They took years of pounding and pushing and pulling and hauling in stride, and simply kept on running.

Tom Rigby's truck was one of those. It was two years older than Tom, himself, and Tom was nearly 80.

He had not bought the truck new, of course. No Rigby had ever had enough cash to purchase a shiny vehicle off the showroom floor. Instead, Tom had saved from his teen years into his twenties, and then he bargained with a neighbor, from two farms away, for the old Ford sitting on blocks in the neighbor's yard.

That was 1965. Tom's truck was 25 years old at the time, and Tom was 23.

He was an able mechanic, as most small-farm operators had to be. If anything in the house, barn, tool shed, or garage broke, farm families did not pick up their party-line telephone and call a repairman. They rolled up their own sleeves and went to work on the problem.

Few had formal training, but most agrarian youngsters had been their own parents' apprentice in a life-long college of practical engineering.

So, 23-year-old Tom Rigby had replaced all the broken and missing parts a little at a time, until eventually he was driving around in his very own pickup truck — a lovely 1940 model with rounded edges and leather seats, reupholstered in gray duct tape.

Tom was in love forever.

That is why, on a particular day in 2018, 76-year-old Tom Rigby and his 78-year-old pickup truck were tooling north on Interstate Highway 75 toward the University of Florida, at Gainesville. The vintage truck's maximum speed was only five miles per hour under the Interstate Highway's posted minimum.

Tom had owned other vehicles in his life — sedans, station wagons, even other trucks — but his affection had always been for the round-edged 1940 pickup.

It wasn't much to brag about on the outside. In fact, nobody had yet come up with a name for whatever color it was. But under the hood, throughout the chassis, and in every centimeter of its tubes, belts, and wiring, that truck was like new.

At least, what "new" meant in 1940. Rigby often said, "Who really needs a radio, or air conditioning, or those computer mapping gizmos?"

When Tom and his beloved pickup slid as quietly as melting butter into a parking space at the University of Florida, a crowd of admiring students swarmed the duo. They always did, when Tom and his truck came to visit a certain professor-friend.

Tom's pickup was a rock-star classic of automobiles. It was

even named *Elvis.* A glittering license plate on its front bumper displayed the name spelled out in flamboyant calligraphy.

♦

Erwin ("Win") Clarkson, Ph.D., was a tenured professor in the University of Florida's Department of Socio-Cultural, Archaeological, Biological, & Linguistic Anthropology — or, as acronym addicts liked to say, the SCABLA (pronounced "SCAH-blah") department.

Some people called it "the department of socio-cultural blah-blah-blah," and that worked as well as anything.

Although the interminable name of his department could put listeners to sleep, Professor Win Clarkson was not boring. In fact, his courses were enriched and enhanced by Win's "interdisciplinary" approach to SCABLA.

Students of Dr. Clarkson often did fieldwork alongside students and teachers from UF's Geological Sciences Department (ancient rocks), History Department (ancient people and events), and the Florida Museum of Natural History (ancient plants and animals).

One result of this collaboration among departments was that anybody who studied about anything ancient, usually ended up listening to Win Clarkson. A Clarkson lecture was universally considered a pleasant and enlightening experience.

Clarkson seemed a gentleman and a gentle man. A trim fellow of about 60, he looked like an archaeologist was supposed to look: sun-leathered skin, bald with white goatee, medium height and generally fit, with a micro-paunch.

He had married and divorced in his thirties and was still friendly with his ex-wife. She had remarried a man who remembered birthdays, anniversaries, groceries, and gasoline for the car.

Once at a university social function, Win had even forgotten his wife's name. That snafu had been the last straw for the soon ex-Mrs. Clarkson.

The new husband would never be the social failure Win had

often been, and for that Win liked, admired, and sometimes wished he could emulate, the replacement spouse.

Dr. Clarkson's ex-wife had been married to ... um ... what's-his-name for more than twenty years, now, and all three were very happy with the arrangement.

For all that Dr. Clarkson appeared to be a quintessential absent-minded professor in social situations, he never forgot a genus, species, paleo-factoid, or morsel of information that was useful to him or his students in the academic pursuits of SCABLA.

Among things Win Clarkson never forgot, the best was: he never forgot a friend. Win also never forgot to *be* a friend, and never failed to help a friend.

One of Win Clarkson's oldest and best friends — though apparently Win's opposite in almost every way — was the farmer, Tom Rigby. Both men were lifelong conservationists, driven to care for the plants, animals, and geology of the natural world around them.

Win's erudition was academic, while Tom's was hands-on and practical, but they thought alike in many ways. Together they were a formidable and affable storehouse of wisdom and knowledge.

Dr. Clarkson was not surprised when Tom Rigby, in his cleanest go-to-town denim overalls, slipped into the last row of Clarkson's class. Rigby removed his cowboy hat and sat back to listen to the lecture.

Win's lectures were popular. Visiting students, parents, or even teachers often stopped by to audit his class informally. The auditorium was large enough to accommodate the multitudes, who signed up every term for whatever Dr. Clarkson happened to be teaching.

"We used to think that the first humans to reach the New World — the Americas, if you will — were the Clovis people," Clarkson was saying when Rigby arrived and settled in.

"Researchers discovered some of the amazing tools of these big-game hunters in New Mexico and dated the Clovis arrival at about 13,500 years ago.

"I say *we used to think*, because some researchers at Texas A&M and, ahem, sorry but it's true, at Florida State..."

A groan went up from the students at this implied praise of UF's archrivals.

"...yes, I know, but credit where credit is due. Michael Waters, at Texas A&M, and Jessi Halligan, at Florida State, used studies of modern and ancient DNA. They more-or-less proved the first humans in North America might have arrived 16,000 or 18,000 years ago — possibly 5,000 years earlier than the Clovis group. Sorry, Clovis fans."

"Awwww," a few students whined theatrically.

"The interesting thing about all this research, young Jedi, is that — *whenever* the first humans came to North America — all the DNA studies and conventional archaeological studies, up to now, have shown the first American humans coming down the Pacific Coast."

He clicked a remote control in his hand and the massive screen at the front of the auditorium lit up with a map of the Pacific Rim, including the Pacific Coast of North America.

With a laser pointer, Clarkson traced the supposed path of early man from Asia, across the temporary land bridge of Alaska's Bering Straits, then southward down the Pacific Coast. He verbalized the course of the journey while tracing it on the map.

Another click of Clarkson's remote changed the map to the Atlantic rim. "But, what about the *other* coast of North America?" he said.

Win shared folkloric, mythological, and traditional stories while tracing his pointer along several different theoretical routes. Tribes of travelers moved from lands of the North Atlantic, to the North American continent, and then either northward or southward until the entire east coast housed humans of one group or another.

Then Clarkson turned a fiercely enthusiastic glare on his students. He leaned forward on his podium, and most of his listeners unconsciously leaned forward in their seats.

Clarkson extended an arm, index finger pointing at the students, and swept the arm across the group, nearly creating a palpable rush of wind.

"YOUR MISSION," he boomed, "SHOULD YOU CHOOSE TO ACCEPT IT…" He lowered his voice to add, "…and you better accept it if you want to maintain your grade point average in my class..."

Students chuckled.

In typical Clarkson fashion, the doctor flicked his remote, and television's classic "Mission Impossible" theme music shook the room.

This time, students laughed out loud.

Satisfied that everyone was paying attention, Clarkson lowered the volume of the music so that he could orate in his stentorian voice: "Your mission, which you will choose to accept, is to use all the intellectual, creative, scientific, and technological tools this great University of Florida affords you, and solve this mystery!

"Those humans on the Pacific Coast 18,000 years ago did not pile into their Corvette Stingray and Route-Sixty-Six it across to the Atlantic Coast. But people got there somehow, and I want you to tell me how, in your research presentation, at the end of this term."

Clarkson silenced the music and spoke in a quieter voice. "The specifications and due dates for the project phases are in your on-line syllabus. Follow instructions carefully.

"I don't need to tell you that the work must be totally your own, with proper attribution to anyone else whose research or opinions you may quote, and I mean quote *briefly*. The penalty for plagiarizing another person's work is expulsion from this university — and that is the State's and the school's policy, not merely mine.

"Expect no mercy. Do not copy. It isn't worth it, no matter how tempting. Your academic life could be over, if you are caught cheating. And you will be caught."

The room was quiet as a granite boulder. Win let his message penetrate the hive-mind of the class before he concluded with the assignment due at next week's lecture.

"Okay, for next time, send me any information you can, ahem, dig up. That's archaeologist humor — and I'll know if you're the one who didn't laugh at my jokes. Send me at least five pages plus bibliography on the Aucilla River sinkhole known as the Page-Ladson site.

"Tell me what scientists are saying about the first people to come to North America and colonize northern Florida — right where we're sitting. Give me the whole who-what-when-where-why in five pages minimum, seven max. My graders and I can't read all night every night.

"Detailed instructions are in the online syllabus. Completed papers are to be emailed to my Assignments inbox before the beginning of Thursday's class next week.

"My T.A.'s will be in their offices to answer further questions if you have them. See you next time."

With that, Clarkson blanked the screen, closed his notes folder, and turned away from the podium.

At this cue, students rose to depart, and in minutes the large auditorium was nearly empty. Only two people remained: Win Clarkson (in his gray three-piece suit) and Tom Rigby (in his overalls).

"Let's go to my office and talk, then you can take me out to lunch!" Clarkson called to Rigby, who was making his way down the long stairs from the back row.

"You're paying," Rigby shouted back. "Everybody knows archaeologists are just glorified treasure hunters with stolen loot hidden under their beds."

A half-hour later, Clarkson and Rigby sat on opposite sides of Clarkson's desk, bent forward until their noses almost met above the center of the paper-strewn surface.

"Congratulations, Tom! This could be a terrific windfall for you," Clarkson said, and both men leaned back in their chairs.

"I sure hope so," Tom said.

"Do you mind if I call my teaching assistants in here and let you tell them your story? They're bright, honest kids. I believe you can trust them to keep your secret. And, they could be useful to us, going forward."

"Fine, call 'em in," said Tom, smiling. "I never get tired of sharing good news."

Clarkson and Rigby had just enough time to make themselves coffee, using the drip-style pot on Clarkson's credenza, before someone knocked on the office door and immediately opened it.

The two people whom Clarkson had described as "kids" turned out to be graduate students in their mid-twenties.

"Tom, I want to introduce you to Felicia Harper and Zhang Dài-Wéi — we call him 'David' —, the smartest T.A.'s I've ever been privileged to have in my department. Felly and David, this guy, swilling my expensive gourmet coffee like it was tap water, is a very old and dear friend, Tom Rigby."

Rigby half-stood and shook hands with the two graduate students, saying with a smile, "Don't listen to him. We're friends, all right, but I ain't so old, and he ain't all that dear."

The assistants chuckled politely and expressed their pleasure at meeting a friend of Professor Clarkson. Clarkson asked the two to bring over a pair of folding chairs from a short stack in the back of the room.

Soon all four people were seated around the desk, and all four noses nearly met in the center of the space as they leaned in to catch every syllable of Rigby's story.

When Rigby stopped talking and sat back in his chair, Clarkson sat back as well. David and Felicia still bent forward toward Rigby. "How deep do you think it is?" asked David.

"Impossible to tell yet," Rigby said. "For one thing, it's still growing a little every day, and I'm not ready to risk my life going down to investigate."

"Is it wet or dry?" said Felicia.

"There's a muddy patch at the bottom center, as of early this morning. I expect we'll see the water rising soon. It's a sure bet there's an underground river under there; that's what's been eating away at the sandy layer beneath the surface soil.

“The topsoil had a lot of clay in it, and the clay held it together until too much of the sand underneath finally got washed away. Then the topsoil collapsed under its own weight and, boom: instant crater."

"So, you don't know yet what's down there," Clarkson said.

"Right. Not yet, anyway. But the history of fossils in this part of the state makes me think it could be something worth some serious money."

"Everybody already has an endless supply of megalodon teeth," David pointed out. "They wouldn't be worth much."

"I've got a hunch there's something bigger than a giant shark's teeth under there," Tom said. "Guy on a farm just a few miles away found the skeleton of a mammoth in a sinkhole a year or two ago.

“I'm thinking there could be mammoth, short-faced bear, giant ground sloth, who knows what. But that other guy's mammoth got stolen within a couple of days of the local papers printing pictures of the new sinkhole — with the curve of a large tusk poking out of the rubble."

"Stolen!" said Felicia.

"Yep."

"Didn't your neighbor have fences or alarms or anything?" came from David. "How did they get in?"

Clarkson intervened at this point. "That's what Tom and I have been discussing. We don't want publicity about any discovery until Tom has a chance to set up some electrified fencing and other security."

"O' course, there ain't been no discovery, yet," said Tom. "But maybe there will be one in a few weeks, or sooner if you guys are willing to help."

Felicia and David talked over each other, assuring Tom of their willingness to join the search.

"Great!" Clarkson proclaimed. "I knew I could count on you two brainiacs. And, you need a little practical digging experience to go along with all that theoretical archaeology and anthropology you've been spouting.

"Now, Tom," he continued, "before you make any million-dollar fossil finds in your new sinkhole, I think it would make an ideal destination for the Audubon canoe trip that's coming up. And my undergrad students are studying the Aucilla sinkhole discovery right now; I know some of them will be eager to see a new sinkhole being born right here, close to home. What do you think?"

"Bring it!" Tom responded. "I'll provide ice and sodas, you tell everybody to bring a lunch, and we'll picnic on the riverbank and then tour the hole."

## Chapter 3 - The Conspiracy

Shepard cooked dinner on odd-numbered days, and today was the ninth. Lasagna (his favorite recipe) sat warming in the oven. He retrieved the pasta dish and added a pan of garlic-buttered Texas Toast to the oven. He was slicing the lasagna when Miranda entered the kitchen in shorts, tee shirt and flip flops, drying her hands on her shirt tail.

"Have you thought about my surprise?" he said as she took glasses from the cupboard and filled them with ice for tea.

"No excitement today, please," she said. "I need time to recover from yesterday's aerial act. Really, I'm surprised you never ran away and joined the circus. I'm still shaking."

He chuckled. "Well, if you're sure...."

"Totally, absolutely, positively, indubitably, irrevocably, undeniably sure."

"I love it when you speak Librarian," he said from behind her. He leaned over her shoulder and kissed her cheek. "Watch the bread, okay? I gotta go reschedule the surprise. Is tomorrow afternoon good for you?"

"Depends on what I catch you doing when I get home from work tomorrow."

"Nothing scary, I promise."

"And it's a good surprise?"

"*Molto bene,* very good," he assured her.

"I guess tomorrow's okay," she allowed, taking a pitcher of tea from the fridge. "But hurry up, I'm starving. If you're not back in five minutes, you'll get yesterday's leftover broccoli casserole, because that lasagna will be long gone."

Shep left the kitchen, and she could hear him talking on the telephone in his bedroom. She couldn't make out the words.

Minutes later the couple was chatting across Shep's kitchen table and enjoying the Italian meal.

"Your surprise would've been cooler with Italian food. Remember that tomorrow night," he said.

"What kind of surprise requires ethnic cuisine?"

"Nice try, but you'll get no more clues out of me. You just have to wait for tomorrow."

Two hours' drive north of Minokee, a society maven, hyphenatedly named Hermione Montgomery-Krausse, dined in glorious state with her administrative assistant, butler, chauffeur, and chef.

Hermione rarely entertained lowly staff members in her formal dining room, but tonight was a special exception. Hermione and her minions were enjoying a working dinner.

They were planning Shepard's wedding.

Shep had no idea his regal matriarch was arranging his nuptials, of course, but he wouldn't have been surprised. Hermione never ceased her attempts to organize and prioritize the life of her only child.

Hermione, the sister of the late Florida governor, Reginald Montgomery, had been disappointed when Shepard did not enter politics right out of law school. Instead, Shep had moved to Minokee — tantamount to living in a yurt in the Mongolian desert — and he had become a local radio personality.

Everyone knows broadcasting is less honorable and more objectionable than being a sanitation worker.

Hermione thought at least he should be on television instead. Nobody would recognize his face on a campaign poster from listening to a radio show.

Television would have been excellent exposure for a handsome, muscular, golden-haired Adonis. He would be elected to any office he sought, if all Montgomery County and the surrounding counties had his glowing image in their mind, along with his familiar name.

Hermione would insist he use his middle name on all campaign materials, naturally. Governor Reginald Jackson Montgomery had used his middle name to identify himself with a distant ancestor, Andrew Jackson, who had become president of the United States.

Shepard Montgomery Krausse should use his middle name to identify with the deceased governor (whose crimes had never become public knowledge), as well as with the family who lent their illustrious name to Montgomery County, Montgomery Memorial Hospital, Montgomery Public Library, Lake Montgomery, Montgomery Highway, Montgomery Industries, and more.

However, Shepard's political future was not the topic of discussion at that night's meeting. Hermione and her loyal servants had placed politics on the back burner to work on Shep and Miranda's personal lives.

Preliminary research was already done, and superbly as always, by Hermione's stunningly aristocratic African-American administrative assistant. Rebecca, the administrative assistant, had compiled a dossier on Miranda Ogilvy almost before the ink had dried on the deed that conveyed to Miranda the pokey Minokee cottage formerly owned by her late aunt.

Hanson, the butler (formerly wrangler of one rambunctious boy, during Shep's childhood), had served the Montgomery-Krausse household nearly four decades now. His spies had befriended the domestic help at the Miami home of Miranda's parents, giving Hanson comprehensive knowledge of the Ogilvy family's habits, customs, relationships, and resources.

The chauffeur, Carlo, had attended Swiss boarding school with Shep and often performed practical tasks for Shepard's mother. For example, the chauffeur had searched Miranda's little house thoroughly (and secretly) to ascertain the librarian possessed no illegal substances or dangerous weapons. Carlo was, in fact, the surprise Shepard had called earlier that evening to reschedule.

Rebecca, Hanson, and Carlo finished their dinner and placed their laptop computers on the table as soon as Chef removed the last course. Minutes later, Chef returned from the kitchen with an electronic tablet for taking notes.

With silver coiffure gleaming and diamond jewelry glinting, Hermione opened her leather-bound appointment diary, indicating that the meeting had come to order.

"I have consulted Rothschild's Tallahassee store, and they are preparing a selection of rings for our approval," she announced. No one mentioned that perhaps Shep and/or Miranda should be consulted on the choice of engagement and wedding rings. No one mentioned that the couple, *not* Hermione, would be wearing the jewelry for the rest of their lives.

"Rebecca, how are the plans for the bridal showers progressing?"

"Very well, Madam," the assistant responded, consulting her laptop. "The guest lists are prepared and the invitations designed. All we need are the dates and times."

"How many guests?" asked Hermione.

Rebecca double-checked her screen before answering. "One hundred fifty at the Jacksonville venue, two hundred at the Tallahassee location, and fifty in Orlando — leaving a hundred vacancies for the Ogilvy family's guests."

"Let's hope they know that many suitable people," Hermione muttered under her breath. "Do you have catering, flowers, and decor hired at each location?"

"Yes, Madam. They will make themselves available on whatever date we select."

"I should hope so, with what we're paying them."

"Yes, Madam."

Hermione turned her attention to Hanson. "Let's discuss the

groomsmen and bridesmaids. I believe we selected six of each, is that correct?

"Yes, Madam," Hanson responded with customary dignity. "A few were reluctant to travel until I advised everyone we would be taking care of transportation, food, wardrobe and lodging for all of them and their plus ones."

"Excellent," Hermione said, nodding. "One must not leave details to chance if one wishes for a spectacular outcome. We will be flying the young ladies to Atlanta when their gowns are ready for fittings?"

"Yes, Madam. The ladies' dresses will be completed two weeks before the wedding. The gentlemen's tuxedos will be tailored to them in Orlando by the same date."

"Not Orlando," Hermione corrected, raising a well-manicured finger. "I've decided to use that adorable tailor shop in Saint Augustine."

"Of course, Madam," said Hanson, and clicked keys on his laptop, making the adjustment.

Hermione then consulted Carlo about limousines for airport transfers and transporting the wedding party from hotels to events to the rehearsal dinner, the bridal breakfast, and the ceremony itself.

She spoke to Rebecca about hotel reservations for at least two dozen members of the wedding party, for garment fittings, bridal showers, and the wedding itself.

Everything seemed perfectly arranged, but for one detail: Shep and Miranda knew nothing about the wedding. In fact, the couple had not even formally announced their engagement to the world.

Hermione's informants had learned of Shep's proposal and Miranda's acceptance a few weeks before, but apparently no date had been set. No one had been told.

Things would have been much easier if Carlo's twin brother, Pietro, was still working as Shepard's companion, driver, and assistant. Pietro would have known everything Shep did, said, and sometimes even thought. And what Pietro knew, Carlo soon knew.

And what Carlo knew, except for a few details nobody's mother should know, Carlo would pass along to Shepard's mother, Hermione.

But Pietro was gone now. Everyone at the table thought it, but no one said it. Carlo would be carrying on alone, and he would begin a new mission when he surprised Miranda tomorrow evening.

♦

The following evening, when Miranda turned her car into her Minokee driveway after work, she took a moment to scan the treetops and light poles as far as she could see. She sighed with relief and dropped her shoulders a quarter inch when she saw no barefoot, blond ape-man perched at the perilous apex of anything.

She collected her small bag of groceries and exited the car, headed for her kitchen. It was Miranda's night to cook, after Shep had provided a delicious lasagna the night before. She was gradually coming to grips with his culinary prowess — and her lack of same.

She didn't realize how much she was dreading preparing a disappointing meal until she saw the typed note wedged in the crook of her screen door. "Dinner at my house tonight," the note said. It was signed with a typed capital "S."

"Yay!" she squealed in her mind, and her worried frown morphed into a happy grin. She hurried inside, shoved her grocery burden into the fridge, and practically skipped to her bedroom to change out of her Stodgy Librarian suit.

Minutes later, feeling fresh and relaxed, Miranda waltzed out her back door and traversed the lawns and hedge to enter the door of Shep's kitchen.

There, she abruptly fainted.

## Chapter 4 - The Return

Miranda began to hear voices nearby as she gradually emerged into consciousness. Beneath her, she felt soft settee cushions instead of a hard, tiled kitchen floor. Someone must have carried her out of Shep's kitchen. Maybe the same someone who was holding her hand, gently stroking her wrist with a thumb.

"This is your fault!" a familiar deep voice resonated off the walls.

"No, no, no, you thoughtless thug! You the one didn't tell her what to expect. You coulda predicted this reaction and prepared her for my return."

The second man had an Italian accent that tugged at her heart. Pietro was dead. Murdered in the car bombing that had nearly killed Shep. "My return," the man had said. His return from the dead?

Yes! That was why she had fainted. She remembered opening Shep's kitchen door and seeing Pietro, at the stove, in his ridiculous apron, cooking as he had cooked every night for years. Pietro's ghost? She had not quite completed that thought when her lights winked out.

"Pietro?" Miranda asked the men's voices, without opening her eyes.

"No, *cara*," the Italian man crooned. "It is I, Carlo. Forgive me if I frightened you."

"I'll get her a glass of water," the deeper voice said, and the hand holding Miranda's began to pull away.

"No! This you fault," snapped Carlo. "I get the water. You stay here and make this right, pretty boy." This last was no compliment, judging by Carlo's tone.

Miranda opened her eyes to see Shepard's concerned face looming over her and another man, in a silly apron, leaving the room. "What?" she murmured, squeezing Shep's hand a little desperately in her confusion. "What? Who? How?"

"Typical librarian. Reciting The Five W's at a time like this."

"Shepard!" She seriously needed answers, and fast.

"It's not Pietro," he soothed. "I'm sorry. I didn't realize what a shock it might be to see Carlo again, under the circumstances. You remember his twin brother, don't you?"

She shook her head, "You talked about him, but I never actually ...."

"Right, you never really met Carlo. I wish you had seen them together; then Carlo's return would've been less ... um ... jolting for you."

She lifted herself to a sitting position, with Shep's strong arms to help, and Carlo, returning from the kitchen, pressed a water glass into her hand as soon as she was safely vertical.

"Pleased to meet you, *cara*," the water bearer said with a Casanova smile. "I am sorry to frighten you. If this brainless oaf had told you ahead of time, instead of playing childish games — 'Surprise! Your dead friend is making dinner!' — our first meeting would have been safer and more pleasant for you."

"I said I was sorry," Shep insisted.

"No, in fact, you did not," Carlo responded calmly.

Shep squeezed Miranda's hand. "I didn't?"

"I don't remember hearing it," she said, "but I can't be sure I heard everything. I was sort of *incommunicado* for a little while."

"Again, *your* fault," Carlo nudged Shep.

For a second, Shep half-turned toward Carlo as if to argue, but he caught himself and turned back to face Miranda. He lifted her hand to his lips and placed a warm, soft kiss on her palm. "I am so, so sorry, Bean. I thought you'd be happy and excited to see

Carlo. I never thought you'd mistake him for," he shied away from the name, " ... his brother. I'm a jerk—"

"Yes, you are," Carlo interjected.

"—and you should make me do penance for scaring you—"

"Yes, you should. A thousand 'Our Fathers'!" said Carlo.

"—and I'll understand if you want to skip dinner with me tonight—"

"No! You want to eat here! I, Carlo, have prepared a masterpiece, one of my mother's greatest recipes. You will dine with us. But, if you do not want to talk to the big, stupid fellow with only muscles between his ears, you can talk to me."

Miranda looked at the two men kneeling beside the sofa where she sat. One radiated shame and regret, the other pride and self-assurance. From the kitchen, a heavenly aroma wafted through the house, transporting her to a *cucina* far away where, years before, a small, rotund woman had taught twin boys to cook.

Miranda smiled for Carlo, and squeezed Shep's hand at the same time. "I think I might talk to both of you," she said, letting her smile fill her voice. "But let's eat first."

♦

The trio had nearly finished consuming Carlo's unforgettable home-cooked Italian dinner, during which no one lost consciousness, when Carlo said something that nearly dropped Shepard right out of his chair.

"So, have you set a date for the wedding?"

Shep's fork clattered onto his plate as he rocked backward.

Miranda choked on her mouthful of iced tea and quickly covered her mouth with her napkin.

Miranda asked, "How did you know about that?" at the same time Shep said, "What wedding?"

"You better get busy looking at your calendar, my friends. Madam is well into a series of planning meetings."

"What?" said Miranda, while Shepard said simply, "No."

"No?" Carlo raised an eyebrow at Miranda and let his voice convey the gesture to Shepard. "Did you ask this lovely lady to marry you?"

"Many times," Shepard said.

Miranda said, "Nobody knows about that!"

Carlo smiled. Madam's spies were never wrong.

"And, pretty lady, did you consent to marry this ignorant savage?" Carlo gestured toward Shep.

"Hey ...!" said Shep.

"Yes," she said.

"So, have you set a date for the wedding?" Carlo repeated, as if the intervening conversation had never happened.

"Well, no, but—" Miranda began.

"This weekend. We're going to be married by a ship's captain," Shepard announced flatly, picked up his dropped fork, and returned to eating dinner calmly. "Simple ceremony. Short and simple. Very simple."

"This weekend!" Miranda cried. "But it's already Wednesday! I can't—"

"Going on a cruise?" Carlo inserted.

"Canoe trip," Shep reported, between bites. "Semi-annual Audubon Society fossil hunting tour on the Sho-ke-okee River."

"Canoeing!" Miranda cried. "Fossil hunting? This is a joke, right? Like when you told me you and Aunt Phyllis used to go bird watching?"

Shep chuckled. "Couldn't believe how long it took you to catch that one. But this one is for real. Phyllis and I went on the Sho-ke-okee canoe trip twice a year."

"Right. And you, Shepard Montgomery Krausse, ... *looked* ... for fossils," Miranda said, sarcastically.

He shook his head. "I was just the brawn. Phyllis was the brains — which, of course, this year will be you, Castor Bean. Bring a field guide. I have everything else."

"You can't get married on a canoe trip," Carlo advised. "There's no ship's captain to marry you."

"I'm not sure they can really do that, anyway," Miranda said.

"We'll have the canoe outfitter marry us."

"You're kidding!"

"Yes, Bean, I'm kidding. The canoe outfitter can't marry us."

"And we're not getting married this weekend."

"Right. We're not getting married this particular weekend. But we are going canoeing. You up for it?"

"Truthfully? I don't know," Miranda said, "but I know I'm not letting you go do something like that alone! It could be dangerous!"

"So, what is the real wedding date?" asked Carlo, bringing the conversation back to his original query. "Madam needs to know."

"No, Madam does not need to know. Madam is not planning the wedding," Shep said, picking up his place setting and carrying it toward the sink.

"That's right," Miranda agreed, taking up her own place setting and following in Shep's wake. "The bride's family is supposed to plan the wedding."

Shep stopped in his tracks, and Miranda ran into him, nearly dropping her dishes.

"You told your parents?" he asked.

"Well, no, but I guess I'll have to tell them eventually."

"Perhaps not," Carlo said in an oddly cautious tone. "I regret to say, I believe Madam may be contacting Doctor and Signorina Ogilvy this week."

"What?" said Shepard, while Miranda simply said, "No!"

♦

After dinner, Shep and Carlo washed, dried, and put away the dishes while Miranda, as the guest of honor and recovering fainter, watched from a comfy chair. Once the kitchen was tidy, Shep held out a hand in Miranda's direction. "Come with me, Castor Bean, and I'll show you your royal barge."

When she rose and took his hand, he led her out the kitchen door and into the evening darkness. In the shadow of the house, away from the few streetlamps of Minokee, she could see a sky so full of stars it looked as if someone had tossed handfuls of white sand across a black tablecloth.

Miranda stopped to look up, and Shep stepped back, to stand beside her.

"Ohhhh, I wish you could see this," she whispered, leaning her head against his shoulder.

"You can see it for me."

"But I don't have the words to share all of it with you, the vastness of it, the power of countless spinning infernos, shining for us out of the distant past," Miranda said.

“Space is so huge!" She spread her arms wide above her head as she went on. "Even at 186,000 miles per second, the nearest star’s light takes more than four years to get here! Many of those stars are so many years away, they don't even exist anymore by the time their light reaches our eyes."

She paused to release a long sigh before she said, “And we walk about beneath them all the time, assuming we are the most important things in the universe."

"Those words will do for a start," he said, and she heard the smile in his voice. He kissed the hair at her temple. "And when you run out of words, Miss Librarian, you can kiss me. That'll give me all the awe and wonder I can handle."

They didn't move from that spot for a few minutes. Then, with his hand resting gently on her elbow, Shep and Miranda strolled across the moonlit backyard to a wood frame workshop in a far corner of the property.

The little building shone a pristine white, and its terra cotta roof tiles peeked from beneath a cascade of massed bougainvillea, covered in magenta flowers.

"Ohhh," sighed Miranda, "it looks like a quaint little cottage right out of a fairy tale."

"But not Hansel and Gretel, right?" he said. "It doesn't look witchy and evil, right?"

"Don't worry. I don't believe in witches."

He scoffed. "You should listen in on one of my mother's bridge parties. You'd change your mind."

"Stop. You love your mother."

"Well, sure, I love my mother. I'm not uncivilized," Shep said. "But I'm also not blind to her faults, I can't believe I even said that, do not respond in any way if you know what's good for you."

"I thought you were going to show me my Cleopatra-ish barge," she said.

"Yes, Your Majesty. Immediately, Your Majesty." He removed the padlock that hung, unlocked, on the workshop's double door, and swung the two panels wide in opposite directions.

Miranda saw only a cave-like black opening. "Um..." she began.

"Oh, sorry!" He reached inside the doorframe, flicked a switch, and light filled the barn-like structure. A canoe rested bottom-up on sawhorses along one wall.

Miranda was awed speechless by the work of art displayed there. Unable to resist, she brushed past Shep to go to the boat and glide her hands over its shining, silk-smooth surface.

"Like it?" said a baritone voice from behind her.

"It's beautiful," she breathed, "but that's not a sufficient description. It's amazing. The lines are so subtle and fluid, like a gently flowing river, and the wood is dark and natural with a texture like rainforest hardwood trees."

"So, you do like it."

"It's not what I expected at all," she said. "I thought canoes were either white, like birch bark canoes pictured in books, or brightly colored Fiberglas and plastic, like the ones at Dick's Sporting Goods."

"I built this one."

She swung around to gape at him. "You made this yourself!"

"Well, my dad and grandpa helped, of course, but they made sure I did my share of the work."

She turned back to the canoe and slid her palm down its sleek keel. "What's it made of?"

"Mahogany and teak, with an infusion of Fiberglas micro beads, and a good coating of clear resin to keep it shiny. I sand it and re-coat it every few years."

"It's absolutely lovely. Is it a good canoe? I mean, does it work as well in the water as it looks on land?"

"You can decide for yourself on Saturday. How much do you know about canoes?"

"I saw 'The Last of the Mohicans' four times."

"Really."

"Yeah, but I confess I know a lot more about handsome, shirtless 'Mohican' actors than I do about the canoes they paddled."

"Ah," he said, carefully without inflection that might be construed as mocking or judgmental or, heaven forbid, jealous. "Well, then, I'll have to give you a crash course before we head out on Saturday."

"Could you not say 'crash,' please? I'm fairly nervous about this venture as it is."

He stepped closer behind her and rested his big hands on her slim shoulders. "Don't be nervous, Castor Bean. All you have to do is steer. I'll provide the forward motion."

## Chapter 5 - The Voyageurs

And so, Saturday morning found Shep and Miranda, Carlo, and neighbor Martha Cleary (an avid Audubon Society member of long standing) waiting outside the canoe outfitter's shop in the nearby town of Turtle Springs.

Shep and Carlo each wore a backpack with water bottles clamped to the sides.

Miranda wore a floppy sunhat, long-sleeved tee shirt, thrift-store jeans and her oldest sneakers. Mrs. Cleary had warned Miranda that walking in waist-deep water — or knee-deep mud — would probably ruin whatever pants and shoes she wore that day.

Martha Cleary wore camouflage khakis that looked like they had survived WWII's Bataan Death March; either that or the scrappy old lady had worn them on a hundred really dicey jungle canoe trips.

Miranda noted that Mrs. Cleary carried no *visible* weapons, only her long-lens bird-watching camera.

Miranda, thinking herself extremely clever, had sealed her cellphone in a Ziplock sandwich bag and hoped to be able to keep the phone dry and also snap some pictures.

If she happened to take a thousand photos of her massive companion in the mirrored sunglasses, but only a dozen pictures of the flora and fauna of Sho-ke-okee River, who cared? Who would even know, since she didn't plan to share her pictures with anyone?

Also waiting in the outfitter's parking lot was a group of ten other paddlers, a professor from the University of Florida, and two grad-school students who served as teaching assistants to the professor.

Two employees of the outfitter shop loaded the canoes (some rented, some personal, like Shep's) onto a specially designed, multi-level trailer. One of the employees would drive a van full of passengers, towing the canoes. The other drove a second van, carrying passengers only.

The vans would drive north to a put-in point about five miles upriver. From there, the canoeists could paddle with the current southward, in a leisurely manner, to a take-out point, where the vans and trailer would be waiting.

The entire trip would take about four hours, including a halfway stop for whatever lunch or snacks the paddlers had brought along.

When the canoes had been secured on their trailer and the paddlers secured in their vans, the small convoy set off down narrow, winding roads through forests and pine barrens.

In the lead van, a bald, sun-leathered man with a white goatee and a micro-paunch stood up behind the driver and faced the passengers.

"Good morning," he said with a smile. He nodded when the passengers spoke a ragged group greeting. "Thank you all for coming and for being here bright and early and ready for adventure. I'm Doctor Erwin Clarkson. I teach an interdisciplinary approach to socio-cultural, archaeological, biological, and linguistic anthropology — quite a mouthful, I know — at the University of Florida in Gainesville. But today, I'm not Doctor Clarkson. Today, I'm just your volunteer tour guide and docent on behalf of the Audubon Society, and you can call me Win."

A chorus of "Hi, Win," "Mornin', Win," "Hello, Win," and even "Nice to meet you," filled the van.

"Now, by show of hands, how many are members of the Audubon Society?"

Some hands went up. Win smiled. He greeted Mrs. Cleary and

a few other long-time acquaintances from Audubon functions.

"How many have been canoeing before?"

Hands went up, but not Miranda's.

"How many have canoed on the Pig River, or the Sho-ke-okee, as our Seminole friends would say?"

Hands went up; one voice called "Go 'Noles!" People laughed.

"Not *those* Seminoles," Win said. "Besides, on this trip it's 'Go 'Gators!' If you want to cheer for the 'Noles, you need a guide from Florida State. This is strictly a University-of-Florida trip." A few laughed again.

"But, speaking of 'gators, we may see a few. They're not interested in us, but it's wise to keep hands and feet inside the boat, just so you don't get mistaken for a bird or fish.

"If you have a fear of snakes, I have to tell you the water moccasins and rattlesnakes are around, but most of the snakes in Florida are of the non-poisonous variety, and they're shy. Watch where you step, but you won't see them if they can help it.

"This is an Audubon trip, so I'll be pointing out as many birds as I can, for you. The people in the first one or two canoes will see more because it's quiet in front of them, and the animals are undisturbed.

Once they can see and hear the bunch of us, many wading birds — like the great blue herons, the snowy egrets, the sandhill cranes — will fly away.

You'll be surprised at how many animals will *not* leave, though, if we stay as quiet as we can and, of course, don't stop, stand up or leave the boat. Enough canoes come through here that some of the local fauna are accustomed to them and will ignore us so long as we keep on going."

The professor paused to sip water from a reusable bottle clamped to his multi-pocketed photographer's vest. "Any questions so far?"

Miranda raised her hand to ask, "Why is it called Pig River?"

"Good question. It's called Pig River because you will probably see — and hear — wild pigs in the woods along the river.

They don't look like cute little Babe, the movie pig, but you can tell they're of the porcine persuasion.

"They're bad-tempered and unpredictable, with sharp tusks. Boars, especially, can be very dangerous, so don't approach them on land.

"The good news is, we've had no reports of wild pigs leaping into canoes. We should be safe."

People chuckled, and Win moved on to discuss proper hydration, sunscreen, mosquito repellant, lunch plans, and other administrative matters. On the second van, the professor's two T.A.'s were delivering a similar orientation lecture to the other paddlers.

Then the professor mentioned something that was not being shared on the second van. The T.A.'s knew about it, but they said nothing.

"We have a really special treat on today's trip," Win said. "My friend, Tommy Rigby, has a farm that runs along the river a ways, and Tommy visited me a few days ago to say a new sinkhole opened up on his land after that hard rain we got last weekend."

People murmured excitedly, and someone said, "How big?"

"About as big around as a good-sized hot tub, but much deeper. And it's still growing, so we'll be careful not to get too near the edge. I hope you realize how special you are. Nobody knows about this hole except Tom Rigby, me, and my two teaching assistants — we call them T.A.'s — who are not even telling the passengers on the second van, because they're sworn to secrecy."

"Why?" someone said.

"Why what?" said Win.

"Why is it such a big secret? I mean, it's only a hole in the ground, right? And Florida is the sinkhole capital of the world. Why would you keep this one a secret?"

"Ah, good question," Win answered with a nod. "Well, partly because this one is on private property, and a lot of people canoe this river. We don't want folks stopping off for a bit of trespassing, and maybe theft or vandalism, on Tom's farm.

“Also, there are often fossils revealed when a hole opens, and people have been known to steal fossils and sell them on the black market."

"Are they really so valuable?" Miranda asked.

"Depends," said Win. "'Saber-toothed tiger' skulls are very popular, as are mammoth tusks."

"In China they grind tusks into aphrodisiac powders, like 'love potions,' right?" a young man asked. His girlfriend elbowed him with a warning glare.

"But, isn't buying and selling tusks illegal?" said Miranda.

"It's against the law to buy and sell the ivory of today's elephant populations," the professor said, “but if you find an animal that has been dead eight or ten thousand years, it's not against the law to sell that ancient, fossil ivory."

"Unless you stole it from someone," Shepard added.

"Exactly," said Win.

"Were there ever mastodons in Florida?" asked the girlfriend of Love Potion Guy.

"There were some, but it's generally believed mastodons stayed farther north, in colder climates. We definitely had the mammoths, which were slightly smaller — though still substantially larger than today's elephants. Mammoths apparently tolerated the southern climate well.

“Of course, the Ice Age kept temperatures a good bit cooler in this area back then. The mammoths were long gone by the time Florida warmed into a subtropical environment."

A few minutes of discussion followed on the varieties of prehistoric animals that had lived in the area, animals living in the area at present, and what sort of fossils they might spot on the bottom of the crystal-clear river.

By that time, the vans had arrived at the put-in point, and soon the canoes were lined up along the riverbank, awaiting their crews.

Behind most of the group, Mrs. Cleary and Carlo shared a canoe, with him paddling and steering from the rear while she sat poised, with her camera and telephoto lens, in the front.

Right behind them, Shep and Miranda shared the handmade, mahogany and teak canoe built by Shep and his family.

After a few minutes of on-shore training on how to help paddle and steer the boat, Miranda took her place in the front. Shep settled into the rear and prepared to provide all the muscle power necessary for smooth, constant forward motion.

At the very back of the line, behind Shep and Miranda, came the canoe carrying the two T.A.'s.

Miranda looked up to see Carlo fasten a small electric device to the gunwale of his canoe. The device emitted a tiny, LED light that blinked on and off in time with a clicking sound.

"How's the volume?" Carlo called.

"Five by five," came Shep's voice in answer.

Miranda swiveled to address Shep. "What is that?"

"Metronome, usually," said Shep, "but today it's a homing beacon. Makes it easy for me to follow Carlo."

"Oh," she said, and turned to face forward again.

The professor's lead canoe began moving downstream, and one by one the eight other canoes followed.

Carlo began singing "Anchors aweigh, my boys! Anchors aweigh," as he put his canoe in motion.

"Quit yer caterwaulin', handsome, or I'll tip you into the river, no matter how dishy y'are," old Mrs. Cleary warned from three feet ahead of him in the boat.

"Yes, *signora* Cleary," Carlo said, pretending to be afraid. Or maybe he was smart enough to actually be afraid. History had shown Mrs. Cleary should not be underestimated.

Shepard began propelling his canoe into the center of the river, behind Carlo and Martha. Instead of using the paddle she had been given, Miranda again spun in her seat and addressed her not-so-secret fiancé. "You don't need me to steer at all, do you! You made that up just to be sure I wouldn't chicken out! You can follow Carlo whether I steer or not!"

"Not if I can't hear the clicker," he said calmly, "which I can't when you're shouting."

"I'm not shouting!" Miranda shouted.

"I also can't hear the clicker if Carlo gets too far ahead of us, which could easily happen. That's when you would step in and save the day, as is your wont."

"My 'wont'?"

"Yeah, it means what you would usually, or nearly always, do if—"

"I know the word. I just didn't expect to hear medieval vocabulary while canoeing through the Everglades."

"The Everglades is a couple hundred miles south of here. And I knew you knew the word, Miss Library. But today you're not a librarian, you're the guidance system on this machine, so turn around and guide. Put that paddle to use for something other than ballast."

She turned around, faced forward, and prepared to dip her paddle into the water. "How did you know I wasn't already 'turned around'?"

"Frankly, that's a little insulting. I have ears, Bean."

"Oh, right."

"Right. Now, please allow me to use said ears to listen for Carlo's clicker, so I'll know you're not about to run us aground or into the next cypress tree."

"Aye, aye, Captain." she said, and began paddling as he had shown her on shore, matching her rhythm to his.

"Thank you, First Mate."

"Future Mate," she corrected.

"And not too far in the future, either," he responded.

Carlo suddenly shouted back to them from several canoe-lengths ahead, "So, have you set a date, yet?"

Miranda tried using her paddle to splash him with river water, but alas his boat was too far away.

For the next two hours, only the gentle splashing of paddles disturbed the relative silence of the river and its forested surroundings. Mrs. Cleary was quick to spot night herons and spread-winged anhinga perched along the shoreline, wild pigs and deer foraging in the woods.

Saying nothing, she'd point them out for Carlo. He would silently point at them for Miranda's benefit, and Miranda would whisper a description to Shepard.

Tall cypress trees formed a leafy dome over the river, splitting the sunlight into pale shafts stretching down between branches like long fingers straining to touch the cool water.

White sand on the bottom of the transparent river reflected the sun's segmented light, mottled with lacy leaf-shadows.

Mockingbirds trilled in chorus with hooting coots and cawing ravens, while Carlo's metronome clicked a soft, steady rhythm. Occasionally, someone's paddle would clunk against the gunwale of a canoe, sending a rich, woody bass note into the music of the river.

Miranda reveled in the aromas of wild magnolias, damp riverside earth, and the barest hint of orange blossoms.

As if reading her mind, Shepard said, "There's an old citrus grove just beyond those trees on the right. The orange-blossom aroma is stronger when the wind is southerly, but even with today's breeze you can tell it's there."

"The wind isn't southerly today, then?"

"Did you learn nothing in the Girl Scouts, Castor Bean? Wet a finger and hold it up. The wind's from the east today. Feel it against your face?"

Miranda closed her eyes and concentrated on the feel of a fragrant breeze brushing across her face as it passed. When she opened her eyes again, she told Shep, "I can see the professor's canoe pulling up onto the left bank up ahead. We must be stopping for lunch."

A tall, barrel-chested, red-haired man in a cowboy hat was waiting on shore to welcome Win Clarkson. Soon, Win introduced the group to Tommy Rigby, owner of the land where they had beached their boats.

Minutes later Miranda was seated on the ground, unpacking

fruit, sandwiches, and water from one of the backpacks Carlo had prepared in the wee hours of the morning.

Actually, she wasn't sitting directly on the ground; Shepard had removed his shirt and placed it on the damp grass for her. She didn't tell him she was okay sitting on damp grass, because, frankly, she was okay with watching Shep without his shirt.

She could tell the other ladies in the group were fine with it, too. All ages. Even septuagenarian Martha Cleary sent Miranda a wink of approval.

Carlo had invited the professor's teaching assistants to have lunch with their group, so that they could get to know the graduate students, who had been on the other van during the trip to the river.

Before long, Carlo and the Asian student, David Zhang, were sharing stories about their mothers back in the old country. Mothers were the same everywhere, it seemed; especially mothers who tried to manage their sons' lives from halfway around the world.

Miranda lost track of the men's conversation when Martha Cleary packed away her lunch gear, stood, and approached Shepard.

"When you finish stuffin' yer face, young'n, I need yer help with somethin' a little ways over yonder."

Shep stuffed the last quarter of a sandwich into his mouth, chipmunk-like, and mumbled around the oral obstruction, "I 'an 'om' 'ow." When he had swallowed most of the mushy mass between his teeth, he stood and repeated, "I can come now."

"I'll put away your stuff," said Miranda when he reached down to pick up his lunch debris. "You go with Martha. And be careful."

"Silly girl," he said, and gave her ponytail a playful tug. Then he took Martha's proffered elbow, and they followed a game trail upriver, into the trees and out of Miranda's sight.

After stowing away the remnants of lunch, including all their trash, which they would take home with them, Miranda struck up a conversation with the second teaching assistant.

Felicia Harper was David Zhang's opposite as west is to east. She was an all-American Barbie-doll blonde female, to his straight-black-haired, almond-eyed Asian male.

She stood four inches taller than he, even when wearing flat, pink tennis shoes on her dainty feet. His feet were long and wide and appeared massive in his neon orange jogging shoes.

Miranda wondered how skilled one would have to be at river trekking, to wear beautiful, new shoes and have no fear of ruining the footwear in a watery mishap. Miranda's shoes were the oldest and shabbiest ones she owned.

She knew her limitations athletically and aquatically. Miranda considered a shoe-drowning disaster to be more than probable, in her case. In fact, capsize was probably inevitable. Shep might even dunk them on purpose, if he felt playful. Or suicidal.

According to Felicia, her relationship with David was proof that opposites attract.

"He caught my eye the first week of the semester, when we were both waiting to be interviewed by Professor Clarkson. He was so polite, tidy, quiet, and witty — so different from the American boys I dated before.

"I figured he would want to date Asian girls, and I knew there were many of them at the university. But when I went in for my interview I got a shock."

Felicia continued, "Professor Clarkson said the other candidate had withdrawn his application when told only one position was available.

"David gave up the job, so the professor would give it to me! I was blown away! Who makes a sacrifice like that for someone they don't even know?"

"That is amazing!" Miranda agreed. "And, David didn't say anything at all to you about it? He must have seen you again on his way out of the interview."

Felicia seemed to gaze starry-eyed at David for a moment, then she turned toward Miranda. "He did not say one single word. He gave me a reserved smile and a hint of a bow — more of a nod, really — and he left. I went right into the professor's office and told him the job should go to the Chinese student who just left."

"You didn't!"

"Crazy, right?"

"What did Professor Clarkson say when you told him that?"

"He nearly fell over backward in his chair, laughing. I was totally in shock. Speechless, staring at the man," Felicia said.

She went on, "When he finally got himself under control, he told me that David had made the same offer. And that's when Professor Clarkson decided he would need *two* teaching assistants this year."

A sincere smile bloomed on Miranda's face. "What a marvelous story you have for telling your grandchildren someday — I mean, if it comes to that. I don't mean to presume ..."

"Oh, presume all you want," Felicia said. "I'm definitely hoping for a serious, long-lasting relationship. But, it's early yet. We've only been dating for three months."

"I wish you all the best," said Miranda.

Felicia said, "Thanks. You're sweet. But, tell me about that blond hunk paddling your canoe." She chuckled. "If *paddling your canoe* is what we're calling it these days." She winked.

♦

Shep and Mrs. Cleary had left the picnic site to walk into the woods. When Martha was certain no one could see or hear them, she told Shep the reason for their stroll.

"I done spotted a osprey nest in the top of one of these trees, and I need you to scoot up there and tell me if there's eggs in it. I'll watch for the adults and let you know if you need to take evasive action."

"Got it," he said, without surprise. He and "Miz Martha" Cleary had been on birding trips in the past. As a child, he had done the same with Miranda's late Aunt Phyllis.

So, when Mrs. Cleary stopped at the base of a tree and placed his hand on the rough bark, he was ready to climb.

She told him, "First limb is about nine feet up at yer three o'clock. I'll tell ya more when ya git there."

Gripping the trunk with hands and feet, he shimmied upward and straddled the first limb in less than a minute. "You know we can't tell Bean about this," he said.

"Ain't that the truth," Mrs. Cleary agreed. "About three feet up, at your eleven o'clock."

Shep moved easily to the next limb and from there on to the top of the tree, with Miz Martha directing him all the way.

When he arrived at the nest, he reached in his pocket and produced a plastic sandwich bag. Using the bag as a glove over his hand, he carefully felt around in the nest until he gently touched two eggs.

He called down to Mrs. Cleary, telling her the number of osprey chicks on the way and the approximate size and weight of each egg.

She wrote the information in the pocket notebook she kept for birding, then she directed Shep back to the ground, branch by branch, just as she had guided him skyward.

When he landed on *terra firma*, Shep took the old lady's elbow, and they strolled back to their friends on the riverbank.

A few minutes after Mrs. Cleary and Shep rejoined their friends on the riverbank, Tom Rigby guided everyone down a game trail, through the woods, and onto the site of a newborn sinkhole.

The paddlers had observed fossil seashells and shark's teeth on the sandy bottom of the glass-clear river. They had even seen one of the relatively rare six-inch Megalodon teeth left behind by the giant sharks of the Ice Age.

Rigby's ragged-edged sinkhole, however, exceeded everything they had seen all day.

The crater was about four yards in diameter, when just a week before it had been only six or eight feet wide.

Grains of sand on the side walls vibrated steadily downward, indicating the hole was still growing wider and deeper.

No one could guess its depth. Intense darkness kept the canoeists from seeing the bottom.

The hole inexorably grew wider and deeper, millimeter by millimeter, with every passing hour.

Rigby pointed his flashlight at the far wall, about nine feet below ground level, to show an uneven vertical slab of mud and tangled vegetation.

"Will you dig for fossils in this hole?" Miranda asked.

Rigby chuckled. "Not till this monster quits eating everything around it," he said.

"What will you do with the fossils, if you find some?" someone called.

"Are they valuable?" another voice asked.

The professor answered, "Depending on a specimen's condition, it could be valuable to a museum for display. Of course, every fossil has value to scientists who want to study it."

Rigby added, "I usually donate my finds to the university. If I had a connection in China, I might be able to sell stuff over there for a tidy sum. Maybe David can introduce me to a rich buyer in China. Whattaya say, David?"

David Zhang laughed along with everyone else and answered with a shake of his head.

After studying the sinkhole for half an hour, and pelting Professor Clarkson and Tom Rigby with questions, the group followed Rigby back to their canoes.

"Y'all don't dawdle, now," Rigby told the paddlers. "My bones is tellin' me there's a doozie of a storm on the way, and you shore don't want to be on no river when it hits. 'Specially if you're in a metal canoe."

He continued, "This state is the lightnin' strike capital of the country, y'know. And Central Florida, where we're standin' right now, is called 'Lightnin' Alley.'"

"We'll make good time from here to our take-out point," Clarkson answered. "Thanks for everything, Tom."

One duo after another, the paddlers called out thanks to their host and pulled away from shore into the river's current.

They would never see two of their comrades again.

## Chapter 6 - The Storm

Farmer Tom Rigby had been right when he predicted stormy weather.

Several square miles of land around Minokee — including Martha Cleary's precious garden — soaked up a heavy rain during the night following the canoe trip.

Martha Cleary named this the Cat Storm. She remembered it that way because in the midst of the storm, bird-loving (therefore, cat-avoiding) Miz Cleary, fell for the sad eyes and matted fur of a half-drowned kitten crying at her door.

No other cat had ever drawn Martha's compassion. This was a singular kitten, however. It did not meow or yowl or mew, as cats are expected to do. Instead, it chirped. So, anyone hearing it might mistake it for a bird.

Thus, Mrs. Cleary opened her door to the storm, expecting to find an injured bird on her porch. By the time she recognized the "bird" had fur, claws, a tail, and enormous, doleful eyes, it was too late for the old softie to harden her heart.

So, the kitten was more-or-less welcomed into the Cleary house, where it was given tuna and a saucer of Half-and-Half coffee whitener (because Miz Martha absolutely did not keep cat food or cream).

She gave the dripping feline a few quick passes with a blow dryer before wrapping it in a soft, thick towel (warm from the clothes dryer). She then placed it in a worn, deep, easy chair, where it slept until morning.

*Wednesday afternoon*

On the fourth day after the canoe trip, Win Clarkson responded to a knock on his office door. "Enter."

Felicia Harper stuck her head around the edge of his door. "Have you talked to Zhang today?"

"No. In fact, I tried to call him, but got no answer. He didn't show up to teach a class this morning, and that's not like him. Do you know if he's ill?"

"I don't know if he's anything. I haven't been able to reach him either, and I haven't seen him since Saturday, and we always talk two or three times a day, and … I'm afraid something's happened to him!"

"Now, calm down, Felly." Clarkson gestured her toward a chair.

She started to close the door behind her as she entered, but Clarkson gestured at her to leave it open.

He waited until she sat. She remained on the edge of the seat, her spine flagpole-erect.

Clarkson said, in his most calming voice, "You and Zhang have been, ah, an item for how long?"

"Just over three months."

"I see. Well, ah, let me put this as delicately as possible. The fact is, um, relationships have their ups and downs; it's only normal—"

She cut him off. "We didn't have a fight, Doctor Clarkson. Everything was fine between us, then he just ... disappeared off the face of the earth. I even went to his apartment, and his roommate hasn't seen or heard from him, either."

Clarkson held up a hand to stop her. Footsteps in the corridor grew louder until a pair of students strode past the open door. Clarkson signaled Felicia to go on talking.

Felicia took a shaky breath and continued, "And, besides, if he just didn't want to see me, that wouldn't keep him from teaching his class this morning. He knew *I* wouldn't bother him; I have my own class at that hour." She covered her face with her hands and began to weep.

Clarkson dug a box of tissues out of a drawer and passed it across the desktop to Felicia.

"We had so many plans!" Felicia mourned loudly. A young man with a backpack looked in as he passed the open door, but he kept walking.

"I can see why you're upset," the professor said, "but let's not make more of the situation than is necessary. Zhang is a loyal, ethical young gentleman. Out of politeness, if nothing else, he would not suddenly shun you after you two had become … um … close, shall we say?

Win continued, "There has to be a logical reason we can't reach him. Perhaps his phone is malfunctioning, or he has had car trouble and is stranded at a repair shop somewhere. Perhaps he told you he had plans out of town, and you either didn't hear him, or it slipped your mind?"

Felicia sniffed, snorted into a tissue, then balled the damp paper into her fist. "I never forgot a single word he ever said to me. I told him I loved him!"

She stood to lean toward the trashcan at the far end of the desk. "And, if he had phone trouble, or car trouble, or any kind of trouble, he would have found a way to call me, I know he would. He wouldn't want me to worry."

The tissue-ball arced gracefully from her hand to the trashcan, and she resumed her seat.

Three girls in shorts and sandals glanced through the doorway when Felicia shouted, "I don't think for one minute that he wanted to break up with me. And even if he did, he would have told me himself. My David is no coward!"

The girls walked on, and Felicia continued. "And he wouldn't miss work without letting you know somehow, sir." She lifted two fresh tissues out of Win's box. "That's how I know something bad has happened to him! What are we going to do?"

Win averted his eyes while Felicia snorted into her tissues. He thought for a moment before saying, "Well, the logical first thing to do is call the campus police. We'll proceed from there, based on what they tell us."

Felicia doubled-sniffed into her wet tissue wad. "Thank you, Doctor Clarkson."

"You're very welcome, Felly. Now, try to calm yourself. It'll be all right. We'll all be laughing about this misunderstanding sooner than you think."

The professor was wrong.

*Thursday morning*

Television weathermen across Central Florida confirmed what Tom Rigby had predicted based on his aching bones. The pros called it a "tropical depression," but it was the same weather Tom had called "a doozie of a storm." The steadily pounding rain continued for several days.

On the morning the rain finally stopped, Shep was pouring himself a cup of coffee, and Carlo was frying bacon, when someone rapped on the kitchen door.

"You'll get it," Carlo said, without looking up.

Shep opened the door with his coffee cup in one hand, and Martha Cleary placed something fuzzy in Shep's non-coffee-holding hand.

"Gotcha somethin'," she said.

Shep weighed the fuzzy object, and it moved against his palm. "What is it?"

Carlo leaned to get a look at the object. "Is a Tribble," he said, "like Star Trek."

"Ain't it obvious?" the old lady said.

"Not to me," Shep said, "or I wouldn't have asked."

"Give us a clue," called Carlo from the stove. "Animal, vegetable, or mineral?"

"Animal."

"It's a puppy!" Carlo guessed.

Shep was pushing the fur ball toward Mrs. Cleary, shaking his head. "No dogs," he said. "No more dogs."

Mrs. Cleary retreated a step, refusing to take back the gift. "It ain't a dog, Chef Boy-Ar-Dee," she said to Carlo. "Dave ain't been gone but six months. Nobody around here's ready for another dog yit."

"Are you saying this is a *cat*?" Shep lifted his hand higher, putting the beast farther away. "I'm not a cat person, Miz Martha. I wouldn't have the first idea what to do with a cat. You're a natural nurturer. It would be better off with you."

"Nope, that horse won't plow. I got birds and bird feeders all over my yard. Dang cat would think it's an all-you-can-eat buffet. And, the first time I caught the little booger with one of my birds in its jaws, I'd have to shoot it nine times to be sure I took every one of its lives. Nope, ain't no cat on earth gonna be 'better off' with me."

Shep sipped his coffee and thought. The kitten had fallen asleep in his raised hand, but he didn't seem to notice.

Carlo broke the silence with, "My brother loved cats."

"He never said that," Shep snapped.

"But did he ever say he did not?"

"Next you'll be telling me *Dave* would want me to have a cat," Shepard snarked.

"Did you ever ask him?" Carlo responded, lifting the bacon onto a plate lined with paper towels.

"That's low, even for you."

"Meh," said Carlo with a shrug, picking up an egg and breaking it into the pan of bacon grease.

Shep sipped coffee again, then said to Mrs. Cleary, "I'm allergic to cats."

"I ain't heard you sneeze, and ya bin holdin' this'n fer a while now."

"It's a slow-onset allergy. Takes a few hours to incubate before symptoms appear, but it's deadly," Shep insisted.

"You know, Madam absolutely despises cats," Carlo said, breaking another egg into the pan.

"My mother? Truly?" said Shep.

"Hates them with a purple passion. Will not go anywhere near one," said Carlo, reaching for another egg.

"Sold!" Shepard announced. "Miz Martha, you've found a home for your cat. Of course, if you happen to find another suitable home for it, just let me know and I'll bring it right over."

"Ain't *my* cat," Mrs. Cleary said. "Cats don't belong to people; it's th'uther way 'round. I'll leave it here and we'll see if it adopts you. If it don't like ya, we'll blow that bridge when we git to it."

"Fair enough," Shep said, swinging his handful of kitten in close to his chest. "Any words of advice?"

"Git a litter box. Soon," she said, and she walked away without another word.

Shep turned from the door as he shut it. "I'll put an old towel at the bottom of that wicker laundry basket, like we did when Dave was a puppy. That oughta hold the little guy at least until after breakfast."

"Hurry up," said Carlo, flipping the eggs. "Breakfast in fifty-five seconds."

When Shep returned to the kitchen a minute later, he carried a wicker basket with a sleeping kitten in it. "We better take him to the vet and be sure he has his shots."

Shep stashed the basket under the table while Carlo plated the eggs and bacon.

"I cannot, not today," Carlo said, and he went to retrieve toast from the toaster. "War council today. Madam has summoned me, and I must obey. Your wedding, remember? Have you set a date yet?"

"I'll get Bean to take us to the vet; she's working the two-to-nine shift today. You have a nice meeting, Traitor," said Shep.

"I am no traitor. I am *double agent.* Is very dangerous work, and I only do it out of friendship, you ungrateful sloth. Is your turn to say grace."

They bowed their heads to pray over the meal. Shepard thanked God for the blessings of the day and for heaven's provision of this meal and of all their needs, beyond what they could ask or think.

In closing, Shepard said, "Amen."

Carlo echoed, "Amen."

*Chirp,* said the basket under the table.

"A religious cat," said Carlo. "That's nice."

After the breakfast dishes were done and the kitchen set to rights, Carlo took leave of Shep and the kitten and drove away to attend Hermione Montgomery-Krausse's war council.

Hermione would have called it a "planning session," but anyone who knew how Shep would react to his mother's plans would know: That meeting was a prelude to war.

Shepard took the kitten outside and placed it in a sandy spot, then stood by while it did its business. When he heard little paws tossing sand over the kitten's deposit, he squatted to pick up the animal, and he walked through the backyard hedge toward Miranda's back door, carrying his fur ball.

Miranda was in the laundry room at one end of her kitchen, loading dirty sheets into Aunt Phyllis's vintage Kenmore washing machine.

The dryer beside it was brand new, with a thousand bells and whistles. Shep had bought the fancy dryer recently, after a near-death experience when he walked neck-first into Miranda's clothesline.

She called "Come in, it's open," when Shepard knocked at her kitchen door. When he entered with a handful of fluff, she said,

"What is that?"

He grinned. "Cost you a kiss to find out."

"Hmmm."

"Well? What are you waiting for, woman? Your prince has come."

"Mm. I'm trying to decide how badly I really want to know."

"Okay, now it's gonna cost you two kisses."

Smiling, she drew close and, on tiptoes, planted a long kiss, followed by a shorter one, on his waiting lips. "Oh, and good morning, incidentally," she said.

"Yes. It. Is!"

"Now you have to answer my question."

"Yes. I. Do." He lifted the hand holding the kitten from against his chest to near where he judged Miranda's face to be. The fur ball uncurled into a tiny beast with big ears and a pink tongue. The beastie extended one hind leg and began to bathe-lick the limb.

"Aw, a kitten," Miranda crooned. She touched its head, and the kitten pushed against her fingers as if requesting a massage. To Shep she said, "And, you suddenly have a kitten because ...?"

"Miz Cleary rescued it from the storm, apparently."

"Good for Mrs. Cleary," she said. "Good for the kitten, too. But, why do *you* have the kitten? Did you *want* a cat?"

"Never thought about a cat. Just knew I didn't want a dog." Neither of them mentioned Dave.

Shep continued, "And then Miz Cleary came to the door this morning and gave me a cat."

"You could've said no."

"I did, at first, but Carlo reminded me of something."

"*Carlo* wanted a cat?" she guessed.

"Nope. He said my mother hates cats. I believe his exact words were, 'She won't go near one.' That's good enough for me."

Miranda thumped him on the arm. "Shame on you! You would use a helpless, innocent kitten just to keep your mother from visiting you? I will not allow you to doom this poor baby to a loveless, lonely existence just so you can have a ... a ... a shrew deterrent!"

Shep pulled the kitten against his chest and covered its ears with his hand. "Shhh! Honey, we said we'd never argue in front of the children," he teased. "First of all, he or she is only staying until he or she decides whether to adopt me, so there's no arbitrary 'doomed existence.'

"Second, it will not be a loveless, lonely existence. I would never abuse or neglect an animal.

“And, speaking of loving care, since you have the morning off today, will you drive us to the veterinary clinic to get the necessary immunizations? And we need to pick up a litter box. Maybe we should do that first."

Shep waited for her answer.

Miranda crossed her arms and tilted her head ten degrees. "Let me get this straight," she said. "You promise to love—"

"I didn't say love."

"Okay, you promise to care for this adorable kitty, but first you want to subject it to torture-by-a-thousand-needles at the vet's clinic."

"Yep, that's about it."

"I'll get my car keys," she said.

The kitten *chirped.*

"I know," Shepard told the cat. "She acts tough, but she's a pushover. You'll like her."

He turned toward Miranda's pantry. "Let's see what Bean has for your breakfast. We'll shop for cat food later today. You be thinking about what you'd like."

A short time later, as Miranda drove Shepard and the kitten to the veterinarian Dave would have recommended, Shep's cellphone chimed in his pocket. He dug it out and answered: "Krausse."

"Good morning, Shep," Win Clarkson said. "How are things in Minokee these days?"

"Hi, Win. We're great, thanks. Enjoyed the canoe trip last Saturday. What's up in 'Gator Country?"

"I just got an email from the university's development office, telling me that your donation was wired to us yesterday evening. I know you'll get one of those fancy letters from the uppity-ups in administration, but I wanted to thank you personally. You've been incredibly generous to us over the years, and this latest contribution to my department is further proof of your benevolence. I thank you from the bottom of my heart."

"Not necessary, Win, it was my pleasure. 'To whom much is given, much is required,' and I've been given more than I deserve a hundred times over. It's a blessing to me that I can afford to support your program. I'll bet you already have plans for the money, right?"

Clarkson chuckled. "Guilty," he said. "I think we'll use part of it for a dig out at Tom Rigby's place. I sent a team with ground penetrating radar out to Tom's place, and they found what looks like a complete mammoth skeleton down in that new sinkhole."

"No kidding!" Shep told Miranda, "Bean, there's a mammoth in Tom Rigby's sinkhole!"

"The one we saw on the canoe trip?"

"How many sinkholes does Tom Rigby have? Of course, it's the one we saw." Into the phone, he said, "Is it the same sinkhole we saw the other day? ... Right. Of course. Well, tell him congratulations from Miranda and me."

"Thanks," said Win. "I can't wait to start signing up students for the dig. This will be terrific field experience for them, and it will be a help to Tom. He's getting too old to be digging up mammoth fossils by himself."

"Listen," said Shep, "I'm sure I don't have to tell you to get your security system in place first thing. Don't wait. A mammoth won't be a secret for long, and fossil poachers will carry half of it away before you can say 'prehistoric.'"

"Oh, I'm way ahead of you there. I've been online this morning, researching motion sensors and alarms and other equipment."

Shep asked, "Is there anything I can do to help?"

"You mean, besides giving us a boatload of money?" Win said. "Oh, wait, you already did that. That's what prompted this call, wasn't it? Did I say thank you yet?"

"I believe so, and I hope I said you're very welcome."

Win did not respond immediately.

Shep waited a slow five seconds before asking, "You still there?"

"Yes. I was, um, thinking there might be something else you could do for me, if you don't mind my asking."

"Anything for you, Win. Ask away."

"Um, if you, um, if you still have the, um, connections you used to have when you were doing Sheep Counters..."

"The radio show?"

"Yeah. I know you don't do it anymore, but you did seem to have, y'know, certain sources..."

"I still have 'em. Win, what's going on? Why do you need my underground sources?"

Miranda said, "What?"

Win said, "My teaching assistant, David Zhang, is missing, and I hoped you could..."

"I'll find him," Shep said.

"You'll find whom?" came from the driver's seat, where Miranda could only hear one side of the conversation.

"Don't worry," said Shep. "Email me the details you have so far. I'll be in touch."

"Worry about what?" Miranda said, her voice rising in pitch and volume.

*Chirp,* said the basket in the back seat.

"Shhh, Bean! You woke the baby," Shep said in a stage whisper.

Miranda stayed quiet while Shep promised to see Win Clarkson soon, signed off on his call, and disconnected.

She stayed quiet for another half-minute, waiting for Shep to speak to her. When he didn't, she sighed in resignation.

Miranda said, "You're not going to tell me what that was

about, are you."

"Nope."

"And, you're not going to tell me about your 'underground sources'?"

"Nope."

"Because the less I know, the safer I'll be? Is that it?"

"Yep."

"Men."

"Ya gotta love us."

Later, on the way home from the veterinary clinic, Shepard brought up the subject of a wedding.

"Bean, do you want your parents to plan you a wedding? Because if you want the bridesmaids, and the candles, and the flowers, and the church organ music, and the whole shebang, you can have it."

He went on, "Don't let me talk you out of it, Castor Bean. We're only getting married once, after all. You should have your wedding exactly as *you* want it."

Miranda reached across and patted his left thigh, and then jerked her hand back to the steering wheel as if she had received an electrical shock. "You're a very sweet man, Shepard Montgomery Krausse."

"I am, aren't I? And good looking, too."

"I agree," she said with a smile.

"And incredibly smart," he suggested.

She scoffed. "You're not so smart if you think a wedding planned by my parents would be any better than the spectacle-of-the-century your mother is probably planning. Neither wedding would be exactly what *I'd* want, I can just about guarantee."

He patted her shoulder. "Good girl. You and I are the only people who matter."

She drove in silence for a few moments and then heard him say, "So, how's this afternoon for you?"

She laughed. "Kinda short notice, doncha think?"

"But, Bean!" He gestured toward the basket in the back seat while he leaned toward Miranda and whispered, "We want to take our vows before the baby gets old enough to understand."

The kitten *chirped.*

"See? He's beginning to understand too much already," Shep whispered.

## Chapter 7 - The Council

*Thursday*

That same afternoon, in the dining room of the Montgomery-Krausse mansion, Shepard's mother had accepted status reports from each member of her staff about every facet of the wedding plan. Before concluding the "planning session" (translation: war council), Hermione Montgomery-Krausse told the attendees her own news.

"I have spoken by telephone with Doctor and Mrs. Ogilvy. Or, more correctly, to Doctor and Doctor Ogilvy. You will not be surprised to hear that Miranda has not announced her engagement to her parents, just as Shepard has not announced his to me.

"Mrs-Doctor Ogilvy and I agree that these two young people are behaving in a slipshod, careless manner that can only end in disaster.

"Therefore, the Ogilvys will be attending our meetings from now on via Skype. Rebecca, you will make the necessary technical arrangements, please."

"Yes, Madam," the administrative assistant responded crisply.

"Holy conspiracy, Batman," murmured Carlo.

Hanson was the only person to hear Carlo's remark. "Indeed," the butler breathed.

"Carlo!" boomed the voice from the head of the table.

"Yes, Madam!"

"Obviously, it would simplify arrangements if we could get a potential wedding date from the happy couple. Have you any news at all on that front?"

"Nothing concrete, I'm afraid, Madam. They refuse to answer my direct questions. I have heard some vague discussions, but nothing definitive."

"Tell me about these 'discussions.'"

"Of course, Madam. *Signor* Shepard mentioned something about being married by a ship's captain—"

"Outrageous!"

"—but *Signorina* Miranda said she did not think such an arrangement would be strictly legal."

"Intelligent young woman," said Hermione. "Any further developments?"

When only silence resulted, Hermione stood and stretched to her full height.

Everyone else at the table stood immediately.

Even though no one was still seated, Hermione seemed to look down on her subjects as if from Mount Olympus. "Inasmuch as the conversation has dwindled into meaningless drivel, this meeting is adjourned. You will receive an email announcing the next meeting."

With that, she made a regal exit, followed closely by Rebecca, the loyal factotum.

Later that afternoon, while Miranda shelved library books in Lake City, Shepard and Carlo sat across a desk from the sheriff of Alachua County, in Gainesville.

Sheriff Connor completed a telephone call and replaced the receiver. He swiveled his chair toward his visitors and rested his elbows on his desk blotter. "Sounds like the campus police have looked into Professor Clarkson's missing-person report, but they haven't found anything that looks like foul play. To them it looks like a homesick foreign student went home to mommy. Happens all the time."

Shepard sighed. "Well, at least they didn't ignore it. Clarkson was worried when nobody he talked to seemed to be concerned."

"They covered all the bases, seems to me," Connor said. "They talked to people, questioned the roommate, couldn't find any reason to suspect the kid had enemies or that he was engaged in illicit activities. His room looks normal, not trashed or anything."

The sheriff's tone was reassuring when he said, "These foreign students skip town without notice sometimes. Some of his stuff is still in his room; he's probably planning to come back in a few days."

Carlo said, "But, they do not tell someone they are leaving? David has a job to do and classes to attend. He would want to be part of the new dig with Doctor Clarkson. You believe he would go away, and say *nothing*?"

Sheriff Connor shrugged. "Who knows? Every culture is different, every family is different, and every kid is unique. One thing I've learned to expect from university students is The Unexpected."

He continued, "And that goes double for students from overseas. Some adjust well to being so far from home, and some don't. If you don't hear from him in a couple weeks, let me know, and my department will follow up on it."

"Thanks, Sheriff. I appreciate your time and your help. I hope you're right about David," Shepard said, rising from his chair.

Carlo rose as well, and casually extended his elbow to Shep.

The sheriff stood and offered a hand for Shepard to shake. Carlo nudged Shep's right arm almost imperceptibly, and Shepard's hand went out toward Sheriff Connor.

With a minor adjustment, Connor met the proffered hand, and the two men shook amicably. Connor followed up with a handshake for Carlo as well.

As the two visitors turned toward the door, Shep asked, "Would it be all right if we poke around a bit, talk to the roommate, maybe look at David's apartment?"

"I don't see why not. I'm sure you can be trusted not to move or remove anything."

"Of course," Shep said.

"Just check in with the campus police," the sheriff cautioned. 'Let 'em know you're there. I'll tell 'em to expect you."

"Thanks, Sheriff. I'll let you know if David turns up," said Shep.

"*When*," Connor said. "Let's say *when* he turns up, not *if*."

"Right," Shep agreed. "We'll hold that thought. Have a good afternoon." Shep followed Carlo out of the sheriff's offices and into the parking lot.

When Carlo stopped beside their car and opened the passenger door, he looked around to be sure no one was near enough to hear. "Do you still want me to alert the grapevine?"

"Absolutely," Shep answered.

## Chapter 8 - The Parents, Part 1

*Saturday. Minokee.*

Although he was a capable adult, Shepard Krausse was inexperienced at the routine task of washing an automobile. This was not because he was lazy or irresponsible, and he certainly was not one to recline and watch TV sports all afternoon.

Shep was inexperienced at the task because he had never had the opportunity to wash his own car. His late friend, Pietro, had taken charge of every vehicle Shepard had ever owned. In fact, Pietro had led the expeditions to purchase Shep's cars, every one of them, to date.

Pietro was always passionate about the maintenance of the machines.

He had been so exacting in the care of Shep's cars that, whenever Shepard tried to wash, polish, Windex, or even vacuum the car, Pietro threw himself between his precious vehicle and the barbarian who would surely ruin its perfection.

Shepard had not even been permitted to empty an ashtray. Of course, since Pietro would never tolerate a habit as filthy as smoking inside "his" car, the ashtrays never needed emptying. Dusting, perhaps, but never emptying. Dusting was forbidden to Shepard, also.

Pietro had died in the car bombing that had also killed Shep's guide dog, Dave. Shepard had not replaced the car in which his dearest friends, virtually his family, had died.

When Carlo arrived home from his brother's funeral in Sicily, he was the perfect person to step into Pietro's stylish, immaculate shoes. Carlo acquired a car on Shep's behalf, and Carlo maintained it as fiercely as had his brother.

In the interim between Pietro's demise and Carlo's arrival, Shepard had bought a car — through an intermediary — but it was not a car for him. He had bought a car for Miranda.

This had several advantages for Shep. First, and most important, Miranda's tiny commuter car had been old, rattle-riven, slow, and unsafe. Her car was so small, a medium-sized Harley Davidson motorcycle could have obliterated her car without even noticing it.

Shep hated to even imagine what a normal car or truck might do to Miranda's little deathtrap. He had nightmares in which her car was permanently wedged into the undercarriage of a tractor-trailer truck that had steamrolled directly over her on I-75, without ever seeing her.

So, Shepard had bought Miranda a full-size luxury automobile capable of eating Harley Davidsons for brunch. The new car was safe, sleek, fast, quiet, beautiful (he was told), and highly visible to tractor-trailer drivers. Shep joked that Miranda's old car would have fit into the trunk of her new one.

Another advantage to Miranda's new car was for Shepard's enjoyment, rather than Miranda's. Miranda was her own driver. As a result, no fastidious chauffeur would be telling Shepard how to take care of this automobile. It was his turn to forbid others (meaning Miranda) from touching "his" car.

When Miranda saw how Shepard reveled in the buckets of soapy water, the squish of sponges, the puddles from the running hose, she did not have the heart to stop him. If Shepard enjoyed washing her car this much, she wanted him to wash it every day. He told her he did not enjoy it quite *that* much, but a weekly bubble-fest in her driveway was highly likely.

At first, Miranda tried to keep the new kitten inside her house while Shep made shallow pools all over the driveway and part of the yard. She stopped imprisoning the strange little feline when she discovered one of its many eccentricities: Water fascinated the little cat. Especially running water.

So, Shepard would lather and slosh and whistle and grin during his weekly carwash routine, and he would leave the garden hose running, on the driveway, for longer than necessary so the cat could play with (or just sit by, adoring) the water. Together, they were a picture of hydro-delight.

That Saturday afternoon, Miranda was cleaning cat hairs from every cranny of her house (and grumbling that she did not even *own* a cat). Meanwhile, Shepard and the offending feline were cleaning almost-no-dirt-at-all from her car, outside in the driveway.

Minokee was hot and humid.

Shep was shirtless, shoeless, soapy, and soaked as he worked on the car. He even had bubbles in his beard, and his ponytail hung in a limp, wet rope between his shoulder blades.

The cat looked more dignified than Shep did, frankly, which was unfortunate because of what happened next.

A dove gray mid-sized car rolled slowly down narrow, tree-arched Magnolia Street and stopped, idling, near the driveway where Shep "worked."

The engine's purr told of fine engineering, and when a window whirred down, the mellow, elegant strains of classical music wafted from a high-quality stereo sound system. This vehicle was not as expensive, prestigious, or large as Miranda's new car, but clearly these people enjoyed excellence.

"Excuse me," a friendly-sounding man called from the car's open window.

"Good morning," Shep called back, smiling.

"It's afternoon," said a woman from within the car. She did not sound as friendly as the man.

"Good afternoon," the man called. "I'll bet you know everyone in this neighborhood. This is Minokee, right?"

"Oh, yes, sir. This is the one and only Minokee, and I've known the people here since I was a kid. Can I help you find someone?"

The man picked up a piece of paper from the dashboard and held it up, not realizing that the laborer in the sunglasses and shorts could not see it. "We have an address," the man said, "but there don't seem to be any street signs or house numbers. How do visitors find anyone here?"

Shep chuckled and kept circling his lathered sponge across the dripping flank of the car. "We don't get too many visitors, actually. And the ones we do get are usually old friends or relatives, and they know their way around. Who are you looking for?"

"My daughter lives in the house that belonged to Phyllis Ogilvy until recently, do you know which house that is?"

"Just turn off your engine, because you're sitting right in front of it." Shep let his sponge splash into the bucket of water at his feet and walked toward the car. "You must be Miranda's parents! I'm so happy to finally meet you, Mister and Missus Ogilvy."

The friendly man turned off his ignition and opened the car door.

Shep was wiping his hands on the back of his shorts as he said, "I'd shake your hand, but I'm a little wet and sticky right now. I'm Shep, by the way. That's my house back there." He gestured over his shoulder with a thumb.

The man was walking around the car to open the woman's door. "Pleased to meet you, Shep. I'm Zeke and this is my wife, Rosario." He offered his hand to the lady emerging from the vehicle.

The lady stood and walked around the car, giving Shep a wide berth and carefully sidestepping puddles. "My husband is Doctor Ezekiel Ogilvy, and I am Doctor Rosario Ogilvy. We are indeed the parents of Miss Miranda Ogilvy. Thank you for your help, young man." She dismissed Shep from her mind and walked with determination toward the front door of Miranda's little house.

Zeke Ogilvy had popped the trunk and was lifting luggage from the car.

Hearing this, Shep offered to help carry bags into the house.

"Oh, no, thank you, Shep. I've got this. Appreciate your help. I'll let you get back to your work there." Zeke chuckled as he shut the trunk. "Feel free to take a layer of road grime off of this one, too, if you've got the time. I'll pay you twice what Miranda's paying you."

He chuckled again and began walking with the luggage toward the house. "Maybe see you again while we're here," he said in parting.

"Pretty sure you will." Shep picked up the hose and gave a squirt in the direction of a high-pitched *burble* from the aquatic kitten. Then, Shep made his way back to the bucket and sponge.

♦

At the same time Shepard was washing a car in Minokee, Carlo was in Gainesville reporting to Professor Clarkson on their meeting the day before with the Alachua County sheriff.

"I'll bet he told you that, with so many thousands of students at this university, we can't be their mamas," said Clarkson. "So, he's not worried when one doesn't show up for a few days. They're adults after all."

Carlo said, "Actually, the sheriff didn't say that, but the campus police certainly did."

"Of course, they did."

Carlo leaned forward in his chair and rested his elbows on Clarkson's desk. "I have to tell you, Professor," Carlo said, "I talked to David Zhang on the canoe trip a week ago, and he did not sound like a young man who was leaving soon for China. David was determined to get his Ph.D.; he even had a position lined up as soon as he got his doctorate."

"I know he was serious about his studies," said Clarkson. "He was serious about the dissertation he was about to finish, and serious about obtaining the University fellowship that will be awarded to a doctoral candidate this year. In fact, David and Felicia are both in the running for the same fellowship."

Carlo angled back in his chair. "So," he said, "if David does not show up to turn in his doctoral dissertation, Felicia would probably get that fellowship. Isn't that sort of a ... motive?"

Win Clarkson chuckled. "Whoa, Carlo. That's a little dramatic, don't you think? This here," he gestured to the college campus outside his window, "is 'Saved by The Bell;' not 'Game of Thrones.'"

"You are right." Carlo shook his head and chuckled under his breath at himself. "I have been binge-watching too much Netflix."

"Yeah, I'd say so." Clarkson joked. '"Felicia has a motive'? To do what, exactly? What could a little girl like that possibly do to 'disappear' a grown man like David Zhang? And please don't ever tell her I called her a 'little girl'! She might develop a motive all right — for a lawsuit!"

Clarkson rose from his chair and extended a hand, which Carlo shook in parting as he stood to go.

"Carlo, I appreciate you driving all the way here on your Saturday to let me know what happened at yesterday's meeting with the sheriff. *I had* to be here today because I have a Saturday class, but I'm sure *you* could have found plenty of other things to do today."

"My pleasure, *Dottor* Clarkson. I had errands over this way, anyhow."

"Let's keep each other advised of any developments, agreed?"

"Absolutely."

As Carlo left the room, the professor sat down to check his emails one more time before leaving to teach his class. He reacted with shock to one of the items in his inbox.

Clarkson punched the speaker button on his desk phone, tapped out a few numbers, and said, "Felly, can you come in here just a minute, please?"

"Of course, sir. Be right there."

Seconds later, Felicia entered Clarkson's office with eyebrows raised in question.

Clarkson answered her silent query with, "I've just received an email from David's mother!"

"In China?"

Win nodded. "I want to tell Shepard Krausse about this, and his man just left. Pop out into the hallway and see if you can catch him, won't you?"

"You betcha!" Felicia was out the door almost before she finished speaking. Moments later she returned, looking downcast and shaking her head to indicate that she had not caught up with Carlo.

"Drat!" said Clarkson. "I've got to get to class, and I'd like Shepard to know this right away. It could change things. Would you be so kind as to forward this message to Shepard Krausse, as well as to the campus police? The police may not be interested, but we should keep them informed, nonetheless."

"Of course, sir, I'll do it right away." Felicia smiled reassuringly as Clarkson tapped keys to forward the China email to Felicia's computer.

"There it is, then," said Clarkson. "It's in your hands. Thank you for saving me this time; I can't be late to another class this semester. I'm setting a very bad example."

They both smiled at his inside joke. Professor Clarkson had a reputation for extreme punctuality.

Clarkson closed his office and proceeded to his class, secure in the knowledge that his teaching assistant would faithfully carry out his request. Shepard Krausse would soon have valuable news from China, which could affect the search for David Zhang.

♦

In Minokee, at that moment, Miranda was standing on a dining room chair, to reach a ceiling fan with her broom. Her front screen door clattered with three quick knocks. She glanced at the screen door, and the sight of her visitors nearly knocked her off her precarious perch.

"Dad! Mother! I didn't kn—!" She paused and forced her

facial muscles to change from astonished grimace to welcoming smile. "What a surprise!"

Miranda did not know exactly how long she stood frozen on the dining room chair, clutching her broom exactly as the old farmer holds his pitchfork in the painting, "American Gothic."

It must have seemed too long to her mother, whose tone was starkly critical when she said, "We would like to come in out of this heat, if it isn't too much trouble."

"Oh!" Miranda leaped from the chair, almost making it all the way from the dining area to the front door in a single bound. She still gripped the broom in one hand when she opened the door. "Sorry. Come in, of course. What a surprise."

"Yes, so you said." Rosario surveyed the room as she entered. Her lips drew downward at the corners.

Zeke squeezed through the door with arms full of luggage, and he leaned down to plant a kiss on Miranda's cheek. "You look lovely, Muffin."

"Ezekiel, put your glasses on. She looks like a scullery maid," Rosario turned to glare at Miranda, "and a poor one, at that."

Zeke ignored his wife. His smile never faltered, and his eyes never left Miranda's. "Where should I put the bags, sweetie?"

"In my room, I guess. I'll show you." She turned to lead her father out of the living room. "I, ah, I don't actually have a 'guest room' *per se*."

"*Quelle surprise*," mumbled Rosario.

Luggage dropped onto the bedroom's old wooden floor, reverberating through the cottage and rattling all the windows. Rosario started and put one hand to her throat.

Miranda was talking to her father as they returned, without her broom, to the living room. "You and Mother can have my room, and I'll sleep on the couch."

Her father said, "Okay," at the same time her mother declared, "Unacceptable!"

Miranda's beauty-pageant smile remained exactly the same size and shape as before, facial muscles thoroughly trained in how to conduct themselves around the matriarch.

"Well," said Miranda, 'why don't you have a seat on the couch while I get you something to drink, and then we can discuss an alternative plan you'll be more comfortable with. I have sweet tea, and I can make coffee or lemonade in a flash, or, of course, there's always ice water. What can I get you?"

"I'll have sweet tea," Zeke said, and sat on the couch.

Miranda's mother said, "We'll both have *un*sweetened tea or, if you don't have that, just water. If it's bottled water. I wouldn't trust the tap water in the middle of this swamp."

Rosario turned toward the couch but froze. "There is some kind of fur on this sofa, Miranda. I hope you haven't acquired an animal!"

"It's only cat hair, and it's from a very clean, healthy cat. It won't hurt you. You arrived before I was finished cleaning. Sorry."

"Does the beast sleep on your bed?" Rosario said, adding a wrinkled nose to her rainbow-shaped lips.

"It isn't my cat, actually."

"Clearly, this animal was in your house, on your sofa. And, I see what looks like a bowl of water on the floor near the back door. Yet you claim it doesn't belong to you?"

Miranda sighed, but kept the smile intact. "My goodness, Mother. You should've been a trial lawyer instead of a mathematician! Such expert interrogation techniques. Trust me, the cat does not belong to me. It lives next door and sometimes visits me."

Ezekiel Ogilvy spoke quietly, but his tone was amazingly commanding for a man who seemed so mild-mannered. "Rosario, be seated, please."

Rosario sat down beside her husband on the couch, still prune-faced with disapproval, not saying anything.

"I'll have the sweet tea, Muffin, and your mother will have water. If she insists, she can boil it herself to remove any swampy microbes."

Rosario crossed her arms across her chest and leaned back

into the sofa cushions, but she said nothing.

"Coming right up," said the smiling Miranda, and she disappeared into the kitchen.

When Miranda was out of sight, Rosario whispered to her husband, "I will not sleep in Phyllis's old mildew-farm of a house. I will not."

"Fine. I'll take you to a hotel. And Rose, keep your criticism of Miranda's home to yourself. You wouldn't be that rude to a stranger, and I expect you to treat our daughter with good manners, at least, even if you can't treat her with affection."

"Thank you," his wife snapped, and then she was wise enough to remain quiet.

Just then, Miranda's back door swung open to the sound of a man's deep voice calling, "Castor Bean?" The half-naked muscle man from the driveway carwash stood glistening on the doorstep.

"In the kitchen. Come on in."

"Not now, thanks. I'm dripping a trail of soapy water everywhere I go. Just wanted to let you know, your car's done."

"Thank you very much! I know it's beautiful," Miranda said.

"No problem. Listen, can you come to the door for a second?"

"Sure. Let me take these drinks to my parents, and I'll be right out." Miranda carried glasses of tea and ice water to the other room and handed them to her parents. "Excuse me for just a minute. There's someone at the back door."

She left them and went to the door, stepped outside, and closed the door behind her. The back door was at the opposite end of the dining area from the living room, and anyone sitting on the sofa could see that door, and Miranda's visitor, quite clearly.

Rosario *hmpfed* and whispered, "It's a mistake to allow the help to take such liberties. He didn't even knock before he opened her door!"

"It's not our business, Rose." Zeke sipped his iced tea and groaned in appreciation. "Ohhh, that's good. Hits the spot."

"You'll gain weight with all the sugar, and you probably won't sleep tonight, because tea is full of caffeine."

"I'll manage," Zeke said.

# Chapter 9 - The Parents, Part 2

In the tiny university office shared by two T.A.'s, Felicia Harper sat alone and typed an email message to Shepard Krausse.

She did not forward the email Professor Clarkson had received from David's mother in China. Instead, she summarized the message in her own words.

She did not send a copy to the campus police.

Without wasting a syllable, Felicia told Shep only what he needed to know.

When she was happy with her composition, she tapped the Send button and watched the message zap out into the ether. Felicia smiled. All was right with her world.

♦

Miranda emerged from her house and closed the kitchen door behind her. She yipped when a pair of strong arms lifted her off the top step, onto the grass, and gathered her against a water-soaked wall of man. She began to laugh, but he cut her off with a kiss, and then another.

Finally, he relaxed his hold, and Miranda stepped back, swiping excess liquid from the front of her clothing. She grinned at Shepard. "You're a louse," she teased. "A very wet louse."

"The better to slosh you with, my dear," he growled.

"I guess you saw my parents are here."

"Yeah, I spoke to them in the driveway. Nice folks."

"Well, Daddy is. Mother has a good heart, I think."

"They raised *you*, Bean, and that makes 'em perfect in my book. Why don't I treat all four of us to dinner in Live Oak tonight? I'll bet you don't have a ton of groceries in your house, and Carlo has the evening off, so cooking at home is out. We can bring back a doggie bag for the kitten."

She wrapped her arms around him and, wet or not, hugged him tightly. "You're just the sweetest man ever."

"That's too bad. I was going for 'heroic.' But if you like 'sweet,' that's what I'll try to be."

She backed up a step and looked into his mirrored sunglasses. "You don't *have* to try, Shepard Krausse. That's why I love you so much."

He kissed her again, but she pushed against his chest, telling him time was up.

"Go home and get dry and dressed," she said, turning him around to face his house. "When you come back, we'll decide where to go for dinner."

"Yes, ma'am," he said, and began walking toward the hedge that divided their properties. He had gone only a few steps when the kitten came flying around the corner of the house and bounded along in Shepard's footsteps.

♦

One of Carlo's errands that afternoon had been to search the two-bedroom student apartment assigned to David Zhang. In the short time since David's disappearance, his possessions had been shoved aside or packed haphazardly into boxes. The room had not been assigned to a new student.

The apartment door was locked, but that was no barrier to someone with Carlo's talents. Likewise, he had no problem at all getting into David's private bedroom and bath.

Once inside, Carlo searched the room, evaluating every dust bunny, shoe print, unsealed box, and even the trails that had been left by furniture or boxes dragged across the floor. A glance in the dresser drawers revealed no clothing, but Carlo found some in a nearby box. In boxes, he found books, bed and bath linens from David's bed, toiletries and *objet d'art* — all of them supposedly David's.

Carlo found neither cellphone nor computer. The mini-fridge held only a few coin-sized bits of lettuce. In one box he found framed, family pictures and personal keepsakes. He thought those things might have been displayed on David's dresser, back before David's "normal life" had become not-normal, and maybe even not-life.

Interpreting the evidence that strangers had entered the room and rearranged its contents, Carlo did not believe this room had been organized by a fastidious young man like David Zhang as he prepared himself for travel. No, even in a great hurry, David would have evacuated that room in an orderly way.

From the condition of David's room, Carlo was convinced the room had been pillaged, and quickly — in case the university would send someone to clear and clean the empty room.

With a hunch, growing stronger every moment, Carlo left David's room and crossed the common living area to a second bedroom, where the roommate resided. Carlo knocked on the door.

Inside, a muffled voice said, "What the heck!"

Carlo knocked again, harder.

"Hold yer horses!" the gruff voice shouted. Drawers slammed, closet doors creaked to a close, and something heavy scraped across the floor to a thumping stop.

Finally, footsteps vibrated the floorboards, the doorknob turned with a metallic scrape, and a man in jeans and a college tee-shirt peered out a narrow opening between door and doorframe.

"Who are you, how'd you get in here, and what do you want?" the man demanded in a voice like a chainsaw.

His visitor was not intimidated. Even an actual chainsaw would not have deterred Carlo Fratelli. Carlo could have done things with a chainsaw that the self-important pup behind the door could not even imagine.

"My name is Carlo. I want to know more about David Zhang. How I got in here is none of your business."

"This ain't Zhang's room, and you ain't no cop with a warrant, so, you got no business knockin' at my door."

The deluded young man thought he would simply close the door and the matter would be ended. The man was way too slow — mentally and physically. His door hit a solid barrier and bounced back, nearly smashing his nose.

The barrier, Carlo's husky right arm, moved into the room, forcing the door and the roommate out of Carlo's path.

"Dude, I do not care who or what you have in here, okay. I am not here about you. I am here to find out what happened to *Signor* David Zhang."

"The guy across the hall?"

"You do not remember your roommate's name?"

"I know he had one of those Chink names; they all sound alike."

Carlo scoffed and looked away from the man, surveying the ill-kept room instead. "When was the last time you saw David, personally?"

"I dunno, man. Him and his Chink friends was coming in and out of here all the time. I mostly didn't know which was which."

Carlo paced the periphery, cataloging every detail of the habitat. Here, he picked up a knick-knack to examine and replace. There, he lifted a dirty shirt to inventory all that was lying beneath it on the unmade bed.

Carlo fingered through the books on the shelf, peeked into the bathroom to note the toiletries and linens, tapped some keys on the laptop computer he found on a chair. Finally, he returned to the entryway and stood facing the man with the chainsaw voice.

The man rasped, "Are you done? 'Cause if you don't get out of here right now Ima call the campus police."

"I think that is an excellent idea," said Carlo. "And, you can explain to them how some of David Zhang's possessions ended up in your room, and some of your old junk ended up in David's room, in boxes."

"You're nuts. I ain't got nothin' of his."

"I think you do. I recognize several things a meticulous man with Asian proclivities would have in his room. Honestly, *signor,* I cannot imagine someone of your ... breeding and ... taste … owning these items."

"Yeah, well, he gave me that stuff, since he was, y'know, leavin' and all."

"Ah," said Carlo. "Funny. I did not realize you and David were that friendly."

"We got along."

"You and David were so close he would give you his expensive personal possessions, and yet you could not remember his name or tell his face from the faces of his friends?" Carlo linked eyes with the roommate and simply waited.

A palm branch swished across the room's window, driven by the breeze outside. Behind the wall, an air conditioning unit ka-thumped into life and began its mechanical rumbling.

The weight of Carlo's stare had crushed men much smarter and stronger than David Zhang's amoral roommate. The young man dropped his gaze and broke the silence.

"Yeah, well, I'll look around real good, and if I have anything of his, I'll put it back."

"That will be much appreciated, ah ... what is your name?"

“Maynard.” The word forced its way out from behind clinched teeth.

“That will be much appreciated, *Signor* Maynard,” Carlo said with a hint of a smile. "I shall return to see how you are doing. Perhaps you will need my help."

The young man edged away, shaking his head in the negative.

Carlo continued. "Until then, if you do happen to hear from David Zhang, please let Professor Clarkson know immediately. You know how to reach Professor Clarkson, no?"

"Sure," said Maynard, switching from head-wagging to head-nodding.

"*Grazie*," said Carlo, and he managed to leave the apartment without slamming a single door.

♦

Miranda returned to her living room and sat down in the easy chair nearest the couch. She told her parents, "My fiancé wants to take us all out to dinner."

Rosario, predictably, sounded off. "I hope you're not taking us to some fish-camp shack with a bait store at one end and a short order cook at the other. Even forgetting hygiene, those places *fry* everything, and you don't want to know what kind of fat they use in their deep fry—"

Zeke cut her off with, "That sounds wonderful. So, it's true then? There really is a fiancé?"

Miranda chuckled. "I thought you knew there was. Isn't that the reason for this surprise vis— *totally welcome* surprise visit?"

"I had to hear it from the young man's mother, instead of from my own, my *only,* daughter. Humiliating."

"Mother, we haven't specifically slighted *you.* We haven't told *anyone.* Only a few close neighbors know I accepted his proposal. We haven't picked a date, or bought an engagement ring, or anything. We would've told you when we felt we actually had something definite to announce."

"Well, *his* mother knew! Thank heaven she had the courtesy to contact me ... us."

Zeke laid a gentle hand on his wife's knee, and she stopped talking. She sent him a poutish look.

"What your mother means is, we can't wait to meet him," said Zeke.

"Oh, you met him!" Miranda said. "Outside, before you came to the door."

Rosario could not restrain herself. "Th— tha— that half-naked, lo— long-haired *laborer,* who was washing your car?"

"Rose—"

"Mother—"

"You can't possibly plan to marry that, that *handyman*! He opened the door just now without even knocking! Oh, no! You haven't given him a key, have you?"

"We don't lock our doors in Minokee. Usually."

"Rose, calm down."

"My heavens, does he even have a job? Zeke, didn't his mother say he had some sort of disability? What was it? He's deaf or something! Can he even support a family? Oh, Great Scott, a family! You're not pregnant!"

"Rose. That's enough."

"Mother, Shepard is not deaf. He is blind, but you can scarcely call him disabled. In fact, he's able to do some things I wish he wouldn't — like climb a streetlamp and change the bulb. He used to be a radio talk show host—"

"*Used to be*? So, he's unemployed!"

"No, Mother. The only person who can fire Shep is Shep. He owns five FM radio stations in four states. He has an undergraduate degree from U.F. and a law degree from an Ivy League university; he just doesn't want to practice law right now."

Miranda's words seemed to have a calming effect upon her mother. Or perhaps her mother remained still because of Zeke's restraining grasp on his wife's knee.

Miranda continued, "I don't know exactly how rich he is, but his family donates buildings to universities and new wings to hospitals. I'm surprised his mother didn't tell you all of this."

"I talked to some assistant, a woman. We were scheduled to meet Mrs. Krausse by Skype in a day or two," said Rosario.

"Shepard's very generous in his own right, as well," said Miranda. "You didn't think I could afford that car outside on a librarian's salary, did you?"

"Nice car," Zeke said. "Sounds like a great guy, Muffin. I trust your judgment."

Rosario's eyebrows rose half an inch. Her eyes showed white all the way around the iris, and her lips opened and closed like a guppy's.

Before her mother could overcome the shock of her father's *approving* Shepard as a future son-in-law, Miranda uttered a quick, "I'd better go shower and dress. Make yourselves at home." And she left the room to prepare for what promised to be a memorable (if not horrible) evening.

♦

Shep entered his house through the back door and went directly down the hall to the second bedroom. He knocked on the closed bedroom door, and someone inside the room cursed sleepily in Italian.

"I'm sorry," Shep told the door. "I realize you got up early and drove all the way to Gainesville and back this morning. And, I know you have the evening off. But I need your help."

"Go away!" came from within the room.

"I need your help getting dressed to go to dinner."

"You can dress yourself, Tarzan. You been doing it for years."

"No, Carlo, I really have to look perfect for this dinner. It's important that I make a good impression."

A tousled Carlo, in pajama pants, opened the door and leaned against the doorjamb. "When do you ever make a bad impression? I would pay to see that. And, what make this dinner more important than Carlo's evening off?"

"It's 'Meet the Parents.' Why are you sleeping at three in the afternoon?

"I have big date for dancing, later tonight, so I build up my strength. *Signorina* Ogilvy's parents must really want to meet you. Madam only telephone them on Thursday, and by Saturday they arrive."

"'Madam telephone them,'" Shep repeated, imitating Carlo's accent. "That explains a lot. Will you help me? … Please? … I'll give you an extra day off."

Then Shep fisted his hands against his waist (in the Mister Clean pose) and scolded, "I won't forget you didn't tell me about that call, by the way. A little heads-up would've been nice. You make a terrible spy."

The kitten stepped from behind Shepard's shoes and looked up at Shep with a loud, *"Meeohrau!"*

Carlo said, "*Grazie*," to the cat. To Shepard he said, "I'm glad *some*body appreciates me around here."

The Italian man gave up his leaning post and straightened his shoulders, ready for action. "You get a shower. I'll prepare your clothes."

Shep surprised Carlo with a rib-crunching bear hug. *"Grazie! Grazie! Mille grazie!"*

"You welcome." Carlo pushed out of the hug. He picked up the kitten and massaged its ears. "Come to the kitchen, my supportive friend. You deserve treats."

"*Mmrrrrrh*," agreed the feline.

Shep turned away and took a step, then he swung back toward Carlo. "Hey, I'll give you a hundred dollars to wash that gray car at the foot of Miranda's driveway."

"Two hundred. It is the important 'Meet the Parents' carwash."

"Okay, two hundred."

"You want wax and carpet-shampoo, three hundred."

"Okay, three hundred."

Carlo began laughing as he carried his fur ball toward the kitchen.

"What's so funny?" asked Shep.

"You so nervous about these people, you forget who you talking to, Einstein. Carlo would do this for nothing! Not for you, of course, but for the *signorina*."

"Oh. Well, then—"

"Three hundred. You already agreed." Carlo laughed all the way down the hall.

Shep shrugged and headed toward the bathroom for his shower. "I would've paid three thousand," he murmured.

♦

Later, while Shepard tied his silk Armani tie, Carlo briefed him on the errands Carlo had run earlier in the day: his status conference with Win Clarkson, the search of David's room, and the encounter with David's xenophobic, sticky-fingered roommate.

"David has not shown up for a class since Wednesday morning. I can find no one who has seen him since last Saturday. *Dottor* Clarkson is worried."

Carlo continued, "The police took an official Missing Person report, but nobody is really doing anything about it. University administration is convinced David went back to China, like other students have done before."

"But you don't think so," Shep said.

Carlo handed Shep a pair of socks, and Shep sat down on the bed to put them on.

The kitten, who was busy cleaning himself on the same bed, looked up and uttered a "*K-k-k-k-k*" warning, in case some human was thinking of asking His Feline Majesty to relocate.

"No, I do not think *Signor* David went home to China," said Carlo. "I sat by him during lunch last Saturday, and we talked. This young man had plans to succeed in a big way, including finishing his Ph.D. at U.F. This was not a kid planning to drop out and run home to Mama."

Shep stepped over to the laptop computer on his dresser. "Let me see if there's any news since you met with Clarkson this morning."

When he opened the laptop, an electronic female voice said, "Good afternoon, Shepard. How can I help you?"

"Read me any messages or emails received from Gainesville, Florida, today."

Seconds later, the electronic voice read aloud an email from

Felicia Harper. In it, Felicia said she was writing on Professor Clarkson's behalf, to summarize an email he received from China.

According to Felicia, David's mother apologized for his leaving Gainesville in such a hurry, he had not stopped to notify anyone.

She said, last Sunday, the Institute of Archaeology of the Chinese Academy of Social Sciences invited David to join a three-month dig, exploring 113 newly-discovered 2000-year-old tombs, near the ancient city of Fudi.

David's mother told them that, unfortunately, David had to be in North China's Hebei province within three days. He barely had time to get to the nearest airport, and after that he was traveling non-stop. The minute he arrived in China, the Institute whisked him off to a remote dig site.

Felicia reported, since David was unable to send email from the site, his mother sent his thanks-for-everything to Professor Clarkson. She also relayed David's promise never to forget his time at the University of Florida.

The message ended. Shep closed his laptop and returned to sit again on the bed.

He finished putting on his socks and reached for the gleaming, Milan-made, Romano Martegani shoes Carlo had plunked down at his feet.

Carlo blew an emphatic puff of air. "We are supposed to believe that this Asian over-achiever works to develop personal, academic, and professional relationships at the University of Florida, and then he run away without a word to anybody? And, why does he do this strange thing? He suddenly wants to be a summer intern, in the middle of nowhere, with a school we never heard of!"

"Yeah," said Shepard. "That kind of behavior would not only be rude, it would be shortsighted, wasteful, and self-defeating. I, for one, do not believe David Zhang is any of those things."

"It would be a dumb thing to do," Carlo added. "And, I do not believe David Zhang is dumb."

"Where do you think he is?"

"Not in China. Nobody called David Zhang traveled out of any airport around here since last Saturday. Our people checked."

"What do you want to do?" Shep asked.

"Call some people, drop your name, find out what really happened."

Shep stood. "Find out what you can — just don't charge me extra for your 'investigative services.' I can barely afford the occasional carwash."

♦

Since the Ogilvys would not be returning to Minokee after dinner, the party of four drove to Live Oak in two cars.

Zeke suggested a men's car (in which he would drive himself and the groom) and a women's car (piloted by the bride, with her mother by her side).

"By her side" does not necessarily mean "on her side," as all brides and mothers know.

Shep was happier about the gender-segregated car trip than Miranda was, but she rolled with the punches.

## Chapter 10 - The Parents, Part 3

*Saturday evening — Dinner in Live Oak*

Conversation in the men's car flowed pleasantly. Zeke began by complimenting Shepard for "looking so dapper this evening."

When Shepard thanked him, Zeke continued, "If you'll indulge an old man, I've always wondered: Is it difficult to attend to your wardrobe when you can't see colors and patterns and such?"

Shepard chuckled. "Some days don't work out quite so well, I admit. I have been known to wear mis-matched outfits, or different colored socks, and such as that, but it rarely happens because Pietr— I mean, Carlo lays out my clothes. He helps me spiff up for special occasions, with a tie and all. Bless him, he was a big help tonight, even though it was his evening off."

"Tell him he did a good job. You look like a million bucks."

"That's exactly the image I wanted to create," said Shep. "Two million bucks would be even better. I am trying to impress my future in-laws."

Zeke gave a short laugh. "Well, future son-in-law, you had me at 'hello,' but I'm only half the battle. You realize Miranda's mother will be a harder sell."

"No problem. I thought about shaving my beard, y'know, thinking mothers generally like clean-cut all-American types."

Zeke looked away from the road ahead long enough for a glimpse of his passenger. "But you decided to keep it."

"Yeah. Carlo and the cat thought a sudden shave would look like I was trying too hard."

"Well, I'm a college professor," said Zeke, "and like most men in my line of work, I appreciate a fine beard. Never let anyone intimidate you into shaving it, if you don't want to."

"Thanks. I'll remember that. But I'll have to be careful not to spill food in it at the table tonight."

"Good thinking," Zeke agreed. "So, 'Carlo and the cat' are your housemates, I gather?"

"The cat is just a cat. Carlo is my roommate and good friend; he's like a brother. He would die for me. … He's not a criminal, but, in all honesty, I should probably tell you. Confidentially, of course …"

"You don't have to tell me anything unless you want to," said Zeke. "If you do decide to share something with me in confidence, however, I can promise you it will never leave this car."

"Thanks," Shep said. "The thing is, it's … remotely … possible that Carlo executed the monster who murdered Carlo's twin brother along with my— along with Dave."

"Good lord, his twin brother! That must have been horrible for Carlo."

"It was beyond horrible — for Carlo and for me. Pietro was my roommate, cook, chauffeur, and counselor, as well as an incredible friend."

Shep inhaled deeply and exhaled slowly. He went on, "Carlo not only punished the murderer, he also forgave *me* for my part in causing the whole tragedy."

Zeke said nothing. He kept his eyes on the road ahead and simply waited until his passenger was able to say more.

After a quiet moment, Shep said, "And, then he stepped in and took his brother's place as the most important person in my life … except for your beautiful daughter, of course."

"Of course," said Zeke. "Dave was your guide dog, Miranda told us. Sounds like he was truly extraordinary."

Shep paused, produced a handkerchief from his pocket, and

wiped his eyes. Then he sniffed and brushed the handkerchief across his nostrils.

"That's true," he said, his voice softer than before. "Dave and I had a unique relationship for seven beautiful years. There could never be another dog like him."

"Is that why you've adopted a cat?"

Shep smiled, and energy returned to his voice. "No, no, no! I'm on probation until the cat decides whether *he* is going to adopt *me*."

Zeke took one hand off the wheel and used it to brush cat hairs off the thigh of his slacks. "I've noticed the cat spends time at my daughter's house. You do the same, I suspect."

"Yes, sir, I do," Shep answered. "But, no sleepovers, Doctor O. I want you to know we've agreed to wait until marriage, as old-fashioned as that sounds."

"Good," said Zeke with a smile. "I like the old fashions."

♦

In the women's car, Rosario was explaining the facts of life while Miranda drove.

"He certainly is good-looking," Miranda's mother was saying. "Of course, men who look like that are accustomed to women falling all over them everywhere they go. It seems only natural to them. One can hardly blame them when they develop a 'roving eye,' so to speak. No pun intended in this case."

Miranda chuckled. "Don't worry, we're not sensitive to blindness jokes around here. In fact, Shepard told me I would never have to worry about him *looking* at other women." She let out a half-second of laughter.

Rosario was not laughing.

"Yes," she said, in a tone that clearly expressed Rosario's doubt about the reliability of Shepard's assurances. She closed her eyes for a solemn second, as if in mourning for her pitifully doomed and deluded daughter.

"It's only a fact of life, Miranda," her mother advised. "You're a wonderful person, dear, but girls who look like you do not marry men who look like Shepard Krausse. It is inevitable that he will stray, perhaps repeatedly."

Miranda's knuckles turned white as her grip tightened on the steering wheel, but her voice vibrated with the quiet authority and absolute courtesy of the professional librarian.

"I appreciate your concern, Mother. But you don't know Shepard well, yet. Why don't we postpone this particular discussion until you have spent time with him and me. You and I can talk about this again when you know him better."

After a pause, Rosario said, "I believe you are right. Neither of us is prepared to have this conversation at the moment."

Miranda drove on, enjoying what she believed to be a friendly silence. In fact, Rosario was merely preparing her next salvo.

All too soon, Rosario blurted, "And, what about the children?"

"Children?"

"Yes. You know, the small people who result from marital relations: Kids. Offspring. Heirs."

"I know what 'children' are. I do *not* know why you are talking about people who don't exist."

"Hopefully, they will exist *someday*," Rosario countered, "unless you plan to deprive me of grandchildren, as a punishment for your … unsatisfying … childhood."

"I would never deprive you of anything, Mother. Tell me what you want to know about these hypothetical children."

"You must realize there is an excellent possibility your children will be disabled, like their father."

Even the experienced, professional librarian required several deep, calming breaths before responding this time.

"Oh, yes," Miranda said evenly. "Only perfect children would merit the esteem of Dr. Rosario Ogilvy. But that's okay, actually. They won't miss out. Because I can assure you, Mother: whatever abilities or disabilities our future child may have, that child will be loved unconditionally by Shepard and, most definitely, by me."

Rosario drew breath to respond, but Miranda continued before her mother could expound.

She told her mother, "I realize this philosophy of unconditional love may not fit into your system of parenting, but perhaps your grandchildren will find something at which to excel and thereby earn their grandmother's affection."

Again Rosario inhaled, but Miranda preempted her, saying, "In my view, Mother, my children would be blessed indeed if they were exactly like their father, in every way."

After that, no one spoke for the remainder of the drive to Live Oak. Miranda, no doubt, appreciated the respite, but she no longer assumed the silence was friendly.

◆

An hour later at the restaurant, when the two couples were being seated with great pomp and *savoir faire* by the *maître d'* and two tuxedoed servers, Miranda leaned close to Shepard's ear and whispered, "How in the world did you get a table *here* on such short notice? Annabelle told me this place has a three-week waiting list!"

Shep turned his head casually and took advantage of her nearness to drop a quick kiss on her forehead. "And, what have I told you in the past about Annabelle?" he whispered.

Miranda had to think a moment to recall Shep's advice to her, several months before, when her library co-worker, Annabelle Sherwood, told Miranda that Shep and Pietro were gay.

She lowered her voice to match his whisper. "I asked you if I should believe Annabelle."

"And I said?"

"You said, 'Almost never.'"

"Exactly," whispered Shep. "And that is still the best advice I have to offer where Miss Annabelle is concerned."

"I must say," Rosario commented from behind her menu, on the other side of their elegantly appointed, linen-draped table. "I did not expect an establishment of this caliber in such a small town."

Miranda responded, "Quality, not quantity, Mother."

Zeke lowered his menu and winked at Miranda. "I suspect our man, Shepard, is accustomed to the best life has to offer."

"That's just what I've been telling Miranda in the car," Rosario added, still not looking at any of them. She studied her menu devotedly as she commented further, "You remember what I said, Miranda, dear."

Miranda lifted her shield-menu and did not agree to remember anything.

The five-tone theme from Steven Spielberg's "Close Encounters of the Third Kind" suddenly played nearby. The eerie tune resounded like a trumpet fanfare amid the subdued sounds in the carpeted-and-upholstered dining room.

"Oh, sorry! That's me." Shepard whipped a cellphone from his pocket.

The music continued to play, now overlaid by a computerized female voice announcing, "Rocket Man is calling."

"Excuse me," Shep said to his tablemates. Into the phone he said, "Hey, Roland, what's up?"

Miranda could barely hear the caller's voice. She peeked over her menu at her parents, across the table. They continued studying the entrees, apparently ignoring the phone conversation.

Miranda sank behind her menu with a sigh of relief.

Rocket Man was saying to Shepard, "Been watching that Maynard guy, per your orders, Chief. I'm reporting the latest development: he had a visitor. A woman. And she came to the back door of the building, like she didn't want to be seen. I got some good shots of her, though. Nobody gets past old Rocket."

Shep smiled. "They sure don't. I can't wait to see the pictures."

"Um … yeah," said Rocket, sounding uncertain. "No offense, Chief, but … how're you gonna ... um … *see* 'em, exactly?"

"No offense taken," Shep said. "That's what Carlo is for. Can you text the pictures to his phone, please? Then he and I can discuss it when I get home tonight."

♦

Midway through the meal, a stately, ebony-skinned, white-coated lady emerged from the restaurant kitchen and approached Shepard's chair. She tapped him lightly on the shoulder, and, when he turned in her direction, she spoke respectfully to him in fluent French.

Miranda had spent years, in Miami's traffic gridlock, listening to foreign language courses in her car. She understood the French woman's conversation well enough to be surprised.

Soon, Shep switched to English and introduced his tablemates to the woman. She was the restaurant's chef, and her name was familiar to Miranda and to Rosario, from the chef's appearances on national television.

While Miranda and her mother sat open-mouthed in shock, the famous chef gracefully acknowledged the introductions and said she hoped the meal would be "satisfactory."

"If it isn't absolutely spectacular, you're fired," Shep quipped with a smile.

"Oh, dear. Not again," the woman responded, in her charmingly accented English, without a hint of concern.

The chef returned to the kitchen. Shep returned to his meal, and Zeke followed Shep's example.

Miranda and Rosario closed their mouths, though their eyes remained wide with amazement.

"Do you know who that was?" Rosario said, looking from Shep to the kitchen door now swinging closed.

Without breaking the rhythm of his eating, Shep said calmly, "Of course I know who she is. My signature is on her paychecks."

"Young man, are you trying to tell me that you own this restaurant?" Rosario's eyes narrowed in suspicion and doubt.

"That's how you got this table on such short notice!" Miranda slapped Shep playfully on the back of his head. "You sneak!"

"Hey, watch it, lady! It'll be *your* fault if I dip my beard in the marinara sauce."

Rosario still was not convinced. "You really own this establishment? A gourmet, five-star dining venue that belongs in New York or Paris? Why have you hidden it here in this obscure, one-horse town?"

Shep put down his fork, blotted his mouth (and his beard, just in case) with his damask napkin, and smiled toward Rosario's voice.

"To answer your three-part question, first item: yes," he said. "I own this establishment. If you need documentation, let me draw your attention to the occupational license posted in the foyer, with my name on the 'proprietor' line.

"Second item: My restaurant belongs in the place where I customarily go to eat. I live in Minokee. The nearest town with appropriate infrastructure is Live Oak. *Ergo*, my restaurant must be in Live Oak.

"Third item: I haven't personally counted the number of horses residing in and around Live Oak, but there are many. If you like, I can have the exact figures emailed to you by the end of business tomorrow."

Still smiling, he waited for Rosario's response.

"Oh," was all she said. Her plate suddenly fascinated her, and her silverware clinked against fine porcelain when she resumed eating.

Shep continued his meal.

Miranda touched his hand. "That was really sweet, what she said about Dave. I guess everybody knew him, didn't they."

Rosario could not resist. "Of what are you speaking, Miranda?"

"I was talking about the chef expressing the entire staff's condolences for Dave's passing."

"When did she say that? I didn't hear anything like that," said Rosario.

Shep moved his hand from beneath Miranda's fingers, until

his palm rested on the back of her hand, and his fingers closed around hers. She understood the gesture and remained silent while he chewed and swallowed the food in his mouth.

Then Shepard addressed Dr. Rosario Ogilvy in a respectful but firm manner. "The conversation — an extremely personal conversation, incidentally — was in French. Miranda overheard because she is sitting so close to me, and she understood because Miranda's French is excellent."

Rosario speared Miranda with a look. "You speak French? When were you ever in France, may I ask?"

"Never," Miranda said quietly.

"I'm going to remedy that," Shepard inserted. "Your daughter is familiar with several languages, Doctor. If I had not met you, I might have been surprised you didn't know. But I have met you. I've learned that Miranda's *many accomplishments* are not foremost in your mind. However, you seem willing to catalog perceived *failures* at the drop of a hat."

"How dare you—" Rosario began.

Zeke, still calmly eating, cut her off with, "Let the man finish, Rose."

"Yes, please," said Shep. "I do not criticize you, Doctor. In my experience, this is the way of mothers — and rightly so. A mother, above all others, is charged with transforming a child into the best possible adult.

"For this purpose, mothers have an organ no other humans have. This organ secretes a hormone compelling mothers to identify (and point out to the child) any need for improvement, in every situation, at every opportunity.

"It's called the Betterment Gland. I know my mother has it — though I am perhaps not the best example of its product. *You* certainly have it. And, it's wonderful."

He raised Miranda's hand to his lips and kissed it before continuing, "Unlike me, your daughter is the best possible example of how a mother's Betterment Gland can produce a kind, lovely, intelligent, strong adult.

"You built this paragon, who has stolen my heart and brought me immeasurable joy. You and your well-developed Betterment Gland — and a little help from Miranda's father, no doubt."

"Hm. No doubt," Zeke commented.

"Doctor Ogilvy and Doctor Ogilvy," Shepard said, holding up Miranda's hand as if she had won a championship bout. "Please allow me to thank you, from the deepest part of my soul, for raising the most beautiful librarian on the entire planet. Probably in the entire solar system."

"Don't forget the entire universe," Miranda joked.

"And, she's humble, too," Shep finished. He released her hand to place his arm around her shoulders and pull her in for a quick hug.

Rosario seemed paralyzed. She sat ramrod straight and looked from Shep to Miranda and back again, moving only her eyes.

"You're welcome," said Zeke, around a mouthful of potato.

"Great!" Shep said. "Now, that's settled, who wants dessert?"

Far from the restaurant, Shepard's friend, Roland, the "Rocket Man," followed directions with military precision and speed. Within minutes of disconnecting the call to Shepard's cellphone, Rocket was texting photographs to Carlo.

Responding to the notification tone from his cellphone, Carlo popped his phone from his back pocket and scrolled through the photos from Rocket Man. He scrolled through them a second time and paused for a moment of reflection. He texted Rocket the message, "GOOD JOB. FORGET MAYNARD, FOLLOW THE WOMAN."

"ON IT," was Rocket's reply.

Carlo scrolled through the photos a third time, slowly, before shutting down the phone and replacing it in his pocket.

At the restaurant in Live Oak, the Krausse-Ogilvy party was finishing their dessert.

"Let me get the bill tonight, won't you?" Zeke said. "Sort of an engagement present for the happy couple."

Rosario hmphed. "Aristotle believed no man could be deemed a 'happy' man until he was dead. Let us not be premature."

"Miranda and I don't need to wait that long," said Shepard told her mother, with a smile. To Zeke, he said, "Doctor Ogilvy, thank you very much for your kind offer. The thought is much appreciated. *Happily*, however," he emphasized the word with a nod in Rosario's direction, "there will be no bill."

"But, thank you, Daddy," said Miranda. "You're sweet to offer. Maybe another time."

"Hmph," came from Rosario. "I don't suppose you own an acceptable hotel in this hamlet, young man?"

Shep's voice was melodious and charming — a noticeable contrast with Rosario's strident tones. "I do not, Doctor, but the question is moot. Much better accommodations await you in my mother's home."

"Oh, Shepard …" Miranda breathed. She stopped when Shepard's hand patted her thigh beneath the tabletop, sending a silent *no-worries* message.

"We cannot possibly descend upon your mother without an invitation," said Rosario.

"I am inviting you now."

"And, if she does not wish to have visitors at this time?"

"You'll have your own wing of the house, with your own servants. You and my mother will never have to meet or speak with one another if you don't want to. However, I know she will be delighted to have an opportunity to know you better. "

Shepard raised his right hand with his index finger extended. In seconds the *maître d'* was bending over Shep's shoulder.

"Yes, *Monsieur* Shepard?"

"Martin, have someone call Hanson and tell him I am

bringing overnight guests, Doctor and Doctor Ogilvy. Ask him to advise Madam that she need not wait up, we will be arriving late, but I'm sure she will want to welcome her guests at breakfast in the morning. … Please. Did I say 'please,' Martin? I meant to, I'm sorry."

"It is always implied, sir. We will be happy to make the call immediately. May I take this opportunity to extend best wishes from myself and all the staff on your upcoming nuptials?"

"This is the worst kept secret in the history of secrecy!" Shepard feigned outrage but spoiled it with his grin. "*Merci*, Martin."

"Yes, thank you, Martin," echoed Miranda.

"And, thank the staff for us as well," Shepard said, and added jokingly, "please."

Miranda's mother tried to intervene. "I really don't think—"

"*Fait accompli*, Rose," Zeke interrupted. "I believe you have been out-maneuvered, my dear. Try to enjoy the novelty of it. And, thank you, Shep, for your hospitality."

Shepard graced the table with a satisfied smile, while beneath the tabletop his hand patted a message on Miranda's thigh: *See? Everything is working out fine.*

Miranda's hand squeezed his, sending her message, *I sure hope you're right.*

♦

By mid-morning of the following day, the three parents were getting to know one another over a luscious brunch in a sunny breakfast room of the Montgomery-Krausse mansion.

Getting up to refill his coffee cup from the gleaming copper urn on the sideboard, Professor Ogilvy glanced out the window and saw a man vigorously washing the Ogilvys' car.

"Who is that washing my car? I'm not complaining, mind you, I'm just curious."

Hermione, buttering a croissant, said, "Is he about six feet tall, black hair, tight pants and olive complexion?"

"Yes."

"It's Carlo. Don't worry, he'll do an excellent job. He used to maintain my cars, when he was my chauffeur."

"Carlo." The professor remembered his conversation with Shep in the car. As he returned to his chair and set down his coffee cup, he said, "This is the man whose brother was killed?"

"Yes. But we've taken care of the criminals involved in that matter." Hermione's tone permitted no further discussion of the murder.

"I'm confused," said the professor. "I thought Carlo was *Shepard*'s chauffeur, housemate and, um, caretaker—"

Hermione froze and interrupted him. "Never use that word with regard to my son, Ezekiel. Carlo is Shepard's friend and assistant. Since my son is not ill or infirm, he has no need of a 'caretaker.'"

"I'm so sorry, I do apologize. I chose the wrong word, absolutely. I only meant to ask whether Carlo lives here or in Minokee."

Hermione returned to her breakfast as if nothing dramatic had occurred. "In Minokee, of course."

"Of course," echoed Rosario, with a stern, sideways, drop-the-subject look at Zeke.

"Of course," agreed Zeke, unconsciously lowering his head under his wife's commanding gaze. "I only wondered why, if he lives in Minokee, he would be washing my car here. That's a long drive just to wash a stranger's car."

Hermione smiled and lifted her chin to proclaim, "I assure you, if Shepard asked him to, Carlo would pick up your car and carry it. My son affects many people that way, although he is hardly aware of it."

"Has he affected my daughter 'that way'?" asked Rosario. "She seems obsessed with him to the point that she has nearly become an ... *extrovert*, if you can imagine, as gauche as that is."

"Rose, please," whispered her husband. To Hermione he said,

"Miranda's mother has difficulty seeing the strength hiding beneath my daughter's calm exterior."

"I know she has 'strengths,' Ezekiel. I'm her mother."

"And, a wonderful job of parenting you two have done," Hermione commended them. "When Shepard was hospitalized after the ... incident ... that killed his friend and the animal, I was very favorably impressed with the effectiveness, courage, and loyalty Miss Ogilvy demonstrated. For all her mouse-like demeanor in the past, she became the dragon at the gates when Shepard was recuperating. Even I was forced to do Miss Ogilvy's bidding until my son went home from the hospital."

Rosario put down her fork, although her omelet was only half eaten. "Dragon! Our Miranda? I find that hard to believe. She has always been too shy for her own good. Do you know, she never even had a school picture taken through all her years of education — and, believe me, we paid for *many* years of it."

"To be fair, she did win several scholarships, Rose. And, there's nothing wrong with being shy," Zeke murmured, forking a strawberry out of his fruit compote."

Rosario disagreed. "There is if it becomes pathological. If the person is unable to function in normal society."

Hermione leaned toward Rosario and patted Rosario's hand where it rested on the heavy white tablecloth. "Have no fear, Doctor. Your daughter is more than merely functional. If I didn't believe she would be an asset to Shepard's career, she wouldn't be marrying him. And, I certainly would not be planning the wedding." She sent the Ogilvys her most reassuring smile.

"Well, thank you for that," Rosario accepted the compliment reluctantly. "And, talking of wedding plans, do you not subscribe to the tradition that the bride's family should ... um ...?"

"Pay for the wedding?" said Hermione.

"Yes," said Zeke. "While we deeply appreciate all the trouble you have taken, even telling us the news when our offspring did not, we want to hold up our end of the stick."

Hermione held her empty coffee cup about two feet above

the table. A uniformed maid appeared from nowhere, took the cup and refilled it from the copper urn, delivered the fresh cup to Hermione, and disappeared as quickly as she had come. Not a word was said.

Hermione sipped her coffee and smiled approvingly. To the Ogilvys, she said, "I have no daughters of my own, and Shepard is my only son. This may be the only wedding in which I will ever have a controlling interest. I would appreciate it very much if you would allow me to indulge myself in spoiling our children with the best of everything for their special day."

It was Rosario's turn to reach out and grasp Hermione's free hand in motherly solidarity. "Of course, we would never want to prevent you from taking a major role in planning the wedding ..."

"And financing the spectacle ..." murmured Zeke, unnoticed.

"...You are most generous to want to do so much for our children. We only ask that you allow us to *share* with you the joy of preparing for the ceremony and reception," Rosario finished.

"Don't forget the honeymoon," Zeke said, poking through his fruit bowl for another melon ball. His sarcasm was lost on the avid women.

"Oh, I have that well in hand," Hermione assured him.

"Then we're agreed? We'll plan the wedding together?" asked Rosario.

"My dear, I wouldn't have it any other way," said Shep's mother.

## Chapter 11 - The Disaster

*Tuesday*

Shepard stepped out of his home office around noon on Tuesday and went to the kitchen for a snack. He passed Carlo coming in the back door with bags of groceries.

"Think I got everything on the *list*," Carlo said, hefting multiple cloth bags onto the kitchen table, clunk-thump, clunk-thump, clunk-clunk-thump.

"I didn't make a list," said Shepard, with his head in the refrigerator.

"That is my point. I do not want to hear complaints about the menu around here if you do not take part in the process."

Shepard lifted his head out of the fridge and took a step back, holding a pitcher of iced tea in one hand. "I'm already part of the process: I consume the end product. If you think about it, that makes me the most important part of the process. Its *raison d'etre*, so to speak."

Carlo was busy emptying bags and putting food in the pantry. He lifted an item from one bag, and Shep reacted to the crackling of the package.

"Potato chips? You never buy potato chips!"

"Zeus wanted them."

"Zeus? We're sacrificing to pagan gods, now? Who the heck is Zeus, and why am I buying his potato chips?"

"*Brrrrrp!*" gurgled the kitten, hopping onto Shepard's shoe.

When nobody moved or spoke, the kitten emitted a slightly more strident, "*Brrrrp!*"

"Give him a minute," Carlo said to the cat. "Sometimes he slow on the uptake."

"*Brrrrp!*"

"You're kidding me!" said Shepard.

"*K-k-k-k-k-k-k-k!*" said the cat from back of its throat.

To Carlo, Shep said, "What makes you think you can name my cat 'Zeus'?"

"First, Doctor Doolittle, he does not consider himself 'your' cat. Second, he knows his own name; he does not need a human to give him some cutesy, embarrassing, kitty name."

Shep set the tea pitcher down on the counter beside the sink. He leaned back against the counter's edge and folded his arms. "Okay, he's not technically 'my' cat; I'm still on probation."

"*Brrrrrrp!*"

"Okay, okay. But really, 'Zeus'? You don't think that's a little ... grandiose?"

"*K-k-k-k-k-k-k!*"

"I meant that in a good way," Shep clarified.

"He know his own name, Hercules. I'm just sayin'."

"And, he told you his name is Zeus."

"Now you catching on."

"And, I guess, he told you he likes potato chips."

"*Brrrrrp!*"

"He says 'yes'." Carlo supplied.

Shep gently wiggled his shoe, where Zeus was comfortably perched. "You are, by far, the weirdest feline I have ever met – and the fastest growing one. I think you've tripled your weight in a week!"

"*K-k-k-k-k-k-k-k!*"

"Okay, maybe not tripled. But definitely doubled. You better not overdo it on the potato chips."

Carlo ripped open the crackly package and poured a handful of chips into the food bowl near the back door.

Zeus deftly untied Shepard's sneaker before hopping off the shoe and trotting to the chip bowl.

"Is that because I called you fat?" quipped Shep, bending down to re-tie his shoelace.

Shep's cellphone played "I'm Getting Married in the Morning," letting him know Miranda was calling. He retrieved the phone from a pocket and answered, "Hello, beautiful."

"Are you on your lunch break?" she asked.

"Yeah. What do you need?"

"Can you come over? I'll make you a sandwich. Unless you're too busy."

"Nope. Just feeding Zeus."

"Okay. See you in a minute." She hung up.

Carlo straightened from petting the cat. "She didn't ask who is Zeus?"

"She's upset!" both men said at once.

"I better get over there," said Shep, and he left Carlo and Zeus to finish storing the groceries.

♦

By the time Shepard arrived at the bottom of Miranda's back steps, she was closing the kitchen door behind her and descending toward him.

The delightful aroma that was singularly Miranda's reached Shepard, and a smile spread across his face. Just as Pavlov's dogs were conditioned to salivate when hearing the food bell, Shepard Krausse was conditioned to walk on air when Miranda came near.

His voice vibrated with happiness. "What are you doing home on a Tuesday? Mind you, any reason at all is fine with me. I could stand having lunch with you every day. Just say the word and you never have to go to work again."

"You're sweet, but you know I like my job. No, I took sick leave today."

Shep's tone changed from contented to concerned. "You're

sick! Do you have a fever?" He found her shoulder with one hand and raised the other hand to feel her forehead.

She gently blocked his arm and pushed it back from her face. "Relax, Nurse Nancy. I should've said I took *personal* leave. That was imprecise of me. I forgot how careful I have to be when speaking to Shepard Krausse, Overlord of Over-reaction."

He subsided, mollified by the smile he heard in her words.

"I made you lunch, since I'm taking you away from your lunch break." She pressed a sandwich into his left hand and a water bottle into his right.

He extended the right hand, saying, "Can you hold this for me? I need both hands for the sandwich."

"Oh, right. Sorry." She took the water bottle.

He sniffed. "Ooh, tuna melt. Nice." He leaned down and hissed her on the top of her head. He used that split second to enjoy the softness of her tresses and the lingering floral scent of her shampoo. "Thank you, Bean."

"You're very welcome," she said. "Let's take a walk."

Miranda laid her hand lightly on Shep's elbow, which was enough to enable him to move with her. She directed him around the house, across narrow, root-corrugated Magnolia Street, and down a familiar path in the woods.

While Shep enjoyed his sandwich, they strolled under the forest canopy, cooled by a green-scented breeze. They brushed by palmetto spikes, cypress boughs, clean-smelling pines, sweet-smelling magnolia trees and, in the treetops, gem-hued orchids.

Shepard took the last bite of his sandwich and dusted crumbs from his hands, using his cargo shorts as his napkin. He held out his hand, and Miranda gave him the water bottle, which he uncapped. After a couple of healthy swigs, he resealed the bottle and stowed it in one of his capacious cargo pockets.

Frogs sang *scritch-scritch, scritch-scritch* in the undergrowth near the couple's feet. Doves *hoo-hooed* above them, and the limber trees *swished* their leaves in farewell when a bird leaped away to a new perch.

From a distance, to the left, a raven *cawed* his question, and another *cawed* the answer from the trees on the right.

Miranda automatically altered their route to take the path leading away from the tree where she and Shep had hidden on the night they had escaped the car bomb only to be chased into the woods by gunmen on foot.

Shepard needed no one to guide him on this familiar route through the woods; he had been taking this path since he was a child.

Miranda had released her touch on his elbow and simply walked beside him. He only needed to move his hand two inches to the left to find her little soft hand and surround it with his large one.

Miranda's hand rested in his like a tiny animal, returned to the safety and warmth of its den. The duo moved so silently down the sandy track, a shy black snake did not even notice them until it was literally in their path. Then, it skittered off with a rustle, into the leaf litter.

Sometimes, Miranda would hug Shep's bicep and lay her head against it. He knew she was ready to talk when she straightened up and moved away so they were no longer touching."

"My mother called," she said.

He said, "Mm," to let her know he was listening.

"You know, I thought when our mothers met face to face, there would be a big argument, two strong personalities in conflict with each other. I was sure all the wedding planning would be put on hold for several months because they stopped speaking to each other."

"But that didn't happen," he guessed.

"Oh, they're best buddies now, partners in crime. *They're* going to plan *our* wedding, *together*."

"Okay."

"They're ganging up on us!"

"Okay..."

"You know what that means!"

"I do?"

"No! Not 'I do.' There won't be any 'I do's'! Shepard, don't you see? I can't marry you!"

## Chapter 12 - The Politics

Shepard froze in mid-step and reclaimed Miranda's hand instantly. She stumbled when she tried to walk on, suddenly tethered to a Krausse-shaped boulder.

"No, Castor Bean. I do not see that. I absolutely do not see that. You said yes. Finally. We're getting married. End of discussion."

She stepped forward, wrapped her arms around his waist, and leaned against his chest. She made no sound, but he soon felt the wetness of tears soaking into his shirt.

"Ohhh, no, don't! Please don't cry, Bean. Whatever you think is the problem, I can fix it. We can fix it together."

She sniffled. She mumbled, "I love you so much," into his damp shirt.

"I know you do. And you know I love you. More than anything. We'll be fine."

She backed up a half step and looked at his face. Her eyes scanned every millimeter from the top of his head to the bottom of his golden, closely trimmed beard.

"No, Shepard. We can't be fine. They won't let us. First, they're going to arrange our wedding and all that goes along with that. Next, they'll try to run the marriage. And, finally, they'll destroy the marriage when things don't work out perfectly. As *they* define 'perfectly.'"

Shep said, "Not a problem. Things *will* work out perfectly. And, nobody but you and I get to define what that is. Trust me,

Bean!"

She said nothing.

He continued, "Look, I've built a business, survived assassination attempts, and brought down criminals all the way up to and including the governor of the state. I think I can *handle* our *parents*."

Miranda would not accept his assertions. She said, "I cannot live my life under the tyrannical scrutiny of people who will never believe I'm good enough for you.

"I'd be waiting every day for the announcement that I'm ruining your career. I'm destroying your life. And, if I really loved you as much as I think I do, I would do the right thing and leave you."

He cupped his hands around her shoulders and held her at arm's length. "Whoa, whoa, whoa there, Bean! First of all, I don't have a 'career' that you can ruin. The only person who can louse up my work is me, so you're in the clear there."

He pulled her gently toward him until she stood beside him, with his arm surrounding her. "Second of all, Miss Miranda Castor Bean Ogilvy – and I'm sure I've made this point before now – you are the pinnacle, the top, the champ, the most wonderful woman in the world. If anybody is 'not good enough,' it would be me. Never you."

"I'm not talking about your career in radio," she said. "I'm talking about your career in politics." She placed her hands on his bicep and tried to shake him.

He didn't move. "Politics!" He threw back his head and laughed.

Miranda watched him, tears drying on her cheeks while the corners of her mouth drooped lower and lower. "You think that's funny?"

"Yes!" He chuckled one last time. "Me in politics! That's a hoot. Really! I'd probably even have to get a haircut."

"If you're not going to take me seriously, we can't discuss this any longer."

"Good!" said Shep. "We should never have been discussing it at all. We're getting married, okay? You want to go do it today? Carlo can drive us to the county courthouse, we can get a license, see the court clerk and a notary, and boom. Done. Let's go."

Taking her hand, he spun on his heel and took a step back the way they had come. He froze when she said, "No."

"What?" he said.

"No. Thank you."

"You mean no, not today. Okay, we c—"

"No, I mean I can't marry you. Not any day. It was silly of me to believe in fairy tale endings. They're not for people like me."

She didn't sound angry or hysterical or weepy in the least. She sounded calm. Empty. Numb. Her voice showed no emotion, no uncertainty, and no sign of backing down.

That voice scared Shepard Krausse like nothing ever had.

So, of course, he lost his temper.

"Why can't you *trust me*!" he shouted, stepping toward her and looming over her. He dropped the hand he had been holding and carefully avoided touching her.

"It's not that—" Miranda tried to say.

He did not even hear her. He was adrenaline-fueled and supersonic by this time. There was no stopping the coming explosion.

His deep voice nearly shook bark off nearby trees. "I thought *you*, of all people, believed in me! Believed in us! Boy, did I get that one wrong! And let me tell you something, Miss Bean—"

"Apparently, I can't stop you!" she snapped, her own anger rising.

"—all my life I've had to prove to people, over and over again, that I was a normal person, with a brain and a heart and goals and talents.

"Day after day, other people just lived life, but I had to *perform*, because people were always watching for a mistake. Watching for me to wear the wrong thing, or look unkempt, or make a mess with my dinner, or step into the path of a bus! Anything!

"If I wanted to live my own life, and take care of myself, and carry out everyday activities like the 'normal' people..."

He emphasized *normal* with a closed fist.

"...if I wanted to go for a run, or date a girl, or buy a radio station, or open a restaurant, I first had to prove that I could do it. So, I did. Because I *can* do it, Miranda! I thought you, of all people, *believed* that from day one!"

She shouted loud enough to make leaves fall from limbs overhead. "You know you don't have to prove anything to me! How dare you accuse me of that kind of petty thinking!"

He yelled, "How dare you imply that I'm defective! I'm not man enough to marry the woman I love and take care of her, protecting her from anyone or anything, including nosy parents, for the rest of our lives!"

"I am not implying you're defective!" she yelled.

For several seconds, all sound abandoned Minokee. Nervous animals strained to hear the next salvo of words reverberate through the trees.

A breeze from the direction of the river cooled the faces of the man and woman. They stood, squared off against one another on the crooked, narrow trail winding between the stopper bushes. The breeze did not cool their anger.

When the shouting did not resume, small creatures began to rustle through the leaves of the forest floor. Mockingbirds once more warbled their sweet songs in the tops of the live oaks.

All the while, Miranda's last words continued to ricochet in the minds of the two people: *I am not implying you're defective!*

In the softest, lowest baritone she had ever heard, Shepard said, "Sure sounds like it to me." He turned toward home, moving slowly.

"Shep—" she began.

He cut her off. "You can't marry me, Miss Ogilvy. You don't even know me."

He kept walking until the trail curved, carrying him out of sight.

Miranda stood absolutely still until she could neither see nor hear him. At a sound in the undergrowth, she looked down and saw Shep's kitten wriggle out from the bushes and come to sit at her feet.

*"Merrrao?"* said the kitten and walked its furry front paws up Miranda's shin.

"I don't know," Miranda answered. "C'mon, I'll give you a ride to my house, and you can go home from there."

Zeus purred like an Oldsmobile when Miranda picked him up and settled him under her chin. He didn't mind at all if she dripped a tear on his head once in a while as she walked.

♦

When Shepard opened his back door a few minutes later, Carlo was jingling keys and drumming fingers on the kitchen table.

"Good, you are back," Carlo said, pushing his chair from the table with an audible scrape. "We need to have a strategy meeting."

**"I'm *sick* of people *telling* me what *I* need to do!"** Shepard's shout rattled the dishes in the cabinets.

Carlo took two deep breaths before responding evenly. "First of all, Miss Congeniality, you need to switch to decaf."

## Chapter 13 - The Strategy, Part 1

Shepard released the tension in his arms and shoulders; he seemed to shrink an inch in height as he relaxed his posture. "I'm sorry. I'm, uh, I'm just a little stressed."

"Well, you gonna get more stressed when I tell you what is happening in the search for David Zhang. Come, I tell you everything in the car on the way to Gainesville. We say nothing to *il professore* about Maynard's visitor, okay?"

"Agreed. I'm not sure of the connections there, yet. And while we're figuring it out, I don't want the woman alerted that she's being watched."

*Tuesday afternoon*

In Professor Win Clarkson's office on the University of Florida campus, Carlo had just finished briefing the professor and Shep on events surrounding David Zhang's disappearance. Carlo looked to the two men for their comments.

"What next?" asked Carlo.

Shepard thought a moment before saying, "What happened to David's stuff from his office here, in this department?"

Clarkson replied, "I haven't touched his office. The police looked at it, but there was no sign of foul play, they said. I don't think the police removed anything, but, if they did, it will all be logged in as evidence."

"Mm," Shep fingered his beard thoughtfully. "If they don't

believe there's been a crime, they wouldn't cart away a truckload of 'evidence.' No, if anything has been removed, I'd bet either David took it with him, or somebody else took it because they knew David wasn't coming back.

"Carlo, search David's office, especially his computer. Read all his e-mails for the last few weeks ... and, I think you'd better do it when his office-mate is out."

"You suspect Felicia of something?" Clarkson said.

"Not necessarily, but we can't rule out anybody right now. Better safe than sorry," Shep told him.

"We should not ignore the roommate, either," said Carlo. "That guy, Maynard, is about as straight as fresh-boiled linguine. He is not smart, either. If he had anything to do with David disappearing, we will catch him in a mistake sooner or later."

Shep stopped stroking his beard. "Professor, I haven't told you, but I've had a guy watching the roommate. It's an old Sheep Counters fan, who used to call my radio show all the time, mostly to report Unidentified Flying Objects. He's a dedicated UFOlogist — which means he sneaks around at night trying to spot aliens and such. I asked him to watch Maynard, and he was on the case faster than you can say 'flying saucer.' I guarantee the subject will never know he's being observed."

Carlo let out a chuckle. "He's called Roland, the Rocket Man."

"Yep, that's him. Rocket Man. Comes complete with night vision gear and infrared cameras and who-knows-what else. I don't ask," said Shepard.

Carlo inserted, "Dude, you know, if Rocket Man watches the roommate, Rocket is going to think the guy is an alien. Because, why would you want to watch him? Unless he has come to pose as human and live among us until the invasion starts?"

Win's eyes widened. "You're not serious! Nobody is that crazy."

"Oh, yes, they are," said Shep.

"You don't know the Sheep Counters," said Carlo. "For several years, thousands of people listened to Shep's broadcast in the wee hours every night, to keep up-to-date on news of aliens and conspiracies and urban legends they swore were true. Fans of 'Sheep Counters with Shep and Dave' believed sincerely in things most people would not imagine."

Clarkson shook his head in disbelief. "I'll take your word for it, but it boggles the mind."

Shep told Carlo, "While I'm thinkin' about it, Rocket would be insulted if I offered to pay him for his 'surveillance activities.' Have my local station make a suitable donation to the Rocket Man website. Call it 'research' expense."

*Wednesday*

Early the following morning, Shepard was already closeted in his home office when Carlo answered a knock on the front door.

"Come in," he said, stepping back and smiling. His smile faltered when Miranda remained outside the threshold and dangled a set of car keys in front of him.

"No, thank you. I'm just dropping these off."

"You do not want to come in and say hello? Shep is in his office—"

"No, thank you. I don't need to talk to Shepard. I just need you to give him these car keys."

Carlo held out a hand, and Miranda dropped the keys into his palm.

"These are the keys to your car?" he said. When she nodded and turned to go, he stopped her with, "Why are you giving Shep the keys to your car? Shall I have it serviced for you? Do you want it washed? Waxed? Painted?"

She turned only halfway toward him, still poised to escape. "I feel it is no longer appropriate for me to keep such an expensive gift, due to the change in our relationship."

"You change you relationship?"

"He didn't tell you?"

"Um, maybe not. You explain to me your side of story."

"No story. We broke up. I can't keep the car. He'll understand."

Carlo wagged his head in the negative. "I am not so sure, but I wait and see for that. Do you need me to drive you to work?

"No, thank you." She shifted her weight as if to step away.

"But, if you give back this car," he jingled the keys, "then, you don't have a car. I know your old car was hauled away to the scrap yard on a flatbed truck. It was my job to be sure it arrived at the yard and went straight into the compactor. Your old car would fit into a lunch box right now."

"I'm borrowing Mrs. Cleary's car until I can shop for a used car after work today."

"Ahm…" Carlo's eyebrows scrunched together.

When he did not continue, Miranda asked, "What?"

"I just was thinking … Have you ever driven *Signora* Cleary's automobile?"

"No, but—"

"Have you even *seen Signora* Cleary's automobile?"

"Well, no, but I'm going over there now—"

"Do you have a Triple-A card in case the car breaks down?"

"Yes, thank you, but it won't break down. Her late husband took excellent care of that car. It's 'just like new,' she told me."

"I hope it is, *signorina. Signor* Cleary, he pass away twenty years ago."

Miranda let this new fact sink in. A shadow of dismay crossed her features, but she banished it and put on her Stalwart Librarian Face.

"Nevertheless, she wouldn't have offered it to me if she didn't believe it would be safe to drive."

"I am sure that is true. Only, promise you will be careful, and, if you need help, you will call Carlo. You have my cell number in you phone?"

"Yes," she said. "Thank you very much."

She walked away.

Carlo closed the front door, bounced the car keys in his hand,

and strode to the door of Shepard's home office.

He gave it a quick rap, then shouted at the closed door. "*Signorina* Miranda was at the door."

"I don't want to talk to her," came from beyond the portal.

"Good. She do not want to talk to you, neither. She just drop off her car keys."

No sound came from behind the door for several seconds.

*"Mao,"* came from inside the office.

"I heard him," Shep answered the cat. Then, to Carlo, he said, "What for? I just washed it on Saturday."

Carlo leaned against the door frame, dangling the keys from one finger. "She say is 'inappropriate' gift, and she gonna buy herself a used car."

*"Merraow,"* Zeus remarked.

Shep answered the cat, "What do you mean 'my fault'? I didn't ask for it back. She should keep it, for Pete's sake. This is totally unnecessary." Then he spoke louder for Carlo. "How will she get to work?"

"You do not want to know," Carlo said. "How come you do not ask me why she say is 'inappropriate'?"

"She says that because she broke up with me, Nosey Parker! But she's wrong. Her idea of what's 'inappropriate' is just … convoluted!"

*"K-k-k-k-k-k!"*

"No, I did not break up with her, Fur Face."

*"K-k-k-k-k-k!"*

"Okay, we both broke up with each other! Happy now?"

The cat said nothing.

"Nobody sounding happy to me," Carlo murmured. To the closed door he said, "I just leave the keys on the rack by the kitchen door. Last hook on the right."

Carlo waited, but no further sounds came from behind the door.

"You welcome," he said, and walked away.

A moment later, the door opened a few inches, and Zeus

sauntered out. He padded past Carlo and through the kitchen, where the purposeful feline swished out the cat portal Carlo had installed in the door.

To the departing kitten, Carlo snarled, "Sure! Run away, coward!"

An hour later, Carlo left for another war council at the Montgomery-Krausse mansion. Before he left in Shep's car, he parked Miranda's rejected vehicle precisely two feet from Shepard's three-feet-wide, outward-opening front door.

Shepard would not be able to ignore the relationship crisis, because he would not be able to go out his front door until the problem with Miranda was resolved.

Two hours after departing Minokee, Carlo was seated at the broad, glistening expanse of mahogany table in Hermione's formal dining room. All the parties from their previous wedding-planning meeting sat in a row on one side of the table. Doctor and Doctor Ogilvy sat, in a row of two, on the opposite side.

Hermione, naturally, presided from her throne at the head of the table.

After perfunctory greetings and a quick introduction of Miranda's parents, Hermione turned to the staff and asked for status reports.

Hanson, the ancient butler, raised a hand as high as his arthritic shoulder would allow. He was third in the row, and reports traditionally began with the first chair, so his gesture caused muted gasps among the other employees.

The Ogilvy's did not gasp. They did not realize the significance of Hanson's gesture.

Hermione did not gasp. As a rule, Madam Montgomery-Krausse did not indulge in vulgar expressions of surprise or alarm.

"Yes, Hanson?" said Madam.

Hanson stood – either a sign of respect or preparation to flee – and cleared his throat. "Ahem … Madam, I have the unhappy duty to inform you that the wedding may not occur as planned."

"Of course, it will occur as planned," Hermione declared. "*I* have planned it."

"Quite so, Madam, but there have been … developments of which Madam is as yet unaware."

"Then make me aware. We are wasting our guests' time."

"Yes, Madam. It will be most expedient if Carlo explains, since he was an eyewitness—"

"More of an *ear*-witness," Carlo muttered.

"—since Carlo witnessed this morning's events." Hanson sat down, his spine perfectly erect and never touching the chair's back.

Carlo stood and looked Hermione directly in the chin, which required less bravado than looking her in the eyes.

"Proceed, please, Carlo," Hermione pronounced.

"Yes, Madam. It began when *Signorina* Miranda came to *Signor* Shepard's house this morning to return the blue Mercedes."

"What do you mean 'return' it?" Hermione asked.

"She said she could no longer keep such an expensive gift, given the current state of, and I quote, 'the relationship'."

The servants gasped in unison, except for Hanson, who had heard the story from Carlo beforehand.

"The relationship!" said Miranda's mother.

"Aw, I loved that car," moaned her father.

Hermione alone remained calm. "And, how did my son respond to that absurd notion?"

"*Signorina* Miranda did not speak to *Signor* Shepard. I conveyed the news to him myself – through a closed office door."

"And, how did he describe 'the state of the relationship'?"

Carlo took a deep breath and lifted his head and shoulders high, looking over Madam's head at this point. "I regret to say he told me they, and I quote, 'broke up.'"

"What!" (Rosario.)

"Indeed." (Hermione.)

"But he was even willing to shave off his beard!" (Zeke.)

Gasp! (The servants.)

"I see," said Hermione. "And, precisely who broke up with

whom? Did he say?"

"It was … unclear, Madam. I only know *Signor* Shepard has not been himself since he went for a walk with *Signorina* Miranda at lunchtime yesterday. *Signor* Shepard would not discuss the details of the break-up."

"Hmm," Hermione said, gazing without focus at the far end of the massive dining room.

"If I may venture an educated guess, Madam," said Carlo.

Hermione looked directly at the chauffeur. "Please do. You know him better than anyone, with the possible exception of your dear brother, of course. But, regrettably, he cannot help us now."

For Hermione Montgomery-Krausse, such a statement amounted to a maudlin display of tearful condolences for the death of his late brother.

"Zeus appears to feel that *Signor* Shepard is to blame. He has left the house," Carlo said. He sat down.

"Who left the house?" came from Rosario. "Did Shepard leave Minokee?"

"Zeus left the house," Hermione clarified.

Rosario' forehead wrinkled and she looked around the table as if for a clue. "Who is Zeus?"

"I'm afraid I don't know, yet," said Hermione.

"Zeus is the cat," Zeke told them.

"Oh." Rosario sounded relieved.

Carlo inserted, "Perhaps I should have reported sooner, Madam: *Signora* Cleary has given *Signor* Shepard a small cat."

"To keep?" Hermione said warily.

"Only on a probationary basis, Madam. The cat may not decide to stay."

"Do you mean to tell me, this animal has been given the authority to determine whether my son, the only heir to the political and financial Montgomery dynasty, is *acceptable* as its owner?"

"If approved, *Signor* Shepard would function as a sort of landlord, Madam. As I understand it, cats do not have 'owners'."

"Great Caesar's ghost! My son has acquired a *feline*?" Hermione sounded far from relieved. "Hanson, bring me a sherry, please."

"I would like one as well," added Rosario.

"Get me a beer, would you?" said Zeke.

For a few minutes, the room was silent except for the clinking of the sherry decanter, the opening of the mini-fridge beneath the room's wet bar, and the soft clunks of two crystal sherry glasses and a beer bottle upon the surface of the great table.

Zeke sipped his beer.

Rosario and Hermione slugged back their sherry in one gulp and daintily replaced their glasses on the table.

"Very well," intoned Hermione. "This adds another facet to our plans. We will need to restore the relationship *as well as* make the wedding arrangements. A subcommittee will be formed. Please leave your name with Rebecca if you wish to serve on that committee.

"Now. Let us continue without further delay. Reports, please."

## Chapter 14 - The Strategy, Part 2

When Carlo returned to Minokee later that afternoon, Shepard was still sequestered in his home office. Zeus was nowhere to be seen or heard.

Carlo liked to cook his way through periods of tension or stress. Within half an hour, he was putting the topmost layer on a pan of his mother's seafood lasagna recipe. Childhood lessons in their mother's *cucina* had not been wasted on the Fratelli boys. *No, signor.*

While the lasagna baked, Carlo went to his room to check his emails for messages from his spies in search of David Zhang.

Rocket Man reported on the movements of the suspicious woman who had been spotted visiting Zhang's scurrilous roommate.

Other minions, scattered about Gainesville and surrounding communities, reported no helpful news.

When Carlo returned to the kitchen, Shepard was bending over a half-open oven door.

"Get away before you ruin something, Fabio!"

"It smells just like your mother's kitchen in here. Hmmm, that aroma pulled me here from my office like a tow rope. Irresistible. When's dinner?"

"*Your* dinner is whenever you throw some leftovers in the microwave."

"Leftovers! But you're making—" Shep sniffed the air, "—lasagna, I think."

"Yes, is lasagna, *Signor* Bloodhound, but is not for you. For you is leftovers."

A short while later, Shep waited by the microwave as a plate of leftovers circled on the carousel inside it.

It must have been torture to listen to Carlo wrapping the fresh-baked lasagna in aluminum foil.

It had to be agony to contemplate decidedly un-fresh leftovers while a cloud of luscious, fresh, Italian scents wafted to all corners of the house.

"At least tell me where you're taking it," he said, when Carlo swung open the kitchen door.

"I am taking to a friend. Of mine. Not of yours, I think."

"Okay, but could you at least remove the roadblock from the front door before you go?"

"No."

"Fine. I'll just continue using the back door if I need to go out. It's been working for me all day."

The microwave beep-beep-beeped. Shep reached, with little enthusiasm, to retrieve his plate.

Carlo went out the door, saying over his shoulder, "Feed the cat, if you can find him."

Carlo carried his steaming dish in oven-mitted hands as he walked across Shepard's backyard, through the dividing hedge, and across Miranda's backyard. He arrived on Miranda's back stoop and knocked at her kitchen door.

A curtain rustled as someone inside screened the visitor. Carlo must have passed inspection, because, in only a moment, Miranda opened the door with a smile and a, "Hi! Come in!"

"*Ciao, bella,*" Carlo said as he entered the house, pecking a kiss on Miranda's cheek. "It is my night to cook dinner, but I think maybe you are not come to our house, so I bring dinner to you."

Miranda lifted a corner of the aluminum foil and inhaled a cloud of Tuscany. "Ahhh," she sighed. "Oh, Carlo. I love you."

"Yes, but not with the all-surpassing passion I truly deserve, I fear," he said with a knowing grin. "Tonight, however, I win you over with my *mamma*'s seafood lasagna recipe. You will quickly forget the buffoon next door and be happy again."

"Nice thought," she said. "Won't you eat with us?"

"No, *grazie*, I have been away all day, and I must steal some 'me time' before sleep. … Excuse me, you said 'eat with *us*'? You have a guest?"

"You could say that. He was waiting for me when I got home from work, and he's been lounging on the couch ever since. Come…"

Carlo followed her around the corner of the kitchen. From there he could see Miranda's couch. The visitor did not stand but raised his head to greet Carlo.

*"Mowrrr."*

Carlo greeted Zeus with a nod. "So, this is where you been hiding since yesterday. I should have known."

*"Merraou."*

Miranda sat on the couch and stroked the kitten's fur. "It's almost like he knew I needed a friend right now."

Zeus purred like a leaf blower.

Carlo had to raise his voice to be heard above the "*RRRRRR.*"

"I am sure he did," Carlo told Miranda. He made eye contact with Zeus as he said, "He will stay with you as long as you need him. You do not have to stay alone, *Bella*."

*"Mrrrrak,"* agreed Zeus.

Carlo remained still. Miranda stroked the cat with one hand and looked away to swipe at a tear with the other. She turned back to Carlo with a weak, valiant, smile.

"Thank you, Carlo – and Zeus. And thank you for your mother's seafood lasagna. I wish you could stay…"

Backing toward the door, Carlo said, "Another time, *signorina.* And you are very welcome. Call me if you need anything. Anything at all."

Carlo took the long way home. He walked down the length of Magnolia Street and around the curve through the moss-draped live oak trees. Then he hiked up Orchid Street to Shep's cottage.

Looking at the Minokee houses with their wide front porches and rocking chairs facing the narrow, tree-canopied road may have given Carlo an idea. The Krausse cottage had a wide covered porch on one side, but no veranda front and back.

The blue Mercedes sat blocking the front door, as it had all day.

Carlo circumnavigated the house and entered the kitchen door. He stepped in only far enough to reach the keys on the nearby rack, then he left again.

In minutes, he entered the house through the front door and tiptoed to the kitchen to replace the keys on the rack. Then Carlo trod audibly down the hall toward his room.

Sarcasm dripped from his lips when he shouted at Shepard's closed door, "How was your dinner?"

Shepard shouted back, "I couldn't find the cat."

Carlo smiled and stepped into his room.

## Chapter 15 - The Heartaches

*Thursday morning.*

The next day, Carlo slept in.

Shepard made his own breakfast of dry cereal. He called the cat's name several times but got no answer. He kicked the empty cat-food bowl on his way to the back door.

A few minutes later, Shep woke Carlo by shoving Carlo's bedroom door open with enough force to whack the knob into the wall.

"Ask me why I now have a really bad bruise on my sternum!" Shepard bellowed.

Carlo rolled up onto one elbow and rested his thoroughly tousled head on his hand. His voice was raspy with sleep. "You say you have a bruise?"

"Yes! And it really hurts. I'm going to have to put ice on it. I'll probably need to go for x-rays. Now, ask me why!"

"I suppose you would get x-rays because you think something is broken or—"

"Not why the x-rays, you clown! Why I have a really bad bruise in the middle of my chest!"

Carlo yawned and mumbled, "Why do you have a really bad bruise in the middle of your chest." He didn't even raise his tone at the end to indicate a question. He probably didn't care about the answer. Or maybe he already knew it.

"I have a *really painful* bruise in the middle of my chest because *some*body blockaded the back door with a very heavy, very hard, automobile with a very nasty *protrusion* aimed exactly at my breastbone!"

"Yeah," Carlo said after another yawn. "That would be the Go 'Gators flag the *signorina* mounted on the side window, you know, back when *Signorina* Miranda was driving that car. … Why did you not go out the front door?"

"Why didn't I—? Because last night when I went to bed, the car was parked at the *front* door, and you know it. You moved it!"

Carlo finally pushed himself to a sitting position. "I moved the front door? That is very funny, *signor.*"

"Not the door! The car! Admit it, you moved the car from the front door to the back door—"

"*Sí,* I did."

"—because you knew I would go out the back door this morning—"

"*Sí*, you did."

"—and you made sure that silly flag would smack me like a Mack truck."

"Well, technically, *you* smacked *it.* The flag did not attack."

Shep took several deep breaths, pressing a hand against his chest, and then took two steps forward and sat down on the edge of Carlo's bed.

After three more calming breaths, the time for shouting was over. Both men now spoke in normal voices.

"And you can stop calling me '*signor.*' We both know you're only pretending to show respect."

"That was not 'pretending,' it was sarcasm. Maybe blind people just do not understand irony."

"Not true. And not fair. Let's not insult all blind people just because you're mad it me."

"*Sí*, I am."

"And, I'm guessing you think you're teaching me a lesson."

"*Sí*, I am. I am showing you how it feels when someone hurts you. When someone hurts your heart."

Carlo poked Shep's sternum with his index finger.

Shep flinched and slid a few inches away on the bed, out of Carlo's reach.

They sat quietly together. Shep moved his hand in massaging circles on his chest.

A dove *coo-cooed* in the crepe myrtle tree outside. The central air conditioning unit, beneath Carlo's bedroom window, *ca-thunked* to life and began its cooling *hmmm.*

Finally, Shepard stood and walked toward the bedroom door. "I'll make you breakfast while you shower. After we eat, we need to meet in the office and go over the reports on the search for David Zhang."

"Okay."

"After I put an ice pack on my new bruise."

"Right. See you later."

♦

Farmer Tom Rigby did not know that David Zhang had gone missing. The farmer went about his daily chores in a relaxed, backwoods-Florida way, without big-city angst or stress. Once in a while he stopped by the sinkhole and studied its walls, mentally measuring the mammoth fossil he saw partially exposed there.

About a week after David's disappearance, Rigby's sinkhole seemed to have stopped growing — at least until the next colossal rain storm. He began making plans to get serious about exploring his new natural asset.

That was what Tom was doing, using a legal pad, at his kitchen table, when someone knocked at the farmhouse front door.

"Come around to the back!" Tom shouted, knowing the house was small enough, and so little insulated, that someone standing on the front porch would easily hear Tom call out from the kitchen.

Sure enough, moments later footfalls thumped on the rickety wooden stoop, and someone rattled the kitchen door with their rapping.

Tom left the table and answered the door. "Well, come on in the house! Good mornin' to ya. What are you doing way out here?"

The visitor entered, smiling. "Surprise! Good morning, Tom."

"Take a seat, take a seat. I got coffee on the stove. Milk or sugar for you?"

"Both, thanks." The visitor sat at the kitchen table and glanced at the notes on Tom's legal pad. "If you've got a few minutes, I want to talk about that mammoth in your sinkhole. I think it could be worth a good bit of money to you."

Tom looked over his shoulder from where he was taking a mug out of a cabinet. "I thought you, of all people, would want me to donate it to the university. That was my plan, anyway."

"That is a good plan," the visitor said, "but hear me out before you sign any papers."

Tom set two mugs on the table between them and sat down.

"I ain't against a little extra cash. Plenty of fixin'-up to do around this place, doncha know. So, if yer talkin', I'm listenin'."

♦

Back in Minokee, Shepard and Carlo had finished breakfast and settled into Shep's little office with fresh cups of coffee. Carlo brought his laptop and opened it on the desk between them.

While Carlo was reading aloud three overnight e-mail messages from his street team, Shep's cellphone played the five-note motif from "Close Encounters of the Third Kind."

"It's Rocket Man," both men said in unison. Shep answered the phone and put it on speaker. After exchanging quick greetings, Rocket reported eagerly.

"Do you know a guy named Rigby?"

"*Tom* Rigby?" Shep asked.

"Got a farm and some woodland on the Pig River."

"That's Tom. We know him, but he had no connection to David Zhang."

"He does now. Guess who's in his house with him right this very minute!"

## Chapter 16 - The Mammon

When Rocket told the men who Tom Rigby's visitor was, they did not reply immediately. After a moment, Carlo murmured, "It has to be about the mammoth."

Shep said, "And, the last time anybody saw David Zhang was the trip to Tom Rigby's sinkhole – where Tom found the bones."

"You want me to stay on the visitor or start watching Rigby?" asked Rocket.

"Stay on the visitor," said Shep.

"Get pictures of them on Rigby's farm together, if you can," Carlo added. "It could be important."

"Roger that," Rocket said, with a crisp salute in his voice.

"Good work, Rocket," Shep told him. "Thanks for calling. Talk soon."

"Right, Chief." Rocket disconnected the call.

"We need to talk to Tom Rigby," Carlo said.

"We will," said Shep, "but we also need to know more about that mammoth, and why certain people have taken an interest in it. Maybe we'll find out the same thing David Zhang must've found out. Then we may be able to find him."

"You think Zhang is dead?"

"I won't know what to think until we've done a little more digging. No pun intended."

♦

Rocket Man snapped several pictures of Tom Rigby's visitor

when the two stood together on Tom's back steps, saying their farewells. Rocket kicked himself for failing to set up his parabolic microphone. He would have given half of his moon rock collection to know what those two were saying.

Rocket would have been even more curious if he had known Tom's visitor was saying, "Has anybody talked to you about David Zhang?"

"David? I met him at the university, and again when that Audubon canoeing group came to see the sinkhole a, it'd be ... two weeks ago Saturday. Don't know nothin' 'bout him, though. And, I ain't seen him since."

"Nobody has. David disappeared after that Audubon trip."

"Well, ain't that the dang'dest thing! What coulda happened to 'im?"

"No idea. But if you hear from him, or hear anything about him, give us a call, okay?"

"Sure, sure. Don't 'spect he'd come here … But then, I wasn't expectin' you today, neither." Tom laughed.

The visitor laughed, too, and initiated a farewell handshake. "That's right. Now, don't say anything to anybody about that mammoth. There are people who know what something like that is worth, and they'd steal it right out from under you, if they knew about it."

"Right you are. Mum's the word," said Tom.

The visitor left, unaware of Rocket Man in pursuit.

After that visit, Tom Rigby began guarding his sinkhole more carefully, especially at night. The very next day, he made arrangements to install a sturdy fence along the Pig River, to keep boaters from taking unauthorized strolls in his woods.

*Friday*

While Tom Rigby spent the day becoming an expert on river-front security fences, Carlo Fratelli spent the day in the Live Oak Public Library, becoming an expert on mammoth fossils.

He could have conducted this same research from home, in Minokee, but anyone might trace the IP address and know Shepard Krausse was asking questions.

Ever since his days in talk radio, Shepard had been famous for uncovering skullduggery and corruption. Someone was always trying to keep Shep from discovering secrets. The last time someone tried to stop an investigation, they had murdered Carlo's brother, Shepard's dog, and nearly Shepard himself.

Carlo was seriously keeping this inquiry anonymous — and far away from Minokee.

So, today he sat at one of the library's reference computers and spoke his findings into his phone's digital voice recorder, for transmission to Shepard.

The posted time limit for use of that computer was thirty minutes, but no one asked Carlo to leave, even after a couple of hours. No one else was waiting to use the machine.

Also, Carlo had formed a close personal relationship with one of the librarians.

He began his recording with the date, time, and place, followed by "These are the results of my research on mammoth fossils."

He estimated the size of the mammoth remains in Rigby's new sinkhole, and he began comparing the prices of mammoth tusks and bones being sold around the world.

"If my estimate is correct, a tusk of this size could sell on the open market for thirty thousand dollars or more, depending on color, rarity of species, degree of stabilization of the fossil, and so forth.

"And tusks come in pairs, so the bones are worth at least sixty thousand dollars, before we even begin valuing the rest of the skeleton.

"One vendor was selling a mammoth's pelvis, stabilized and mounted, as 'paleo art,' and not merely an artifact. He wanted $30,000. One large tusk was valued at $75,000 by a well-known art gallery."

Carlo stopped the recorder long enough to turn a page in his handwritten notes. He continued dictation: "A well-preserved mammoth tooth, although a fairly common item, might still sell for three thousand dollars each. I calculate there could well be four molars in Tom's sinkhole.

"Remember, that land would have been marsh or shallow water at the time of the mammoths, so it is likely more than one animal got stuck in bottom silt or deep mud and died there."

Carlo discussed the skull and the tusks. He considered spinal vertebrae, ribs, leg bones, every large bone he could find for sale on one website or another.

"In summary," he recorded, "the mammoth in Rigby's sinkhole could possibly be worth as much as three hundred thousand dollars."

He slouched back in his chair with a sigh, thought for a moment, then resumed recording.

"I think we can agree there are people who would make someone disappear for a lot less than that. Even people who would not kill outright, would happily step over the body of *someone else's* victim, to get to three hundred thousand dollars.

"Tom Rigby seems like an honest man. He says he will donate the mammoth to the university, but if he gives the fossil away, *somebody* loses out on three hundred thousand dollars.

"The last time we saw David Zhang was at that sinkhole, and Zhang has disappeared. Was he a roadblock to someone who wants that fossil? Or has he gone into hiding because he plans to get that fossil, himself?

"Either way, Tom Rigby could be in danger as long as he is the barrier to selling those bones. We need to tell this to Tom, and we need to tell him to watch his back.

"End of recording

# Chapter 17 - The Boyfriend

*Saturday*

Miranda was stowing her purse in the bottom drawer of a file cabinet in the library office when a strange and wonderful thing happened. Annabelle Sherwood, Miranda's man-hunting coworker, actually acknowledged Miranda's presence.

Miranda seldom heard more than "Going on break" from Annabelle, in the course of a normal workday. But this Saturday morning, the sexy, deep-cleavaged, short-skirted, spike-heeled siren initiated an entire conversation with her wren-like, bespectacled, invisible, librarian colleague.

"Oh, hey, Marion, while you were out, um … somewhere … not here … yesterday, your friend came in. I told him you were out, but he said he'd rather talk to me. So, he did."

Then Annabelle continued in a husky, *sexier* voice (which Miranda had never thought was even *possible*). "I mean, he really *spoke to me*, if you know what I mean."

"My friend?"

"Remember that gorgeous hunk of man I thought was gay, but you said he wasn't? Boy, were you right! Whoo!"

"Annabelle, you know, I was here all day yesterday. I could've talked to him myself."

"Really? Huh. Didn't see you anywhere. Sorry. Anyway, as I said, he wanted to talk to little ol' *moi.*"

"I see. Well, uh, lucky you, I guess," Miranda murmured.

"He's different from most men, isn't he?" Annabelle said.

"I used to think so."

Annabelle continued, "You know what really impressed me the most about him? Not that he was tall, and built, and dressed like a European prince — although he was all that —"

"He always is," Miranda said.

"— but what really touched me was that he didn't care about my *looks*!"

"No, he wouldn't," Miranda said.

"Nobody ever liked me for my personality before."

"Imagine that. And you such a people person. Giving, giving, giving," said Miranda.

"I know," Annabelle said, "but people never learn that about me because they only care about my, um, dimensions."

Miranda inserted, "And the hair and the makeup."

"Yeah, exactly. And the clothes."

"Or lack of," Miranda said.

"Exactly! You get it," Annabelle crowed. "But your friend, wow! He looked me right in the *eye* ... I think — he was wearing fabulous Italian sunglasses — but I'm pretty sure he focused in the direction of my *face."*

"And, that's a rare experience for you," Miranda said.

"You know it. Most men want to tell me I'm beautiful, or I'm graceful, or my dress fits in all the right places, my hair is like silk, blah, blah, blah."

"You must get so bored," Miranda said.

"I know, right? But your friend. Wow. You know the first thing he said to me?"

"You smell wonderful," Miranda said, a little wistfully.

"I *smelled* beauti— how did you know that?" Annabelle looked stunned.

"Just guessing," Miranda said.

"Well, you got it in one. And the way he said it! Honestly, that voice. My heart just—"

"Melted."

"—I was gonna say my heart caught fire, but yeah, melted is good, too." Annabelle sighed She practically swooned. "I can't believe what I once believed about him."

"Funny what we'll believe, especially if we want it badly enough," Miranda said.

Annabelle had come to the conclusion of her narrative. "Anyway, Mary Ann, I just want to thank you. If your friend had not come in here, and if you hadn't told me he wasn't a homo, I might never have gotten to know him. I owe you for that."

"Just name your first child 'Miranda,'" said Miranda.

"Or we could name it after you," Annabelle suggested. "That would be nice, wouldn't it?"

*Saturday evening*

Shep and Carlo had spent part of their Saturday on the river. They were returning the canoe to its rack in Shep's workshop when Miranda marched through the hedge from her yard into theirs. Thumping noises from the shed drew her in that direction.

The men did not hear her soft tread on the grass, and they both started when she proclaimed from the doorway behind them, "I gotta hand it to you! You are unbelievable!"

Carlo froze in place.

Shep dropped an oar.

Carlo commented, "She's right. I am unbelievable. But it sounds like a bad thing, the way she says it, so I do not think she means me. I am incredible in good ways only."

"I'm talking to Golden Boy there!"

"Yep," said Carlo to Shep. "That would be you."

Shep rotated slowly 180 degrees, so that he faced Miranda's voice. "Unbelievable in what way?" he said quietly.

"I thought you were a man of integrity, honor, faithfulness, or, at the very least, good manners."

"I thought the same. From your tone, I gather that ... I thought wrong?"

"How could you!"

"Um, … sorry, but I'm going to need some sort of context before I try to answer that question."

"It's rhetorical, Casanova."

"Are you talking to Carlo?"

"Very funny. I'm talking to you, you ... you great, big ... *flirt!*"

Shep suppressed a smile. "That's a pretty serious accusation, Bean. I'd like to hear the evidence against me before you lynch me."

"Oh, I've got evidence! I've got it straight from the filly's mouth."

"I see. And did the filly call me by name?"

"She didn't have to use your name. She described you perfectly. We both knew exactly of whom she was speaking."

"May I hear this description, please?"

"Tall, well-built, handsome, — actually, I think she said 'gorgeous' — definitely *not* gay, wore expensive designer sunglasses, told her she smelled good, didn't seem to care about her looks, had a sexy voice..."

Shep spent a five-count absorbing the list of traits ascribed to him. "Well, it seems a little extreme, but I guess it could be me. I'd be a fool to say I didn't want to be described that way. Who gave you this description, may I ask?"

"As if you didn't know."

"Pretend I don't. Maybe I flirt with so many women in a day that I can't remember all my romantic encounters. Consider that."

"You don't get to mock me! Not when you go putting the make on another woman less than a week after breaking our engagement — and my heart, by the way."

"What other woman, please?"

"Annabelle, of course! As you well know!"

"You flirted with *my girlfriend*!" Carlo shouted, shocked.

"*Your* girlfriend!" Miranda yelped.

"Your *girlfriend?*" Shep blurted.

"Did she really describe me the way you said?" Carlo asked, a satisfied grin spreading across his face. Then the grin fell flat. "Wait, did she say she thought I was gay? Why would she think I was gay?"

Shep said, "Not you, buddy. Pietro. She thought Pietro was gay."

"My brother was not gay. Why did she think my brother was gay?"

"Pietro and I pretended to be a gay couple whenever we visited the library," Shep explained. "We didn't want that literary love goddess aiming her attentions at us."

Carlo stared at Shep for a moment. "You must have been very good at acting!"

"Thanks."

"But not necessary, my friend. You are not her type. She likes the dark, dangerously attractive man, not the golden, goody-goody boy. You are cotton candy, and she prefers me, Carlo — I am a thick juicy steak. No offense, candy boy."

"None taken. I think you and the delightfully predatory Annabelle will make a lovely couple."

Miranda had gaped in shock during the men's brief interchange, but now she roused herself to say, "Carlo, are you telling me it was you at the library yesterday? Not Shepard?"

"I was there, *signorina*," Carlo said.

"And I definitely was not, Castor Bean," Shepard said. "Even if it had been me putting the moves on Annabelle — who is not my type either, I might add, although in deference to Carlo I imagine she is a nice person — even if it had been me, flirting with her ... why would you care? You broke up with me."

"*You* said I couldn't marry you."

"You said it first."

"But you said it last, and that counts the most."

"Well, regardless of who said what, I think you owe me an apology for accusing me of pursuing other women."

"Only one woman."

"Nonetheless, I want you to admit you were wrong, and you

accused me falsely."

"I apologize, I was wrong, I accused you falsely. Is that all?"

" I want my cat back. I know Zeus hangs out at your house, and I want you to send him home. I'm the one who feeds him; he shouldn't take sides against me."

"No, *I am* the one who feeds him," said Carlo. "He can take any side he wants."

"I'll pass on your message, if I see him," Miranda said, "but I think you know Zeus doesn't take orders from anybody, least of all me. Goodnight."

"*Ciao*," said Carlo to her back as she paced away from them, toward the hedge.

"Sleep well, Bean," Shep murmured under his breath.

## Chapter 18 - The Ritual

*Sunday morning*

Carlo entered Shep's bedroom and threw the covers off the sleeping man's bed. "Get up, Jabba! The Hutt family is go for a morning run."

Shep yawned and rolled over. "Lucky me, I don't belong to the Hutt family."

"Lucky you, you just been adopted. On your feet. Stretching starts in three and a half minutes. Shorts on the dresser, shoes and socks under the chair."

"Where's my shirt?"

"No shirt. The ladies been waiting for months for you to show up at morning coffee time, so you give them a bonus today: no shirt. And I don't care if we have a freak blizzard! You deserve a little frostbite for lazy-ing around so long for no good reason."

"I have a good reason, Simon Legree. I need Dav— … I need a running buddy who can see."

"That is me. Carlo is new running buddy. I been practicing for the past few weeks, while you been sleeping 'til the cows come home. Plus, you still got you cane. You navigate just fine."

Seeing no increase in activity from the bed, Carlo said, "Get dressed. I take it easy on you; we walk most of the way today."

Shep rolled over again. "I'll pay you to go back to bed instead."

"No good. I do not take money for making you run — or

walk, but walk fast. I do it for the joy of making you suffer."

"Even if I suffer more than you," Carlo continued, "is worth it. Meet you in the kitchen. Only two and a half minutes left now.'

♦

Running together was not much different from canoeing together, as it turned out. Shep followed Carlo's lead, stayed slightly behind, and listened to Carlo's footfalls. Carlo gave verbal notice if he changed course or pace unexpectedly, and they kept their speed low on the first day, since Shep was out of shape.

At first, Shep's excuse for not running every morning was the burns on his lower legs, from the car bombing. That was six months in the past, and his burns were virtually healed.

Scar tissue on Shep's lower legs pulled at first, with an uncomfortable, unaccustomed tautness, but there was almost no pain. As Shep ran, his somnolent muscles and resistant skin began to stretch and relax, benefiting from the exercise.

Shep's mood benefited, too, as the running released long-imprisoned endorphins into his grateful system. He had not realized that this feeling of wellbeing was yet another thing he had been missing. He had cheated his body, mind, and spirit by neglecting his dawn trot through the lush smells, sounds, and breezes of Minokee's forested lanes.

With the endorphins flooding his body and brain came an epiphany. Even though he could never regain the loving, strengthening relationships he had lost when his car exploded, some of the best gifts in life might yet be found — in new ways, with new relationships.

No, life would never again be the same as before Shep's closest friends had been murdered, but Shep finally began to believe life could someday be bearable. Maybe even enjoyable, albeit in a different way.

After running a couple miles on forest trails along the Minokee community's perimeter, Carlo took pity on the panting

Shep and slowed their pace to a brisk walk. Just before the men turned a corner onto the road that would lead them past a cluster of five cypress-clad bungalows on Magnolia Street, Carlo stopped Shep and touched his arm.

"This is it," said Carlo. "For the next two minutes you not tired, not sore, not lonesome, not thirsty and sweaty — well, they might not mind if you a little bit sweaty — but you gonna give these ladies the Shepard Krausse they been dreaming of since that explosion scared everybody senseless. For the next two minutes, you gonna be living proof that God is in His heaven and all is right in the world. Got it?"

Shep nodded.

"Say it."

"Not tired, kinda sweaty, all's right with the world. Sweetness and light."

"*Molto bene.*"

"Think Bean is there?" asked Shepard.

"Want me to tell you, if she is?" said Carlo. "You want to stop for her?"

"No, no need to say anything. If she's there, I'll know. Either way, I won't be stopping. There's nothing to say."

Carlo said, "You are the boss."

Shepard actually laughed. "Oh, so *I'm* the one who decided to go running this morning! Good to know."

Carlo grinned and clapped Shepard on the shoulder. "Ready?"

"As I'll ever be."

"Showtime!" Carlo turned and led the way toward Magnolia Street's coffee ritual, with Shepard running strongly, close behind.

When they turned the corner, Zeus leaped into the street from atop Miranda's garden fence. The kitten bounded across the pavement and fell into step, loping beside Shep.

"*Mmrrrrt*," chirped Zeus.

"Morning, stranger," Shep said with a smile. "Thanks for coming."

"*Buon giorno*, Zeus," Carlo added.

A moment later the runners were nearly concussed by the *BLAAAAAAT!* of an air horn nearby. The horn's blare was still reverberating in the atmosphere around them when they heard an old woman shout, "Git yerselfs out here fast! He's back! And it's a no-shirt day!"

Three screen doors slammed – one from the direction of the horn and two from the opposite side of the street. The Magnolia Street ladies were assembled. Let the morning ritual recommence, after months of hiatus.

"They're waiting for you," said Carlo. "Remember, you not tired, you not sore, you not sad. Just smile and wave."

"I know what to do," Shep said.

"*Myreao?*"

"Of course, you can come. Look smart," Shep told the cat.

Moments later, a three-unit parade jogged down the middle of shady, green, delicately-scented Magnolia Street. Four elderly ladies in house dresses stood at their front porch railings, a coffee cup in one hand, and waved to Carlo and Zeus.

Waving communicated nothing to Shep, however, so the ladies also whooped and hollered and shouted greetings to Shep as if they had not seen him in a long time. And they had not, really. This was the first time Shep had made a morning run in months.

Nobody mentioned it was also the first time in years Shep had run without his dog, Dave, to guide him.

Carlo and Shep waved at the ladies, angling from one side of the street to the other and back to the center. They continued on to the end of Magnolia Street, then turned right and disappeared from sight, progressing toward Orchid Street and home.

Carlo reacted to the *bang-bang-bang* of screen doors slamming on the street they had left behind. "What, only three went back inside?"

"Miz Cleary stays on the porch pretty much all the time," Shep answered. He dropped to a walk and tried not to pant too obviously. "That's enough for today. Don't want to overdo it."

Carlo jogged in a circle around his slower companion before

taking a place walking beside him. "You must feel pretty good after a big welcome like that."

"Sweet ladies. … How did they know we'd be there this particular morning?"

"Are you kidding?" Carlo told him. "They been posting a lookout *every* morning. Sometimes all four of them be out there in their rocking chairs, with the morning coffee. …Sometimes the *signorina* Miranda be out there with her coffee, too, before she go off to work."

"But not today."

"No. Not today."

"*Mao-yao.*" Zeus made a U-turn and padded back toward Magnolia Street.

"Thanks, buddy," Shep called after him.

They walked past several Orchid Street houses without a word. There was no ritual on Orchid Street, only on Magnolia.

As the two men angled off the street and toward Shep's cottage, Carlo said, "After church today, let's canoe out to Tom Rigby's farm."

"Sounds like a plan."

## Chapter 19 - The Money

*Sunday afternoon.*

The Minokee houses were the only private residences grandfathered in when Little Cypress National Forest was established in the 1940's.

Existing mostly in isolation, Minokee residents adopted a slower pace of life out of necessity. Civilization of any significance – that is, significant enough to have, say, a traffic light – was a long way from the dozen ancient cottages nestled in between the cypress trees and alligators of Minokee.

No interstate highway or multi-lane turnpike passed through Little Cypress National Forest.

A county road, with a forgotten name, wound from the forest boundary, around and between ponds, trees, and sinkholes for several shady miles, to end at Minokee.

That single, narrow, asphalt ribbon was barely wide enough for two compact sedans to squeeze past one another.

This was no problem, because the odds of two vehicles being on the same Minokee road, at the same moment, were no better than the odds of winning the Florida lottery (usually about one in umpteen million).

The cottages sat clustered in a hammock with only two, one-car-wide roads. Magnolia Street ran west to east, then angled sharply to the right, and right again, and connected to Orchid Street, which ran east to west.

Driving from Minokee to anywhere took a long time, at low speeds, on circuitous routes.

Shep and Carlo would have had to drive many miles westward to reach backroads, which would then take them in the opposite direction many more miles, in order to visit Tom Rigby's farm.

Pig River was shorter and faster. Rigby's farm was an easy glide downstream through Little Cypress. Carlo and Shep would return to Minokee by simply turning upstream and paddling against the current.

They had canoed this river for years, in both directions, and had the impressive shoulder, arm, and back muscles to prove it.

On Sunday afternoon, the two friends shared a single canoe, and their pace was very different from the easy, ambling rate of Clarkson's Audubon cruise two weeks before.

That trip had taken a lazy four hours to reach Rigby's farm.

Today, two fit young men propelled their craft like a collegiate crew on uppers.

Their flying rhythm faltered only slightly when Zeus crawled out from under a thwart and perched himself on the bow of the boat, mewing the feline equivalent of "I'm king of the world!"

The oars paused for a split second, but rowing resumed when Shep said simply, "He sure does like water."

"Weird," said Carlo. "What kind of cat he is, you reckon? He still a kitten, but he getting huge."

*"Mrratt!"*

Shep said, "He's not calling you fat. Don't be so sensitive."

"Right," Carlo agreed. "And, look at that mane he getting. Soon people will think you keeping a lion."

*"MerrrrOARH!"* Zeus gave his best imitation of a roar.

"Everybody is a comedian," Carlo muttered. He steered the canoe away from a low-hanging tree limb on the left, and they rowed toward a limb on the right that was slightly higher.

Shepard said, "Speaking of funny business, Rocket tells me rumors are spreading that Tom Rigby will be coming into some money. Suddenly, he's ordering equipment and materials the farm has been doing without for a long time."

They brushed under the limb hanging off the righthand bank, and Shep stopped speaking to wipe a spider web off his face and spit it out of his mouth.

"Sorry," Carlo said. "I did not see that one."

"Me neither," said Shep and spat one more time. "Anyway, it's funny that Rigby starts spending tons of money *now*, just when he's supposedly getting ready to donate a three-hundred-thousand-dollar mammoth fossil to the university."

"I got something funnier than that for you," Carlo said. "My spies around Gainesville tell me Maynard has been selling things to raise drug money."

"That's not unusual. We know he's been busted in the past for possession, and we know he's a thief."

"*Si*, but the things he is selling right now are not Maynard's usual merchandise," said Carlo. "Is higher quality and in much better taste. Maynard leans more toward car radios and DVR's. Now, he selling jade art and high-class Asian clothing."

Shep said, "David Zhang's possessions."

"*Si*, but one thing he has not sold is a laptop computer. I think, if Maynard wants money and he has something of value, like a laptop, he would not keep it for sentimental reasons," Carlo said. "He has not sold the computer, because he does not have it."

Shep thought for a few moments.

Zeus batted at a cluster of red berries hanging over the river on a slender stalk that bounced in the breeze.

"What if he hasn't sold the laptop because his usual clientele can't afford it?" Shep said.

"So, we come back to how much is that computer worth?"

"And that depends on what is on the computer and how useful it is to the person who wants it," Shep concluded.

No one spoke further. Both men concentrated on their paddling. Shep's unique, hand-crafted canoe moved so fast it could almost have pulled water skiers.

The trio arrived at Tom Rigby's property in less than an hour.

They beached the canoe at the spot where they had enjoyed a picnic lunch two weeks before. That had been the day they first met David and Felicia, the professor's teaching assistants.

It was the time they met Tom Rigby, visited Tom's sinkhole, and saw part of a tusk protruding from the earth, just a tantalizing two or three meters below ground level.

It was also the last time anybody saw David Zhang.

"A few weeks," Carlo mused. "In such a short time, David has gone missing, and many people are behaving strangely. I am thinking about Tom Rigby and David's professor, David's fellow teaching assistant, and David's roommate."

He went on, "And, I am thinking, if mammoth bones are worth three hundred thousand dollars, how much is David Zhang's laptop worth?"

"Good question." Shep knelt on the shore beside the bow of the canoe. "Especially since his doctoral dissertation is probably on it. …Come on, if you're comin'!"

Zeus hopped from the gunwale of the boat to a comfy perch on Shepard's shoulder. Shepard stood, took the elbow Carlo offered, and the two men walked into the woods.

"Does Felicia have the laptop?" said Shep as they dodged palmetto spikes and cypress knees. "Could she pass David's research off as her own and win the fellowship from the university? How much would that be worth, factoring in the boost it could be to someone's future career?"

Carlo pointed out, "Don't forget, according to Rocket, Maynard is getting late-night, back-door visits from someone connected to David, even though Maynard told me he didn't know any of David's acquaintances."

"Does Maynard have David's laptop?"

Carlo reflexively shook his head, even though his friend could not see him. "I did not find it when I searched his room, but maybe he already hid it someplace else."

Shep did not nod, although he understood and agreed with the statement. He seldom used nodding and head-wagging; the habits were not ingrained in him as they were in his sighted friends.

"Has Maynard come into a sum of money lately? Above what he's selling the small items for? Ask one of your hackers to get us a screenshot of the activity on Maynard's bank accounts," Shep said. "Maybe he wouldn't want to keep a large amount of cash just stuffed under his mattress."

Carlo brought them to a stop.

A three-foot corn snake slithered across the narrow trail they were following.

"Traffic," said Carlo. Then he started walking again.

Carlo continued. "Okay. Felicia and Maynard. Definitely something going on there, but maybe they too obvious. We also have to look at people who do not look suspicious, right?"

"Whom do you suggest, Inspector Frattelli?"

"*Il Profesore* Clarkson. On the surface he is a college professor of many years, respected and admired in academic circles, never even had a parking ticket in his whole life."

"So, he doesn't look suspicious," Shep said.

"*Si.* But also consider: Tom Rigby follows Clarkson's advice on anything about archaeology."

Carlo continued, "Could Clarkson be looking to score some cash — maybe split the profits or receive a commission — when Tom sells the bones?" He stopped their forward motion. "Here is a stream."

Carlo stepped behind Shep and, palms on Shep's shoulders, aimed him at the path ahead. Then he lifted Zeus from Shepard's shoulder and said, "About four feet across. Less than two feet deep, but lots of tricky rocks on the bottom."

Shepard jump-stepped across the bubbling creek in their path. Carlo did the same and placed the cat again on Shep's shoulder. The trio resumed their hike. All with dry feet.

Continuing their conversation, Shep said, "Clarkson seems upright and law-abiding, but he *is* nearing retirement age and may not have saved much of a nest egg on a teacher's salary."

"*Si.* Maybe he has realized people are living longer these days.

He needs his money to last as long as he does," said Carlo. "What if he retires and then lives to be a hundred and two, but the money runs out at age ninety, or even ninety-eight? A man could get pretty hungry those last few years."

Shep rubbed behind Zeus's ears with one hand as they walked. "So, we're looking at Felicia and Maynard, and potentially Doctor Clarkson. That brings us to Tom Rigby. Hopefully, we'll know what's going on with him after we talk with him face-to-face in a few minutes."

"We are at the sinkhole," Carlo said, stopping a few safe feet away from the edge, which was a sheer drop-off into a cavern of uncertain depth.

"What do you see in the surrounding scrub?" Shep asked his friend.

Carlo scanned the clearing and trees around the hole. "I see a pile of fence posts, some bags of concrete mix in a wheelbarrow, and some coils of barbed wire. And, I see a box that looks like electrified wire, like you'd run along your fence to discourage animals."

"Hm," said Shep. "So, Tom is anxious about unwanted visitors. Why is that? He didn't seem so nervous three weeks ago. What has changed?"

"Maybe Tom found out that his fossil could be worth a *lot* of money?" mused Carlo. "I would like to know who told him that."

A languid Zeus stood up from his shoulder perch and chirped in Shepard's ear. Shep knelt on one knee, and Zeus trotted down Shep's back and off into the trees.

"I guess nature calls," said Carlo.

"I hope he doesn't come across any wild pigs in these woods."

Carlo chuckled. "If he does, I think I feel sorry for the pigs. That little cat already put the fear of God into every animal within five miles of Minokee."

"Yeah, but wild boars are big, strong, and mean, and their tusks are sharp." Shep thought a moment. "All these piles of fencing stuff … Has anything actually been installed, or does it look like just supplies and materials, stacked up for later?"

Carlo scanned the woods in a complete circle around them and the sinkhole. "No. I see where they have marked the fence line with orange spray paint on the ground. Looks like they sprayed an orange 'X' wherever they want a posthole. In fact, I see the posthole digger sticking out of the ground over there about twenty yards, like somebody quit work in the middle of something. Maybe got interrupted."

Shep inhaled deeply through his nose before he said, "I don't remember it smelling so damp in this spot last time we were here. Are we close to a large amount of standing water?"

"Stay here," said Carlo and dropped to all fours. He crept carefully to the edge of the sinkhole and looked over the side. "The hole has been filling with water. Impossible to say how deep it goes."

"Probably goes all the way down to the underground river that caused the land to collapse. Can you still see the fossils?"

Carlo backed up from the edge and stood, dusting mud and gravel from his jeans. "Oh, yeah. The bones are on the north wall, about nine feet down from ground level, where we're standing. The surface of the water is about six feet below that, but it could still be rising."

"Hm," Shep said. "Let's go talk to Tom."

He called over his shoulder toward the place Zeus had rustled off into the woods. "Zeus, we're going on to the house now. Be careful out there."

From someplace in the trees above them came a distant "*merraou*."

"That's good," said Carlo. "No pigs up there."

As their hike brought them closer and closer to the farmhouse, Carlo described to Shep many signs of disrepair, weathering, and neglect around the farmyard and outbuildings.

Shep said, "So, the place needs a lot of maintenance and restoration. That won't be cheap. At Tom's age, he can't do all the work himself, like he would have years ago. He'll have to hire workmen and buy parts, or maybe new tools."

"Maybe *Tom* is the one who realize he did not save enough for the years when he is too old to farm," said Carlo. "Is he already in those years, now?"

"Maybe. So, we agree that the rumors of Tom buying a lot of stuff lately appear to be true. The stuff is here to be seen."

*"Sí."*

"Too bad there were no rumors about where the money is coming from."

Minutes later, the duo's path led out of the woods and onto the acre of lawn surrounding Rigby's ancient farmhouse. They crossed shin-high grass to the back stoop of the house, and Carlo rapped on the peeling paint of the battered wooden door.

The door swung open at his touch.

Seeing no one waiting to invite them in, Carlo called out, "*Signor* Rigby? *Signor* Rigby! Is Carlo Fratelli and Shepard Krausse!"

Shep and Carlo waited, but nobody answered.

"*Signor* Tom Rigby!" Carlo called again. To his companion, he said, "He should be home from church by now; is way after lunchtime. And, Shepard, there is a pickup truck tagged 'Elvis' in the tractor shed. If Tom Rigby's famous truck is here, he should be somewhere here, too."

Shep said, "I don't know how to explain it, but the house feels … empty, y'know? Maybe it's the echo, but it gives me the creeps."

"Something is not right," Carlo agreed. "I keep thinking of that posthole tool abandoned in the woods. I think Tom is one of those guys who puts his tools away when he is finish with them. Good farmers are like that."

"See anything from here?"

"I can see the kitchen table," said Carlo. "Papers are scattered there. Breakfast dishes drying beside the sink. Two coffee cups, but only one plate."

"Let's go in," said Shep.

Carlo edged the door open wider and, with Shepard at his elbow, entered the house.

Once inside, Shep pulled his white cane from his pocket and telescoped it to its full length with a few quick snaps. "I'll poke around the other rooms, in case he's asleep or something. You take a look at those papers on the table."

"Good. Be careful, my friend."

"Yup," Shep said, and he began cane-tapping his way through the rooms of the house. In a few minutes, he returned to the kitchen. "There's nobody here."

"There was somebody," said Carlo. The loose pages spread across the table made faint crinkling sounds when he jabbed them with his forefinger. "I do not know Tom Rigby's handwriting, but I can see that two different people have written notes on these papers."

Shep seemed to be thinking out loud when he said, "If we assume one of them is Tom, since it's Tom's house and Tom's table, then who is the second person?"

"Could be the visitor Rocket followed here. Unless Tom is a more social man than I thought, he probably does not have a lot of visitors. And it has been only a short time since Rocket's target was here, we know."

Shepard placed a palm down atop the papers as if to glean information by osmosis. "Can you guess if either handwriting is a woman's? I don't know ... little hearts dotting the *I*'s or some such thing?"

Carlo pushed papers around, revealing first one and then another of the penciled notations. "No. Everything is block-printed. Plain. Could be anyone."

No one spoke for the next minute or so. A blue jay squawked outside the kitchen window. A jet engine's drone drifted down from the stratosphere, a wisp of sound from tremendous altitude.

Through the beat-up open door, a zephyr pushed the scent of distant orange blossoms into the room and cooled the air of the warm kitchen.

Carlo said, "What do you want to do?"

Shep seemed to gather his thoughts for a moment more, then

he said, "Send Rocket a text and find out where Felicia and Maynard are. He should be following one of them, and, if we're lucky, the two of them are together."

*"Sí."* Carlo took out his phone and began tapping keys. "I keep thinking of that deep hole full of water out there."

"Me, too."

"Should we tell the police Tom is missing?"

"We don't actually *know* he's missing," Shep said. "I don't particularly want just anybody to know we're out here poking around. And, I don't think we can trust anybody much, until we know what's going on and how all these people are connected."

Carlo's phone signaled an answer to his text. He read the screen. "Rocket says Maynard and Felicia are on Interstate Ten, headed toward Jacksonville. He's four cars behind them."

"Good. Tell him to stick with them. You and I will head upstream."

"*Sí,* I would like to be off the river before dark."

"I guess we need to round up that crazy cat."

More than one blue jay suddenly squawked up a racket outside.

"That will be Zeus coming now," said Carlo, and he stepped to the sink to look out the kitchen window. "The birds are dive-bombing him. It is time for us to go."

"Bring those papers with you," Shep said. "If Tom's visitor returns, they might take away something. And, if you don't mind, I think it would be good if you'd go to Gainesville tomorrow morning and spend some time with Win Clarkson. Tell him what we've found and see how he reacts."

## Chapter 20 - The Subcommittee

*Monday morning*

Miranda was more than a little surprised when Dr. Rosario Ogilvy marched up to the library's circulation desk at nine in the morning and uttered a crisp, "Hello, Miranda."

"Mother! Um, … good morning…. Is Daddy with you?"

"He is parking the car. I had him drop me off at the front door, since suitable parking is too far away to walk in this abominable heat."

Rosario surveyed the library's interior with a regal turn of her head. "How many branch libraries do you have? This is obviously one of the smaller ones."

"There's *one* public library in Live Oak. This is it. This is where Dad's sister, my Aunt Phyllis, worked for many years."

"This is the only library in town?" Rosario might have wrinkled her nose, if she were willing to expend that much energy on such an insignificant subject. "Well, I didn't come to discuss your unfortunate career decisions today."

"How nice for me," said Miranda pleasantly. "Hi, Daddy!"

Zeke Ogilvy came to stand beside his wife. He leaned across the circulation desk to kiss Miranda on the cheek. "Hi, beautiful."

"Mother was just telling me she doesn't want to discuss my 'unfortunate career choices.'"

"Really? How nice for you."

"That's what I said." Miranda exchanged a smile of

commiseration with her dad.

To her mother, she said, "So, what did you want to discuss, Mother? I have a coffee break in about fifteen minutes, if you'd like to talk privately. We can use one of the conference rooms."

"Thank you, dear, but I can't stay long. I have a hair appointment. I only wanted to remind you that you must consider the plans of others sometimes, in addition to your own personal wishes."

Miranda glanced at her father, but he only shook his head with a wry smile that seemed to say, "I'm not involved in this."

"I'm sorry, Mother, what are you talking about? I am considerate of others."

Rosario proclaimed: "You don't realize how much time and money has been invested by many people to secure an acceptable future for you and Hermione's boy."

"'Hermione's *boy*?' Is that what you're calling Shepard now?"

"Don't be overly sensitive," said Rosario. "It isn't meant to be demeaning."

"So, I'm over-sensitive *and* inconsiderate? And, yes, I'm afraid being called 'Hermione's boy' would offend most adult males."

"Fine," Rosario said. "Then don't tell *Shepard* I said it. I'll refrain in future."

"I don't tell him anything. I'm not speaking to him, actually."

Rosario jabbed a forefinger toward Miranda. "That's exactly what I'm talking about. Your father and I—"

"Please leave me out of this," Zeke murmured.

"Very well … *Hermione and I* are convinced the two of you will make a perfect match. It will be a great boost to his political aspirations, and you'll be able to stop working in this pitiful little building and be a full-time First La— I mean, a full-time supportive wife."

Miranda looked around the library and found no patrons or employees close enough to overhear. She took a deep, centering breath and kept her tone pleasant and low.

"First of all, Shepard has no such 'aspirations,'" Miranda said.

"And, secondly, I have no plans to quit my job. I'm a career librarian, Mother. There's no shame in it. You act like I sell flowers on street corners and eat dinner at soup kitchens."

"And steal hubcaps for spending money," Zeke added.

Rosario did not bother to lower her voice. "Ezekiel, if you want to be left out of it, then stay out of it! Miranda, I can see that you're in no mood to discuss this right now, and I have a hair appointment at 'Millie's Beauty Mill' somewhere on this street."

A scoffing sound escaped Rosario's pursed lips before she continued, "Heaven only knows how *that* is going to turn out. No doubt my stylist will have a fit when I get back to Miami."

"No doubt," Miranda and Zeke said in unison.

Rosario ignored them. "I hope you'll think about what I've said. I'll talk to you later. Ezekiel, are you coming?"

"In just a minute," Zeke told her. "I have a research project for Miranda. I'll catch up with you at the 'Beauty Mill.' I wouldn't miss this for the world."

To Miranda, he winked as he said, "Want to come with me and observe, Baby Girl? No? Well, I'll text you a picture if things go horribly wrong."

Rosario gave them a look that said she found no humor in their exchange. She left the library without a word to either of them.

When Rosario had gone, Zeke said to Miranda, "Try to cut your mother a little slack. We've recently been appointed to a very important subcommittee, and it's got her stressed to the max."

"What kind of 'subcommittee'?"

"Doesn't matter. Can you help me with some research for a friend?"

"Sure, what do you need?"

"While we're here, I've been catching up with my old friend, Win Clarkson, at the University of Florida – he says you two have met. Well, he has an odd situation. He tells me his teaching assistant, an Asian young man called David Zhang, has gone missing."

Miranda reacted with wide eyes. "I know David! I met him on a canoe trip Professor Clarkson led, a few weeks ago. I met the other T.A., too. Letitia, is it?"

"Felicia," said Zeke. "Felicia Harper. Apparently, the two were dating fairly seriously, but Felicia hasn't heard from David, either."

"Have they called the police?"

"Oh, yes, definitely. The authorities at the university and in the city and county are unconcerned. They say international students sometimes get homesick and return to their country, often suddenly and without notice. There is no evidence of foul play. David's family has not contacted the university saying they haven't heard from him. The consensus is that he must be in China. Full stop."

"But you don't think he is in China?"

"No, and neither does Win. Nor Shepard."

Miranda's eyes suddenly drilled directly into Zeke's. "What does Shepard have to do with this? Is this some feeble plot to get me together with Shepard? Because it won't work. We're through being manipulated."

Zeke reached for her hand and held it in his right while stroking it with his left. "At ease, Corporal. This has nothing to do with the maternal generals at Wedding H.Q. This is a recon mission from me to you. The only person you report to is me. Nobody's mother needs to know anything about it. Except maybe David's, if he really is missing."

Miranda's shoulders lowered from full alert, and she covered her dad's soothing hand with her own. "Sorry. Shell-shocked from all the wedding pressure, I guess."

"Perfectly understandable," Zeke said. "All I want is any background information you can find on David and Felicia. You tell me, and I'll pass the data on to Win and to Shep – because Shep, apparently, is trying to help find David. That's all."

"And I don't have to talk to Shepard!"

"Absolutely not. Unless you want to, of course."

She wagged her head *No.*

Miranda took a note paper and tiny pencil from a box on the circulation counter and pushed them across the oak countertop toward her father. "Write down the names and anything else that might get me started. I'll get back to you with a status report tonight."

Minutes later, Ezekiel Ogilvy sauntered into Millie's Beauty Mill and sat down in a plastic lobby chair next to his wife.

Rosario looked up from an antique copy of Vogue magazine and raised an eyebrow at him in query.

"Mission accomplished, General," was all he said.

*Late Monday afternoon*

Shep had been sitting in his home office with the door closed since 4:40 a.m.

He had not eaten the French toast breakfast Carlo had prepared before leaving for Gainesville, but he had consumed numerous cups of coffee from the pot on the office credenza.

When he didn't emerge from his man cave for lunch, Carlo would have assumed Shep was engaged in one of his marathon conference calls with radio station managers. But Carlo was not at home.

Shep might be researching conspiracy theories on the Internet, for the Sheep Counters late-night call-in show he had formerly hosted. A new announcer had taken over the hosting duties.

Although Shep had not returned to the midnight microphone, he still had a flare for encouraging conspiracy theorists, and he often compiled material for the show's new host to use.

Carlo would have been concerned about Shep's reclusiveness, if Carlo had known that Shep spent more than twelve hours not using his computer at all. He also made no telephone calls, sent no memoranda to his station managers, and provided no conspiracy fodder to the new shepherd of the late-night Sheep Counters.

Shep had spent twelve silent hours with his chair tilted back, his feet on his desk, his coffee cup in his hands, and his face toward the window.

He couldn't see out the window, of course. In fact, there were days when he worked in his office all day without ever opening the curtains.

On this day, he had opened the curtains before the sun came up, then sat waiting until he could feel its warmth on his face.

He had raised the window glass to feel a whisper of breeze and hear the birds sing to one another from the branches of gracefully arching, moss-shawled old trees.

Zeus hopped onto the window sill from the backyard. Shep heard the kitten batting at the window screen. Then the cat "*merroaw-ow-ow*"-ed until Shep lifted the screen to let it in. Zeus dropped softly onto Shep's desk.

"You're welcome," Shep quipped.

"*K-k-k-k-k-k.*"

"I know you've been spending the night at her place. You think we don't notice you disappearing just before she gets home from work? I bet you curl up in her lap and get all snuggly! But all you do for me is leave sandy footprints all over my desk!"

"*K-k-k-k-k.*"

" I'm tired of you snapping at me like everything's my fault, when it isn't." Shep leaned toward where the cat was sitting on the corner of his desk.

The cat stretched its neck until it touched Shep's nose with its own.

Suddenly Shep sat back in his chair as if stung. "I can't believe it!"

*"Mwahr?"*

"Oh, don't play innocent with me, you traitor. Lemon chicken! Bean made her lemon chicken recipe, and *you* ate it!"

*"Mwaht!"*

"Yes, you did! I can smell it on your breath!"

Shep sat a moment. Then he leaned forward again, and Zeus

did the same, until they were nose-touching. Shep slowly relaxed back into his chair and sighed. "I love Bean's lemon chicken."

Zeus jumped from the desktop to the floor and sauntered to the closed door. "*Ahwr-wao-err*," he said.

Shep pushed off with his feet and let his chair roll toward the door. He turned the knob and opened the door exactly feline-wide. "If you're looking for Carlo, he's not home. I sent him to Gainesville for the day. …Oh, sure, him you like. Fine. Just remember, to err is human; to forgive is feline.'"

"*Mwaht*," said Zeus.

"Well, it should be."

Zeus gave Shepard a curt swish of the tail and cruised out of the office, heading for the food bowl in the kitchen.

Shep rolled the chair back to the desk and again turned his face to the window. He didn't need to see to know what was out there. The view from Shep's home office was Miranda Ogilvy's cedar-sided, vine-cloaked little house.

♦

Half an hour later, when Miranda arrived home from work, she was surprised to find no fur-ball-with-attitude waiting on her back steps. She set her purse inside on the kitchen counter and went back outside to stroll around the yard, looking for the mighty Zeus.

As she circled the house, Martha Cleary's porch came into view, with Mrs. Cleary reigning over the kingdom of Minokee from her rocking throne.

Miranda waved to Mrs. Cleary, calling, "Good evening! You haven't seen Zeus, have you? He's usually waiting at my back door."

"Evenin'," the old lady responded with no break in her rocker's rhythm. "Seems like ya oughta be askin' the boys at the house over yonder." A bony finger extended toward Shepard's house, beyond Miranda's back hedge.

When Miranda didn't answer, Mrs. Cleary nodded knowingly. "Y'all ain't speakin' these days, I reckon."

Miranda remained silent, but the sudden switch of her gaze toward her toes communicated agreement.

"Ain't my bidniss, o'course," Mrs. Cleary said. "Anyhow, Zeus knows he ain't welcome over here among my birds. Prolly the cat done made up with Shep, 'cause Zeus is smart."

"If I wuz you," she continued, "I'd mosey on over there and do some makin' up of my own. 'Course, as I said, ain't none of my bidniss."

When Miranda didn't answer, Martha changed the subject. Sort of.

"How's that old Caddy running fer ya. Getting' ya back an' forth to town okay?"

"Yes, ma'am. Thank you."

"Thought you wuz goin' ta git a new car fer y'self. What ya waitin' fer?"

"I don't know. Busy, I guess. Do you need the Caddy back?"

"Naw, I don't need nuthin'. I'm jest curious if you can say the same?"

Mrs. Cleary's tone indicated she expected no answer to that question.

Miranda waited, but only the creaking of the distant rocking chair on ancient wooden boards reached her ears. Miz-Martha-the-Oracle had spoken. The interview was ended.

Lifting her eyes from the ground, Miranda waved weakly and mumbled, "Thanks," toward the old woman across the street.

## Chapter 21 - The Papers

Daylight yielded its place to oncoming darkness. Only the day's dusky-pink coattail lingered above tree-shaded Minokee when Miranda entered her kitchen a few minutes later.

The clock declared evening dinner time. Miranda inventoried the possibilities, out of habit.

She still had several dishes in the refrigerator — meals that Carlo had cooked and delivered to her during the past week.

She had thrown out last night's lemon chicken, since she had no appetite, and it would probably kill Zeus if she let him eat the whole thing.

She did not have a feline dinner companion today, and — continuing her pattern of many days — she had no desire to eat.

Instead of preparing and eating dinner, Miranda put on a pot of water for tea and sat down to call her father with a report on her day's research.

She told Zeke about looking at the previous academic experience of both Felicia Harper and David Zhang.

Both had attended respected undergraduate schools and achieved excellent grade point averages.

Both came from what amounted to middle class families in their respective countries, and neither had a lot of money.

Felicia had a scholarship from the State of Florida that paid her tuition and materials, but not room and board.

David had an international scholarship that was a bit more generous, but he had to pay his own expenses of traveling to and from China or communicating with friends and family there.

"They sound evenly matched," said her father. "It's impossible to guess which one might win the post-doctoral fellowship once they submit their dissertations."

"Actually, I think it's more than possible, Dad. Of course, I don't have access to the research notes or drafts for their doctoral dissertations, but I was able to read their masters' theses, and I think there might be a critical difference between Felicia and David."

"Are you kidding? You actually saw the master's thesis for each of these people? How in the world did you get hold of something like that?"

"You're spending too much time in the Pleistocene Era with your giant ground sloths, Professor. Here in the twenty-first century, Dad, everything is on the Internet, if you know how to look for it. And I am a librarian. We specialize in knowing how to find information – printed or electronic."

Ezekiel took a moment to absorb Miranda's statement, and he smiled. "Have I told you lately how proud I am of you?"

"No, in fact, I don't think you have," she said pleasantly. "If it's any consolation, though, I'm sure you've told me a million times in the past —and that's about nine hundred ninety-nine thousand more times than Mother has said anything complimentary."

Zeke's smile faded a little, and his brow wrinkled. "You know that's a reflection of who *she* is, right? Not who *you* are. You're wonderful, whether anybody tells you so or not."

"I know, Dad. Thanks for the affirmation, though. Always good to hear."

"You're welcome, Muffin."

"Daddy! I'm not twelve anymore!"

"Oh, sorry. *Miss* Muffin. Or is it *Doctor* Muffin? Did I miss anything these past few years? Oh, wait. I did miss that whole boyfriend, engagement, broken-engagement episode. I don't suppose there's any news on that front?"

Miranda was quiet, but only for a second. "We were talking about the masters' theses of David Zhang and Felicia Harper."

"Okay. I'm listening."

"Felicia's vocabulary and writing style are what you'd expect from an average undergrad," said Miranda. "She presents facts and draws rational conclusions, but there's no spark."

Miranda went on to specify, "The syntax is awkward. The words don't flow. The thoughts don't resonate. Compared to an excellent thesis – David's thesis, for instance – Felicia's paper is academically crude."

"It can't be that bad," her father said. "She earned her master's degree with it."

"True," said Miranda. "If you read it as a stand-alone, not comparing it to anyone else's work, it's okay. There are no glaring mistakes, the paper is formatted well, the facts seem correct, and the conclusions make sense."

"But?"

"But nobody exists in a vacuum, Dad. In the competition for the university's doctoral fellowship in paleontology, Felicia has a rival. David Zhang's paper will be compared with Felicia's, and Felicia will not come out ahead, in my opinion."

"Really," Zeke said. "You seem to feel strongly about your opinion."

"I guess I do."

"Then I think you better tell me more," her father told her.

Miranda's tea kettle whistled for her attention, so she excused herself and left her chair to make a cup of tea. She put her phone on speaker and talked to her father from across the room, while she fussed with water, tea bag, cup and spoon.

She told her father that David Zhang was a gifted writer, especially for someone writing in a second language. Although his subject matter was scientific, and full of geological and mathematical vocabulary, he expressed complex concepts in terms most lay readers would comprehend.

Miranda felt that David's paper was more than informative, it was actually enjoyable and, in parts, almost poetic. As a purely academic document, it was remarkable for its panache.

"In my opinion," she said, "anybody who read both of these papers would swoon over David's and forget Felicia's entirely. If their doctoral dissertations are anything like their masters' theses, Felicia doesn't have a prayer of winning that fellowship."

Miranda concluded, "Heck, they'll probably give David the fellowship, nominate him for the Nobel Prize, and make him president of the university."

Zeke laughed out loud. Then he said, "They probably won't make him university president, but if you're right, they'd undoubtedly give him the fellowship."

"I'm right."

"I trust your judgment." Zeke thought for a few moments before saying, "I think Win Clarkson needs to know this. If he can see us tomorrow morning, would you be free to drive to Gainesville with me?"

"Will … anybody else … be there?"

"I'll make sure it's just you, me, and Win. Nobody else. Unless you want me to invite somebody else?"

"No! … I mean, … I think we should discuss this privately, especially since I'm just speculating. Tuesday is my comp day this week, for working Saturday, so I'm good to go."

Zeke said he would contact Win Clarkson to set up a meeting. He would text Miranda later with an exact meeting time and place.

Miranda said she would meet her father at the library in Live Oak and drive them to Gainesville.

Zeke did not ask his daughter to come to the mansion of Hermione Montgomery-Krausse, where he was staying. Miranda did not volunteer to go there.

*Tuesday morning*

Miranda and her father arrived at the University of Florida campus in the middle of the morning.

Win Clarkson was expecting them. He had arranged for his teaching assistant, Felicia, to cover his classes for the next few hours, but he had not told her with whom he was meeting.

Zeke and Win both listened as Miranda laid out the findings she had reported to her father by phone the night before.

She finished by stating firmly her belief that David Zhang would almost certainly be awarded the paleontology fellowship on the basis of his doctoral dissertation and oral defense.

"Thank you for doing all that work on David's and my behalf," Clarkson told her. "I think you could be right about David's advantage in the competition for the fellowship."

He went on, "But remember, Felicia would not have read David's master's thesis. That was done before he came to this university. And, I'm sure he would not allow her to see his drafts or research for his doctoral dissertation – especially since she's his competition for the fellowship."

"Oh," said Miranda, relaxing her posture somewhat. "Then maybe there's nothing to worry about. Felicia might be oblivious to the odds against her in the competition, so she would have no reason to try to sabotage David."

Win lifted himself from his chair and began pacing the carpet behind his desk. "Don't let me mislead you. I didn't say I'm not worried. Carlo Fratelli was here yesterday, and he told me some things that really started me thinking."

"Carlo was here?" said Miranda.

"What sorts of things?" Zeke asked.

Win told them that Shep and Carlo had enlisted several of their former Sheep Counters investigators in and around the university. One man in particular had been watching Felicia, and he had photographed her in suspicious circumstances.

"Suspicious how?" said Zeke.

"Late night, back-door visits to David's former roommate – a man who had told Carlo that he knew none of David's friends."

"But Felicia and David were dating," Miranda put in. "She told me, herself, that they were getting serious. Surely the roommate would have known her, if she spent much time with David. You would think she would be at their apartment frequently."

She continued, "I don't want to judge them, because I don't have any knowledge of their intimate behavior, but it is true a lot of couples sleep together before marriage. If Felicia spent nights with David, I don't see how David's roommate could not know her."

Win nodded. "I'm afraid there is more. David's laptop computer has not been found."

Zeke said, "Maybe he took it with him. He may even have worked on his dissertation on the long plane trip to China."

Win shook his head slowly. "Looks like there was no plane trip. There is no record of anyone using David's identification, or matching David's description, leaving Florida by any public transportation near the time David went missing.

"Also, David's bedroom and study space seemed to contain everything he could be expected to take with him, if he left. Or, at least, it used to contain David's possessions."

"It doesn't now?" asked Miranda. "What happened?"

"Maynard happened," Clarkson told them. "Maynard, the roommate, has been arrested with drugs in the past, and he has recently been selling jade art and Asian clothing that Carlo believes are David's. Carlo saw them when he searched David's apartment, and it's a good thing he searched it early on. After two weeks now, it may have been cleared out by university cleaners."

"Oh, dear," Zeke said.

"Yes, 'oh, dear,'" Win echoed. "So, we have Felicia meeting secretly with a thief and druggie who claims not to know her. And there's more. Carlo's spy followed Felicia to Tom Rigby's house. I can't think of a reason on this earth why she should go out there and talk with Tom, herself."

Zeke said, "Did you ask Tom what they talked about? Why she went to see him? Maybe it was something to do with research for her dissertation."

"That could be," said Win. "There could be some totally

innocent reason for Felicia to visit Tom, but why didn't either of them mention it to me? That would have been a normal thing to do, right? 'Professor, I'm going to see your friend. Is there anything you'd like me to tell him for you?' or 'Win, I talked with one of your students. She spoke very highly of you.' Assuming she would, of course."

Miranda leaned forward to ask, "Nobody said anything?"

"Not a word."

"Did you specifically ask them, after you learned of the visit?"

"Felicia has managed to avoid me; we've been communicating solely by e-mails. I called Tom several times. There's no answer, and he doesn't return my calls."

Clarkson went on, "That's perhaps the most worrisome part. Tom would never avoid me. Whatever he's doing, there's nothing he couldn't tell me. We've been friends long enough for him to know that."

Zeke fingered the tip of his goatee absently and seemed to be thinking deeply. After some moments, he lifted his head toward Win. "If Maynard is dealing in stolen goods connected to David's disappearance, then Felicia's visit to Maynard looks bad."

Miranda said, "How? I mean, besides Maynard lying about knowing her."

"You have to ask yourself," Zeke said, "was she receiving some of David's belongings from Maynard – like the missing laptop? Or was she conspiring with Maynard to do something to David?"

Miranda's eyes widened with alarm. "'Do something to David'? What do you think they would do? Granted, these people seem to be capable of criminal activity, but would they go so far as to hurt David? Or kidnap him? Maybe to get at his laptop?"

"How far do we think they would go to keep him from finishing his dissertation?" murmured Clarkson.

"And not only David," Zeke said. "I'm concerned about Tom, as well. Would they want something from Tom? Something they could steal, like they stole from David? And if they went so far as to harm David, would they harm Tom, as well?"

"It worries me that I can't seem to find him," Win Clarkson said. "And I can think of only one thing Tom Rigby has that would interest both a thieving drug addict strapped for cash and a poor graduate student in paleontology."

"The mammoth fossil," breathed Miranda.

A fog of silence settled onto the room. Miranda and Win might have been picturing a dark, water-filled crater near Rigby's house.

Win stopped pacing and slumped into his chair as if too tired to support his own weight.

Seconds passed, then Zeke spoke in a more positive tone. "Look at us, jumping to all sorts of conclusions. What do we really know? Felicia *may* have been cheating on her fiancé with his roommate. David's roommate helped himself to some sellable knick-knacks after David left. Tom Rigby hasn't returned a few recent phone calls. Am I right?"

"All I really found out was that David is a better writer than Felicia is," Miranda agreed. "Being a boring writer is not good, but it's not a crime."

Win leaned back in his chair and steepled his hands in front of his chest. "We could be assuming the worst for no reason, other than we watch too much television."

"Or listen to too many conspiracy theories on late-night talk radio," murmured Miranda."

Zeke slapped his knees with both hands and stood energetically from his chair. "Let me take you two lovely people to lunch. We'll talk about *my* specialty: The mighty megatherium – elephant-sized ground sloths – around which there is absolutely no drama, at least that I know of. And, when we get back, there will probably be a phone message from Tom, and we'll all feel pretty silly."

# Chapter 22 - The Abyss

*Tuesday night*

It was late in the day, and dusk overlaid the forest. Shep and Carlo had returned to the farm, seeking news of Tom Rigby. They searched for the farmer as thoroughly as they could, while moving as quickly as possible through the trees and brush.

No one wanted to be poking around the Pig River woods after dark. They hoped to be in their canoe, on the river and near home before the woods came alive with night hunters.

When they reached the sinkhole, they argued about who would go down and search, and who would stay at ground level to watch for danger.

"You crazy if you think I send blind guy down into black hole to 'look around' for a body – or whatever else is down there!"

"So, you plan to leave the blind guy up top to be the 'lookout'?" was Shep's retort. "And besides, which one of us is accustomed to navigating in places where you can't see, huh?"

In the moment of silence that followed, an owl flew low over their heads and faded into the trees a few feet away.

The moon-call of a coyote drifted to them on a breeze from the west, and another coyote answered from the south.

Something way back down the trail, near the river, let out a grunt that was nearly a roar. It could have been a wild boar or a bull 'gator.

"We're wasting time," Shep said at last.

Carlo capitulated with a sigh and guided Shep to the edge of the hole. He handed one end of a rope to Shepard and prepared to secure the other end to the nearest sturdy tree.

"Give me one of your waterproof flashlights," Shep said, tying the rope around himself.

"What you gonna do with a flashlight, may I ask?" said Carlo, carrying the light to his friend even as he spoke.

"It's so you can see where I am down there in the dark."

Carlo ran the rope through the flashlight's D-ring and handed the rope-end back to Shep, who was creating himself a rope harness.

When Shep was finished, the light dangled from his harness. Carlo looped the slack rope around himself and tied the end to a tree.

With Carlo helping support his weight, in case the unstable sides of the pit should give way suddenly, Shep eased down into the hole to search for any evidence of what had happened to Tom Rigby, or Rigby's mammoth.

Carlo saw the swinging flashlight's beam reflected on the top of black water four yards below his friend.

Back in Gainesville, after a pleasant lunch with Zeke and Miranda Ogilvy, Win Clarkson had promised to notify his friends of any news from Tom Rigby.

The first stars winked into view above, and Win Clarkson's phone rang. When he answered, Carlo said, "Win, we found him." Clarkson knew from the timbre of the voice that this was not good news.

Win was not really surprised to hear Shep and Carlo were at the sinkhole. If Tom Rigby were to disappear, the sinkhole was the most likely place to look for him.

Win asked hesitantly, "Is he … is Tom all right?"

Carlo was quiet a heartbeat too long. "I'm sorry, Win."

Win sighed. "Should I call the police?" he said.

"We don't want to do anything more until you get here –

except maybe set up some ropes and belaying anchors to make it easier to get to him," Carlo told the professor.

"Right," Win said without enthusiasm. "I'll leave now. Be there in an hour or less, if I don't get pulled over for speeding. Because I definitely will be speeding."

"Understood," Carlo said. "Bring lights and a blanket. We'll see you soon."

Because darkness was draping its black cloak swiftly over the land, Shep and Carlo worked while they waited for Clarkson to make his hour-long drive to join them. They fetched ropes and tools from Rigby's farmyard shed and prepared for a second grim foray into the watery pit.

True to his word, Win Clarkson joined them less than an hour later and found them roped up and waiting for him.

Then, while Clarkson stood on the edge of the sinkhole, he watched Carlo strain to control a long rope wrapped around his waist, lowering Shep into the dark pit. Soon, only a flashlight's beam could be seen, bobbing around where the far end of the rope should be. Carlo paid out the rope, inch by inch, until Shep's voice rose from the darkness, "Stop!"

Shepard must have found footing on the side of the hole, above the waterline, because the rope went slack. The flashlight Carlo had tied to Shep's belt moved around in odd patterns, like Shep was trying to examine something from many different angles.

It was important for him to determine that it really was Tom's body, but he did not want to disturb anything that could be evidence. He took a deep breath and went down.

Running his hands gently over the body under the water, Shep determined it wore denim overalls. He also discovered that the body was anchored beneath the water's surface by a heavy object tied to its ankles.

"Win!" Shep called from the deeps. "I think you should call the police now. Tell 'em we think we've found Tom's body, and we won't move him until they get here."

While Win Clarkson telephoned the authorities, Shep pulled

the rope tight and called to Carlo. Carlo belayed while Shep climbed out of the sinkhole.

Moments later, Win held the phone away from his mouth and said, "They want to know if we think it's foul play or just an accident."

"I don't think it was an accident," Shepard answered somberly, wringing water out of his ponytail.

"Why not?" Carlo whispered.

"Because the back of his head is smashed in, and the dent is shaped like the bowl of a shovel."

"*Merraow*," said Carlo's backpack.

"No, you can't come out. It's dangerous out here," Shepard answered. "And, not only because of the pigs," he murmured to himself.

Clarkson relayed Shep's answers to the police. When Clarkson disconnected the police call, he immediately phoned, Zeke Ogilvy. He told Zeke the mystery of Rigby's whereabouts had been solved – and not happily.

Zeke thanked Win for the update and offered sincere condolences for Clarkson's loss of a comrade.

After receiving Clarkson's call, Zeke phoned his daughter and relayed the news to her. He provided as much detail as Clarkson had given him, but Zeke's information did not satisfy Miranda.

"Call him back and tell him I'll be there in under ninety minutes," Miranda told her father.

"Wait just a minute," Zeke said, "you can't go zipping around on that pitiful road through the swamps at night!"

"It's the same road that's there in the daytime, Daddy, and I'll be careful."

"But it's pitch black out there. There are no street lights for miles and miles."

"That's because street lights confuse the nesting turtles," she pointed out.

"Yes, on the shore of the ocean, but we're seventy miles from the nearest ocean. And, it doesn't matter *why* there are no lights, you can't deny there are *no lights*."

When she did not answer, her father argued further, "The asphalt is black, the sky is black, the roadside is black, the bridges are black, the rivers and canals are black. And your family will be wearing black to your funeral after we find your car underwater at sun-up tomorrow."

Still, his daughter said nothing.

"Just wait at home," he said, "and we'll call you the minute there's any news."

"I'm going," she said.

Zeke blew a strong puff of air. "Why can't you be sensible about this!"

"Because Shepard is out there in the woods, in the dark, possibly with a murderer. I will not leave him there alone."

# Chapter 23 - The Responder

Zeke began, "He's not alone, Muffin, there are people with h—"

"Not the right people," Miranda said, and she disconnected the call.

Miranda pushed the old red Cadillac – and her guardian angels – to the limit during her dash from Minokee to the Rigby farm.

She ploughed deep tire tracks into the muddy shoulder of the near-invisible, winding road each time she barely made it around a curve.

No doubt, people who drove that stretch of road the following morning would think a raving drunk in a Sherman tank had passed that way during the night, driving part-time on the asphalt and part-time in the well churned mud of the road shoulder.

When the Cadillac finally skidded to a stop at Rigby's farmhouse, so many vehicles and people covered the lawn that no one even noticed Miranda's arrival.

Police cars from two different jurisdictions parked beside a fire truck, a search-and-rescue van, an ambulance, and a car with a UF faculty parking sticker on the window. That one must belong to Win Clarkson.

Red lights and blue lights strobed and spun, streaking the house and yard with colors that were bright, but certainly not festive.

Miranda parked her car, grabbed the flashlight she had laid on the passenger seat, and snagged her daypack.

The pack contained water, protein bars, cat treats, and first aid supplies. Okay, maybe the first aid supplies were superfluous, considering the number of emergency vehicles on the lawn, but Miranda was not stopping to unpack now.

Even though Miranda had never been to the Rigby house, and had never hiked to the sinkhole except from the river, she had no trouble following the people and lights to the center of activity in the middle of the woods.

The police had cordoned off the sinkhole with yellow crime-scene tape, and a corpse had been zipped into a black body bag, laid out on a blanket. Officers were talking in solemn tones to Shepard and Carlo, separately, and also to Win Clarkson. Firemen and paramedics were gathering their equipment and supplies, preparing to depart.

Instead of forging into the milling crowd, Miranda stepped into the shadow of a fat, old oak, turned off her flashlight, and blended into the darkness to listen.

She heard enough to know the dead body was indeed Tom Rigby, and his death was considered a homicide. Shep and Carlo had been at the farm looking for clues to Tom's disappearance when they searched the sinkhole and found his remains.

Win Clarkson reminded the police officers that his teaching assistant, David Zhang had been missing for weeks and was last seen on a trip to this very sinkhole. Now, Win was worried that David, too, would be found dead.

The question needing an answer was, "Why?".

Carlo told the police about the mammoth skeleton and its monetary value. He thought it was relevant that both David and Tom had connections to the mammoth.

A police officer asked Shepard about the value of the fossil, and Shepard confirmed Carlo's figures. Shep was hesitant to name the mammoth as a motive for murder, however.

"Would people kill one another just to be able to sell some mammoth bones?" Shep said. "They're not really rare. They're not worth millions. No, the bones might be part of it, but there's more going on here. I still think we need to find David Zhang's laptop computer, if we want to know the whole story."

Miranda watched over Shepard from the shadows until the authorities seemed to be finishing up. In the wee hours of the morning, she crept back down the dirt path to the farmyard, got in the red Caddy, and left without anyone knowing she was ever there.

In less than twenty-four hours, Shepard Krausse would be charged with murder.

## Chapter 24 - The Suspect

*Wednesday morning*

Miranda was at her desk, preparing to enter a new shipment of books into the digital catalog, when the phone rang. She looked up from her chair to see that Annabelle was entertaining a gentlemen patron at the end of the circulation desk nearest the telephone. No phone ever distracted Annabelle when a male was within arm's length.

Miranda punched the flashing button on her desk phone and answered. "Live Oak Public Library, Miss Ogilvy speaking. How may I help you?"

"Bean, it's me. Listen—"

"I can't talk now. First of all, I'm officially Not Speaking To You; and, secondly, I have about a hundred new books to catalog before the end of the day—"

"Miranda, I've been arrested. You're my one phone call. If you hang up on me now, I'll spend the rest of my life in undeserved misery, like Jean Valjean in *Les Miserables.* Or worse, like the old guy in the cell next door to the Count of Monte Cristo."

"Is this a joke? Because, if it is—"

"No joke. I'm in the slammer, and I need your help. Look, I realize you have no reason to—"

"I'll be right there. Don't talk to anyone 'til I get there. See you soon."

"Bean!"

"What?"

"Don't you want to know where I am?"

"Oh. Okay, let me get a pen."

♦

Miranda had to stop in Minokee to change clothes and collect some essentials before racing on to the town of Luz, Florida, population 934.

Luz was a town with one off-brand gas station, which was actually the front of a general store that included the town's laundromat and pizzeria. The decidedly non-bustling town of Luz boasted a remote branch office of the Alachua County Sheriff. The sheriff's office in Luz consisted of a one-room office, with one jail cell against the back wall.

Miranda walked into the office to find a lanky, twenty-something, cocoa-skinned young man in a deputy's uniform, seated at a desk.

The Stetson he wore seemed to spread a yard wide, like a tourist-trap sombrero, emphasizing his thin face and frame.

When Miranda suddenly appeared in his doorway, the young man spilled a dollop of coffee on his scuffed oak desk. He set down his mug, hauled his booted feet off the desktop, and stood up.

Tyrell Krothers's mother had raised him well, and good manners were the very least she would have expected of her son. Mrs. Krothers would have been proud of Tyrell today.

He knew a real lady when he saw one, and his visitor could not be mistaken for anything else. He offered his hand, and she shook it with confidence and cordiality.

"Miranda Ogilvy," she said, "to meet with the accused."

"Yes, ma'am. I'm Deputy Tyrell Krothers. Been expecting you."

"Is that him?" she said in her best lawyer voice. She didn't know how a real lawyer would sound addressing a novice deputy in a one-room sheriff's office. She tried to imitate Perry Mason, the late-fifties television attorney, whom she knew from grainy black-and-white reruns.

If her TV-lawyer voice failed her, she would fall back on the classic Official Librarian Demeanor. It could intimidate almost anyone, and certainly should impress an inexperienced small-town lawman.

Deputy Krothers turned to confirm that her extended finger was pointing at his only prisoner, who was napping on a cot in the cell, on his back with arms crossed on his chest. The blond man's shoulders were wider than the cot, and his feet hung over the end.

"Yes, ma'am. That is Shepard Krausse, in the flesh. I could hardly believe it when he walked in the door, told me his name, and turned hisself in. I was a big fan of Sheep Counters with Shep and Dave. Terrible what happened to Dave."

Miranda said, "Yes, terrible. Thank goodness the perpetrators were brought to justice. May I go in and speak with him privately, now, please?"

"Oh, sure, sure." A wooden drawer squeaked, and metal clattered as Deputy Krothers retrieved a heavy keyring from the old desk. The iron ring held an amazing number of keys for a small office with only one cell.

Krothers took a step toward the cell as if to lead the way, then he stopped and turned back to Miranda. "I'll need to look in your briefcase, ma'am, if you want to take it in with you."

"Of course." Miranda plopped her imposing faux leather black case on the deputy's desk. The behemoth briefcase was the size of a picnic cooler that would hold lunch for twelve people.

She opened the combination lock and spread the top of the case wide.

The deputy looked inside but withdrew the hand he had nearly inserted. "Is that what I think it is?"

"Yes. Is there a problem, Deputy Krothers?"

"Well, I don't actually recall a specific statute that mentions it, but it don't seem right somehow."

Miranda lowered her lawyer voice to a soft, confiding tone. "Deputy Krothers, you are aware that the accused has a disability..."

Krothers nodded.

"...and that his long-time service dog has died."

Krothers nodded again and murmured, "Terrible."

"This is the solution to that problem," she concluded.

Krothers took a closer look at the contents of the briefcase. "Are you kidding me?"

Miranda shook her head solemnly.

"Seems kinda small..."

"Nevertheless..." She waited through a moment of silence as Krothers studied the case's cargo. "If you like, I can provide you a copy of the pertinent subsection and paragraph of the Americans with Disabilities Act for your records," she added, managing to sound friendly and vaguely threatening at the same time.

Deputy Krothers looked the lawyerly lady right in the eye and lied his heart out. "Oh, no, ma'am, that won't be necessary. I'm familiar with the statute, of course. Y'all come right on in."

He turned and walked seven feet to the cell door, which he opened with a flourish.

"Thank you, Deputy Krothers." Miranda closed the briefcase, left it unlocked, and carried it with her through the cell door. Once inside, she set the case on the concrete floor, turned it on its side, and opened the latch.

"Okay. Go on," she said.

A bullet of fur exploded out of the briefcase and onto the sleeping prisoner's chest. Then the alleged service animal wrapped itself around the alleged felon's neck and began purring like a beehive gone amok.

The man awoke, clasped the kitten gently with both hands and said, "What the—?"

*"Mrrrratt!"* the kitten said, and, "*K-k-k-k-k-k.*

"Zeus!" The man held the kitten closely, sat up, and swung his feet to the floor. "What are you doing here, little buddy?"

Zeus began washing Shep's face with a pink, sand-paper tongue. Possibly, the ever-pragmatic Zeus merely liked the salty taste of the man's silent tears. Nonetheless, it comforted the prisoner.

"How did you get here?" Shep asked the cat, nuzzling its head and neck as it nuzzled him in turn. "Surely you didn't come alone. Is Bean with you?"

Miranda said, "His Majesty, the King of Olympus, permitted this lowly human to drive him here. He said he had an important meeting."

Tyrell Krothers stood motionless in the open cell door, watching the most surreal attorney-client conference he had ever witnessed. He came to himself and backed out of the cell doorway, closing it with an echoing steel-on-steel clang, and turning the key in the lock.

"Y'all take all the time you need. I'll be right outside, in the porch chair. Yell if you need anything or when you get finished talking."

"Do you want us to come get you if the phone rings, or can you hear it from out there?" asked Miranda.

"It hardly ever rings," Krothers said. He clattered the handful of keys into the squeaky desk drawer and walked out the front door.

Shep held the kitten in place against his throat with one hand and, with the other, patted the open space beside him on the cot. "Take a seat, Bean. Thanks for coming on short notice."

She sat, smoothed her skirt to cover her knees, and slid off her shoes with a sigh.

Shep heard clompety-clomp. "Did you just take off your shoes, Miss Proper Librarian? And in a public place, no less? Honestly, Bean, I'm shocked!"

Miranda exhaled in relief as she massaged one foot with the other. "I borrowed them from Annabelle. They're about ten inches high, and I never wear a heel higher than half an inch. I barely got to this building from my car without toppling like a felled pine."

"Why would you do that?"

"Because I can't walk on my toes like a prima ballerina."

"No, I mean why are you wearing Annabelle's skyscraper heels that you can't even walk in? You could break your pretty neck, Bean!

"I wanted to look taller and more like a professional."

"A professional *what*?"

"An attorney, of course. How else was I supposed to get a private meeting with a prisoner?"

"Why didn't you bring a real lawyer? You could get in big trouble impersonating an officer of the court."

"To answer your questions in order, first: I didn't know what kind of lawyer to bring, or which ones to avoid, since I'm pretty sure you somehow got yourself jailed in the huge metropolis of Luz, instead of a bigger city, because you don't want your mother or her lawyers to know.

"Second, I did not impersonate an officer of the court, I just walked in and asked to see the accused. Deputy Krothers assumed the rest."

She went on, "I would like to point out, also, that *you* actually *are* an officer of the court, Mister Non-Practicing Lawyer Man, and it seems to me *you* are the one who is in big trouble. Not me. I shall be leaving this charming iron room shortly, and you, I believe, shall not."

"Right on all counts," Shep admitted.

"I know. Now, before I can do anything to get you out of here, I need to know what crime these silly people think you committed."

"You don't think I committed the crime?"

"Oh, please, Shepard Montgomery Krausse! Zeus is a more likely criminal than you."

*"Aorrrow!"*

"It was just a figure of speech. I apologize if I offended."

"I think I'm offended, too," said Shepard. "I could commit a crime if I wanted to. I'm capable. Is that just one more ability I need to prove to you?"

"There is *nothing* you need to prove to me. *You* said that in the heat of anger, and we both knew then -- and know now -- that you misjudged me. *I know* you are capable. I also know you are not a criminal. Now, quit wasting time. What are you supposed to have done?"

He lowered the kitten from his throat to his lap, where the cat reclined and purred beneath Shep's stroking fingers.

"You know that David Zhang has been missing for three weeks, right?"

"Yes," she said. "So, what? Why arrest you, of all people?"

Shepard explained, "Seems I'm the last person to talk to David Zhang — *two* days ago. Somebody turned in David's cellphone to the police with an anonymous tip that they should look at who David last talked to. The call history showed him calling my cellphone several times since he went missing — and they weren't short calls. Some of them lasted several minutes."

"So David Zhang is alive!" said Miranda.

Shep said, "Maybe. The anonymous tipper told the police they found the cellphone in a trashcan in Jacksonville. There was blood on it."

"David's blood?"

"They're testing it. Guess we'll know soon."

Miranda asked, "Did you talk to David on the phone since the canoe trip?"

"Absolutely not."

"Great! No problem. Just show them your cellphone, and they'll see those calls never happened."

Shep's tone lowered as he delivered bad news: "They took my phone, Bean. They said they did find calls on it from David's number. But I swear, I never heard from him. I haven't talked to David Zhang since we left Pig River that day. And yet, the facts seem to say that somebody used my phone to talk to him."

"Who could have access to your phone?"

"Nobody! That's just it, Bean. Nobody could've gotten hold of my phone. Pietro and Dave died because I misplaced my phone that night. That phone has not been out of my pocket since. I even sleep with it. Nobody has talked on my cellphone but me."

Shep took a breath before continuing. "I have no idea who set me up, but I'm starting to think they wouldn't go to this much trouble framing me unless..."

"Unless David is dead," she finished for him.

Shep gave an affirmative "Mm-hm." After a second's pause, he said, "I'll be very interested to know whose blood is on Zhang's cellphone."

Miranda folded her hands in her lap and stared at the concrete floor as if piecing a puzzle together in her head. After some moments, she asked, "How did you get here, to the town of Blink-And-You-Missed-It, Florida?"

"I had the police scanner on in my home office — old radio station news-gathering habit. Imagine my surprise when I heard a BOLO on myself!

"I grabbed my cane and was halfway to your house when I heard cars with sirens skid to a stop in front of my house. I knew you weren't home, so I bypassed your house and went straight to Martha's.

"She drove me to Luz – in your car, by the way — and dropped me off at the sheriff's door. I turned myself in."

Miranda said, "And the sheriff did not notify the press."

Shep's cheeks dimpled with his smile. "Tyrell was kind enough to keep it out of the press and off my mother's radar, at least for the moment. Lucky for me, he was a fan."

"Yeah. Lucky." Miranda blew a stream of air. "Hoo! You really do need a lawyer!"

"Yes, ma'am. And, I don't think the height of their heels will be important, in the long run, even though I appreciate your sacrifice. Hope your toes aren't permanently damaged."

"Whom do I call?"

He gave her the name of a friend from law school. She said

she would find them.

He did not have to ask her to keep his secret from Hermione Montgomery-Krausse or any of madam's acquaintances or employees — including Carlo Fratelli, who, fortunately, had not been home when the police arrived.

Then, placing the kitten in Miranda's lap, Shep knelt beside the cot where they had been sitting. He massaged Miranda's feet and her calf muscles until he felt some tension dissipate.

Then he lifted her shoes one at a time, examined them with his hands and sent Miranda a teasing smile, that was almost a leer, but not enough of one to cause offense to a lady. He eased her shoes onto her feet and rose, offering her a hand to stand.

"Careful tip-toeing to the car," he said.

In answer she hugged him tightly about the waist, pressing her face against his sternum as if desperate to hear his heart beating. The kitten watched from the cot.

"Thanks for coming, Castor Bean," his deep voice hummed from deep within his chest.

*"K-k-k-k-k-k-k!"* came from the direction of the cot.

Shep chuckled. "And thanks for bringing Zeus, although I know he didn't give you a choice. He's a talented and experienced stowaway, I can swear to that."

Miranda had been silent since receiving his instructions about obtaining an attorney. She released him from her hug, picked up her briefcase, and placed it on the cot. Zeus obligingly crawled inside then poked his head up and looked at Shepard.

*"Merrewyah,"* yowled Zeus.

"I will," Shep answered. "You take care of our Castor Bean while I'm away."

*"Myek,"* Zeus chirped, then he ducked down inside the briefcase.

Miranda closed and lifted the briefcase, faced the door, and squared her shoulders. When she remained silent, Shep called for Deputy Krothers.

The deputy re-entered the office, unlocked the cell door, and nodded his farewell to the lady with the briefcase. No one said a word while Miranda left the building, Shep returned to the cot and lay down on his back, and Krothers returned to his desk after locking the iron door.

♦

Miranda was chagrinned, but not surprised, that the attorney Shep had requested turned out to be an attractive female.

Ursula Norland, Esquire, had attended law school with Shepard Krausse and, in fact, had been one of Shep's regular readers.

He hired a team of readers every semester, and they rotated through his study room on a schedule, each taking up where the previous reader had left off, to read aloud all the texts necessary for a law student to cover.

The texts were many, and the cases to be researched were endless, and next to none were available on recording for visually impaired students.

Miranda knew that the twins, Pietro and Carlo, had also served as readers throughout Shepard's college and law school days.

No doubt, dozens of former readers existed, and certainly a significant number of them would be female and attractive.

In such ways did life often stink, in the view of plain, invisible, spinster librarians.

Nevertheless, Miranda called attorney Norland and explained Shep's situation and need for discretion. Ms. Norland understood immediately, having long known Shepard's family and their standing in the community.

Norland went to work without delay.

That afternoon, the lady lawyer met with the Luz, Florida, Sheriff's Department, in the form of Deputy Tyrell Krothers.

The lady provided faxes from the Florida Department of Law Enforcement Crime Lab, stating that the blood found on David

Zhang's cellphone was not David's and not Shepard's. It was not even human blood, but was from a rodent.

Calls to Shep's number were listed on David's phone, but there were no fingerprints on the phone — not even David's — which might well indicate that someone else had made those calls, using David's stolen phone, in an attempt to place Shep under suspicion.

On the other hand, the calls may never have occurred at all. Attorney Norland produced a sworn affidavit from a respected telecommunications engineer, describing in detail how an expert hacker could have inserted false calls into Shep's call record — and David's.

Finally, since there was no evidence that David Zhang was a crime victim — with the possible exception of the theft of his phone — there was no murder with which to charge Shepard Montgomery Krausse.

There was no question of charging Shep with Tom Rigby's murder, because Shepard had a solid alibi for the estimated time of death.

Deputy Krothers personally agreed with Ms. Norland's rationale and the facts as she presented them -- presented them in her lilting Jamaican accent. Krothers was a goner the first time she opened her mouth.

After a quick and cordial phone call to a judge who had jurisdiction in the case, all the parties concurred that, in fact, there was no case.

The judge sent his best regards to Shepard's dear mother.

The deputy released Shepard from custody and received an autograph from the head Sheep Counter.

Attorney Norland did not quite say no to Deputy Krothers's dinner invitation for some future evening.

During the long drive from Luz to Minokee, Ursula Norland and her old college buddy, Shepard Krausse, reminisced about their university years.

When Ursula dropped Shep off at his front door with a

sisterly kiss on the cheek, she reminded him not to let his guard down. "Whoever faked those calls to your phone is still out there, and they may try again to do you harm. They may even get you arrested again, if new evidence of a crime comes to light. Watch your back."

"Will do," he said, unfolding his cane and turning toward his house.

Once inside, he went into his home office and telephoned Miranda. When she answered, he said, "Thanks, Bean. I'm home, safe and sound and no worse for wear, except for being tired and hungry. All charges were dropped, and they gave me back my phone. You really came through for me today, and I owe you big time."

"You don't owe me anything. I'm glad I could help. Did you and, um…"

"Ursula?"

"…Ms. Norland enjoy renewing your acquaintance?"

"We caught up a bit in the car, but this wasn't exactly a happy social occasion, Bean."

"She's very pretty."

"Good for her. Does all this mean you're speaking to me again, now?"

Miranda did not answer immediately. After some moments of silence, she said, "I don't know."

"Okay. I understand. But, just know that *I'm* speaking to *you* again, in case someday you're ready to do the same. We don't have to get married, but we don't have to be strangers, either. Just give it some thought."

"I will," she said. "Goodnight."

"'Night, Castor Bean. Sleep well."

They disconnected the call without a clue that they would be speaking a great deal indeed within just a few hours.

## Chapter 25 - The Shadow

*Thursday*

Zeus spent Wednesday night with Miranda. Whether he was still punishing Shep, or diligently guarding Shep's lady, or just liked Miranda's cooking, nobody knew. He was a complicated feline.

The cat knew that Miranda was awake, and had been for some time, even though dawn was still several hours away. Zeus complained when Miranda tossed and turned, repeatedly dislodging him from a carefully arranged nest among her covers.

Since it seemed Miranda had become nocturnal, Zeus accepted it. He jumped off the bed and padded across the rug to Miranda's dresser.

Gracefully he sailed onto the dresser top, where he selected a page out of the papers Miranda had stacked there yesterday.

With the page anchored in his teeth by one corner, and flapping behind him like a superhero's cape, Zeus dropped deftly to the floor and returned to the bed.

He did not return to his nest near Miranda's feet. Instead, he sauntered across her stomach and ribs to sit on her chest and poke the page at her chin.

With one hand Miranda lifted the paper from Zeus's fangs and held it up in front of her face. "Do you realize it's three o'clock in the morning, mister?"

*"Myoark."*

"Right. You don't wear a watch." She reached out with her

free hand and turned on the bedside lamp. With the light, she could see what was on the page. "This is part of the research I did for Dad and Professor Clarkson."

*"Myeert."*

"You're right," said Miranda, looking over the page in her hand. "Since I'm not sleeping anyway, I should be using this time for something constructive."

Zeus hopped down from the bed and trotted to the bedroom door. There he stopped and looked back over his shoulder at Miranda.

She sat up and swung her legs over the side of the bed. "Okay, okay. I'll put on a pot of coffee."

*"Myerrk moae."*

"And feed the cat." Slipping her feet into her slippers, she followed Zeus to the kitchen.

Within minutes, Miranda was savoring a mug of fresh coffee, and Zeus was happily nose-down in his food bowl.

The stack of papers from Miranda's bedroom dresser now sprawled across the kitchen table. Miranda paged through her research notes, shifting them into loose piles.

Zeus finished his snack, washed his face and paws, and bounced from the floor, to a chair, to the tabletop.

Miranda continued reading page after page while Zeus tiptoed among the scattered papers without disturbing the piles.

Miranda had just set a document atop a pile on her right. When she reached toward a pile on her left, Zeus promptly sat on her target.

"Excuse me, sir," said Miranda, gently sweeping the cat to one side of the papers. "There's something under there I need."

She pulled a document from beneath the pile and set about reading it.

Zeus stood and walked back to the pile and sat on it again.

"Sorry, kiddo, I need to get under there again." Miranda carefully edged Zeus off the papers, took a document from the bottom of the pile, and moved the pile to another part of the table.

"There," she said and patted the space where the pile (and Zeus) had been sitting. "You can have that spot now."

While Miranda perused the research notes, Zeus stood and moseyed across the table to the pile Miranda had moved. He sat on it.

A moment later, the librarian looked up and noticed the cat's new location. "What is up with you?" she said, easing the papers out from under him. This time, she placed that pile of papers on the seat of the nearest empty dining chair.

*"Maorrar,"* said Zeus, and he crossed the table to hop down into the chair. This time, however, he didn't sit on the pile of papers. He nosed through them until he found a particular page, then he lifted it in his teeth and looked at Miranda.

She sat back in her chair and dropped the page she had been reading onto the table. "Are you kidding me?"

*"Mmwmrrw,"* Zeus said without opening his mouth.

"Unbelievable," murmured the librarian, taking the page from the cat. "I do not believe I'm doing this."

The paper had two sets of fang marks: one from when Zeus brought it to Miranda's bed earlier, and one from his lifting it out of the chair.

"Okay, since you insist," she said, and she began to read.

Zeus curled up in the chair and went to sleep. His work here was done, for the time being at least.

♦

By four o'clock Thursday morning, Miranda had organized her research notes into several manila file folders and stacked them on a chair in her bedroom. One folder she left on the kitchen table for further reference.

Then a yawning Miranda picked up Zeus from his sleeping place in the kitchen, and the two of them returned to Miranda's bed. They slept soundly another couple of hours.

Miranda had showered, dressed, and made breakfast before

the Minokee morning coffee ritual began.

All four of the elderly ladies on Magnolia Street sipped their coffee and rocked in their porch chairs, awaiting their morning adrenaline rush. Shepard Krausse and his jogging companion raised these ladies to life every morning just by passing by and exchanging greetings with the fans.

Miranda felt the adrenaline jolt as well, though she was not waiting outside on her porch for the dawn parade this morning. She stood behind the curtains at her living room window, where she could sip her coffee and watch the road without revealing her hunger for a glimpse of the blond runner.

She did not know what had caused Shepard's recent return to his running regime, but whatever the cause, she was grateful. The daily reenactment of the Magnolia Street coffee ritual proved that life was proceeding toward a new normal, long overdue, as the tragedy of some months before slowly lost its grip on Minokee's residents.

Carlo, Shepard, and Zeus passed by, greetings were exchanged with the porch ladies, the trio disappeared around a corner, and the ritual ended.

Miranda gave Shepard and Carlo time to return home from their morning run, shower and dress, and prepare themselves for their daily activities. When she judged that the hour had come when Shep would be starting work in his home office, she took her manila folder and went to visit her neighbor.

Zeus was waiting on Miranda's back steps, and he trotted beside her across the yard.

Carlo answered the kitchen door of the Krausse home. Miranda greeted him with a friendly hug and warm smile. She stepped into the kitchen with the ease of intimate acquaintance, and Zeus followed on her heels.

"I need to talk to Shep," she told Carlo.

*"Merrwak!"* her companion agreed.

"On one condition," said Carlo, and he stepped to the key rack on the wall beside the kitchen door. He lifted a set of car keys and held them up in front of Miranda's face. "You take these back. That car is yours, and nobody else is gonna touch it as long as you live. Plus, Martha's car will bankrupt you just paying for fuel every day."

"I'll get an affordable car."

"Really? And, why it take so long for you to find one?"

"It's important to find exactly what I need."

"Take this one," he jangled the keys before her nose. "You driving this car is exactly what Shepard needs. Whose need means more to you? Be honest."

Miranda lowered her gaze to the floor for a moment. When she looked up again, she took the keys from Carlo's fingers. "Thank you. Now, can I see him?"

*"Merwao."*

"I mean, can…*we*…see him?"

"In the office. You know the way."

Miranda kept as quiet as possible when she walked to the office door and eased it open. She stayed in the hallway, looking into the room, but Zeus strolled in.

Shepard was not at his desk, as she had expected. He was sitting facing the office window, feet up on the sill. A cup of coffee, no longer steaming, sat neglected on a corner of his desk.

Zeus crossed to Shep's chair and hopped lightly into his lap.

"Good morning," Shep said, fondling the cat's ears and rubbing its back.

Carlo must have gone out the back door at that moment, because Miranda felt a wisp of breeze brush past her from the kitchen and continue across Shep's chair. She saw Shep's head jerk up and swivel towards the doorway.

"Bean?"

When she remained quiet, he said again, "Bean? Is that you?"

"It's me."

His feet dropped to the floor and his chair spun in her direction. "Why aren't you at work? Is everything— Are you all right?"

"I'm fine. I was up all night, so I took a personal day. For someone who hasn't taken a vacation in years, I'm sure making up for it since I moved here. I wanted to talk to you."

"Bean, I'm sorry."

"Oh, … well, I can come back at a better time—"

"No, I'm not sorry you want to talk. I want to talk, too. I meant, I'm sorry I've been such a selfish Cretin. I'm sorry I said a lot of stupid things to y—"

"Shepard, I enjoy a good, long apology as much as the next person, but can I get a rain check on this one? I do want to hear all of it, and maybe more than once, but I need to talk to you about something else right now. Okay?"

He grinned. "Rain check? Like, for the next time I see you?"

She grinned, too, knowing he would hear it in her voice. "Yeah, for the next time you see me."

"Deal," he said. "Sit down. Let's talk."

A few minutes later, Miranda finished describing to Shep the paper Zeus had brought to her attention before dawn.

"It was a page from David's master's thesis," she said. "The one I found online when I was researching David's background. Most of the thesis was academic prose, as you would expect, but the page Zeus brought to me was different."

"How different?"

"It wasn't only text, it included a photograph … of David, sitting on the sandy ground of a dig site, typing on his laptop computer."

"The same laptop computer that we haven't been able to find."

"Right," said Miranda. "But we may not need to find it, after all!"

Shep stroked his beard absently before he said, "Okay, you lost me. Zeus brought you a page from David's thesis, but it was not just text, it had a picture of David. Therefore, we *don't* need to find David's missing computer?"

"Right."

"Uh-huh. So, … exactly how did you come to this conclusion? Walk me through the logic here."

Miranda hoisted herself onto the edge of Shep's desk, facing the chair where he sat. Her toes brushed his shins just below the knee, which placed her eyes level with his. She held her manila folder in her lap, with the photo page laid on top of it.

Shep rubbed the cat's ears and raised his voice to be heard above Zeus's sonorous purrs. "I'm listening."

"We know Zeus is smart, right?" she said.

Shep whispered, "Please don't say that in front of him. He's already insufferably condescending to all of us."

"My point is, even though he is," she dropped to a whisper, "S-M-A-R-T, he still can't read."

"Not as far as I know."

"So, since he can't read, what made him pick that particular page out of all my research papers? He brought it to me in the middle of the night, and then he kept bothering me until he got me to take it and look at it."

Shep thought a moment. "It wasn't the words on the page. Could that page have smelled funny to him?"

"I don't think so," Miranda pulled the sheet out of the folder and held it close to Shepard's nose. "Does it smell funny to you?"

Shep smiled. "A: I have a pretty good sense of smell, but not as good as a cat. And, B: since you walked through that door, I haven't been able to smell anything but you. You smell terrific, by the way."

"Thanks, but I need you to focus right now. It wasn't the words and it wasn't the smell. I think it was the picture."

"Hm. Describe that photograph again."

"The bottom one-third of the picture shows acres and acres of desert sand dunes, rolling in waves like a beige ocean. The top two-thirds of the photo shows a wide, blue sky … and one cotton-puff cloud. *That's* what Zeus was trying to tell me."

She placed the photo back in her manila folder and leaned forward, resting her elbows and forearms on her lap.

Shep had dropped his chin toward his chest while he listened, but he jerked upright when she said the last words. "The cloud," he said.

Miranda nodded automatically. "David was fastidious about his appearance, his apartment, his desk, everything. He would've been careful about his data, too. I'm betting everything on that laptop is backed up on the Cloud."

"Unbelievable," Shep said.

"No, it isn't. Everybody backs up to the Cloud these days."

"Oh, of course, I know that. I just have a hard time believing Zeus figured it out and showed it to you," he said. "If that's true, he'll be impossible to live with."

"I'm sort of in denial about the Twilight Zone aspects of the whole situation." Miranda admitted. "I'll bet you know someone who could hack into David's Cloud storage."

Shep grinned. "You'd win that bet. I know several Sheep Counters who specialize in hacking into corporate and government data bases, looking for captured aliens or conspiracies. We'll need as much personal information as we can get about David Zhang, to help with finding his passwords and such."

Miranda slapped the manila folder on her lap. It sounded solid, because it contained a solid inch-thick stack of papers. "I pulled a bunch of info from my background research. We're ready."

"Well, okay, then," Shep crowed, "let's start making some calls!"

By the time Shepard reached his target hacker by phone, it was after nine o'clock that Thursday morning.

The drive to Minokee took about two hours from virtually anywhere in Central Florida, so Shep's friend arrived just in time to join them for lunch.

Carlo served his signature pasta salad to the humans, and Miranda provided leftover tuna casserole – reheated, of course – for Zeus.

Lunch was surreal for Miranda, who had never before joined

conspiracy theorists for a prolonged discussion. She could not be certain whether Shep and Carlo believed what they were saying, but their guest certainly seemed confident that every crazy word spoken was gospel truth.

Miranda had decided to think of their guest as an *It.* With its skinny jeans, loose sweatshirt, and half-shaved hairdo, the visitor might have been a girl, a young woman. Or *it* might have been a beardless boy, a young man with slender build and tenor voice.

Even *its* name was no help, because – predictably – real names were verboten in conspiracy circles. The visitor called itself *Shadow.*

Since Shadow was of African-American complexion, Miranda balked when Shepard told her the nickname.

"Are you sure you want me to call you that?" Miranda asked carefully. "I feel like I'm making some awful, racist joke."

Shadow laughed. "Thanks for caring, but that really is my handle, my screen name. Not because I'm black, but because I can get in and out of any computer system without leaving even a shadow. And that's not me bragging, that's only the truth."

"Okay, then … Shadow. Nice to meet you," said Miranda.

"You didn't. I was never here," said Shadow.

That introduction had been Miranda's first clue that lunch conversation would be unconventional, at the very least. She was not wrong.

It has been said that C. S. Lewis, writer of the Narnia Chronicles, and J.R.R. Tolkien, writer of *The Hobbit* and the *Lord of the Rings* novels, had been known to spend hours at a pub table, in solemn conversations. When asked once what their deep discussions were about on one particular day, they answered matter-of-factly, "Dragons."

Compared to the discussion at Shepard's table that noon, talk of dragons would have been as mundane as making a grocery list.

Shadow and Shepard, the former head Sheep Counter, conversed in sincere tones about polar bears conspiring to take over Canadian villages.

They included Carlo and Miranda in talking of multiple extraterrestrial encounters, government agencies that were secret even from the president, public elementary schools practicing mind control, and more.

The ultimate incongruity came when Shadow agreed to help them hack into David Zhang's Cloud storage, even though Shadow believed without doubt that the information would not help them find David. Shadow said David clearly had been abducted by aliens. Really.

Nobody at the table said a word to contradict Shadow's strongly held belief.

After lunch, Carlo insisted on doing the kitchen clean-up and sent the other three to Shep's office to conspire together.

Miranda provided the folder of personal information she had assembled about David Zhang.

After thoroughly briefing Shadow on the sorts of information they hoped to find, Shep and Miranda sat back and let the hacker get to work.

Finding David's account on the Cloud was child's play. Getting access to all his folders, however, required discovering his passwords. With his typical attention to detail, David had placed several obstacles in the way of unauthorized users. Once or twice, a word or phrase in Chinese barred the way. That was when Shep called in Carlo, who had studied Chinese for three years in college.

Shadow assured Shep and Miranda that improbable tasks took only seconds, but impossible ones took a little longer. After ninety minutes of trying words and names from David's life – some in English and some in Chinese – Miranda asked if they would have to give up.

Shep and Shadow laughed out loud.

Minutes later, Shadow uncovered a different online translation of a Chinese term that seemed to be one of David's favorites.

"Shut the front door!" crowed Shadow -- and typed in the new translation. Immediately *its* computer screen bloomed with rows and rows of stored document titles.

They now had access to David Zhang's e-mails, research

notes, thesis outline, and the first draft of David's doctoral dissertation.

Shadow shared the access information with Shepard's and Miranda's computers before accepting their effusive thanks and taking its leave.

*It* left with a refrigerator dish full of Carlo's tasty leftovers. *It* also took with *it* a cash contribution from Shep, for a secret save-the-world-from-UFO's organization, of which Shadow was an administrator.

Characteristically, Shadow would not exit from the front door of Shepard's house. The Orchid Street house might be watched. (Nobody said, "By whom?".)

The androgynous hacker slipped out the back door and dashed in a half-crouch through the hedge and across several lawns to where *its* motorcycle was hidden, in roadside bushes along Magnolia Street.

The distant roar of the motorcycle was fading away when Carlo poked his head in at the office door. "Elvis has left the building," he said. "I guess that means you got what you needed?"

"We got a lot," said Shep. "I need a few hours to go through it to see if there's anything that will help."

"Need me to read?"

"Nah, thanks. I'll let the computer read it to me. And Bean is here if I get stuck on something. You'll stay … right, Bean?"

Miranda looked at Carlo and wagged her head. Carlo contradicted her with a nod of his own.

"Um…," she said, "I thought I would go back to my house and use my desktop computer to send Doctor Clarkson a copy of what we found, so he can look through it, too. Maybe he can spot a motive for someone to harm David. Something we, as outsiders, might miss."

"Good idea," Shep said. "And, then you'll come back, right?"

"Um…well, actually…I was sort of plan—"

"I am making tiramisu for dessert tonight," Carlo interrupted.

Miranda's shoulders slumped in defeat. "That's a dirty trick.

It's not fair that you know my weaknesses. I don't have anything that gives me power over you."

"You're kidding, right?" said Shep. "Go. Send your message to Clarkson, and we'll see you back here at ..."

"Dinner at five," Carlo put in.

"...back here at five. And tell Zeus he's eating here tonight. Don't let him talk you into cooking for him. Okay?"

"Okay. See you then," she said. She gathered up her papers and folder and left.

Carlo had to step into the room to open the door wider for her exit. When she had gone, he whispered, "High five!"

Shep raised a hand, and the two men slapped palms.

## Chapter 26 - The Engagement

*Friday morning*

The three people meeting in Win Clarkson's office had not slept much for two nights in a row. Shepard, Miranda, and Win had each stayed up until early pre-dawn hours, going over the documents uncovered by Shep's hacker friend on Thursday afternoon. Miranda took another personal day off from the library, after a second night with no sleep.

When they gathered at an agreed time Friday morning, they consumed cup after cup of coffee from the pot on the professor's credenza. The caffeine may have been superfluous, however; their nervous worries alone probably would have kept them awake and alert.

Shepard recounted for Win the events of Shep's arrest and incarceration as a murder suspect, and the false evidence someone had planted using David Zhang's cellphone.

"That is absolutely unbelievable!" said Clarkson. "Who would go to all that trouble to incriminate *you*, of all people? They had to know their scheme would fall apart in the long run. The Montgomery-Krausse lawyers would guarantee it, even if the evidence weren't so flimsy."

"I'm glad it didn't get as far as my mother's lawyers, but I agree the attempt to frame me for abduction or murder is an extreme measure. I'm sorry to say it, Win, but it really makes me think David is dead. Especially after what happened to Tom

Rigby."

Clarkson shook his head slowly. He removed his glasses and wiped his eyes with a tissue from the box on the corner of his desk. "I'm not ready to believe that yet. There's still hope we'll find David alive somehow."

Shep said, "I think we can all agree he is not on some short-notice university dig in China."

"What do you mean? What university dig?" Clarkson said, replacing his glasses and leaning forward.

"The one he mentioned in his email," Shep answered.

"You got an email from David?"

"*I* didn't; *you* did. Felicia wrote me about it. I'll play it for you." Shep's laptop was already open on the edge of Win's desk, and in moments Shep had located his archived message from Felicia Harper. After a series of voice commands from Shep, his computer read the message aloud.

The voice told Win and Miranda the same story it had initially told Shepard: David wrote that he was leaving in a hurry to accept a position with a dig in China, time was short, sorry to leave, thanks for everything, goodbye.

"I never got a message like that!" Clarkson almost shouted. "I never got any message at all from David himself. All I ever got was that email from his mother, saying that she was worried about him because neither she nor his fiancée had heard from him. He'd even missed a Skype date, and that almost never happened. I had Felicia forward it to you, remember?"

"I didn't get it. She must have sent a fake summary instead."

Miranda began snatching tissues from the desktop box and daubing at her skirt.

Shep reacted to the sounds. "You okay, Bean?"

"When you said, 'his fiancée,' I spilled coffee on myself." She tossed damp tissues into a nearby trashcan. "David had a *fiancée* … in *China*?

"According to his mother," Clarkson answered. "I admit, it surprised me, too. I always had the impression from Felicia that she and David were spending time together, socially."

Miranda sat back in her chair. "Hmh!"

"What, Bean?"

"At the picnic, at Tom Rigby's place, … remember what she said?"

"I didn't hear her say anything. As I recall, I went with Miz Martha to check out a— to do some bird-watching. So, I could've missed something."

"She wanted you to climb something, didn't she! What was it, a rock? A tree?"

"We were investigating a nest she thought might have eggs in it."

"So, it was a tree."

"Right."

"And you *sneaked* off to do this because …"

"I know you don't like me climbing, so …"

"Listen, mister: I *don't like* you climbing, but I *hate* you lying to me! See the difference?"

"Right."

"We'll talk about this later," she promised.

Clarkson gestured to Miranda to continue her story. "At the picnic, Felicia told you something about David's fiancée?"

"That's just it, she didn't," said Miranda. "In fact, it was exactly the opposite. Felicia told me point blank, in so many words, that she, Felicia, was engaged to David – or about to be engaged to David. I forget how she phrased it exactly, but in Felicia's version, she and David were an item. There was no mention of a fiancée in China."

Win said, "Maybe she didn't know about the fiancée in China."

"Didn't you just say how close the two of them were? Surely, if David was engaged to be married, Felicia would've known about it," said Shep. "Unless you think he would hide it from her because he was interested in Felicia."

Win shook his head. When Shepard didn't respond, Win

spoke up, "No, I can't see David lying or cheating. He was a man of excellent character."

"Was?" murmured Miranda. "That's how we're really thinking of David now, isn't it! *Was*. Not *is*."

The room went silent under the weight of Miranda's conclusion.

Win got up and fetched the coffee pot. He refilled all three cups, replaced the pot on the credenza, and dropped into his desk chair. The chair gave a sad squeak.

Shep took a sip of the freshened coffee before he said, "Could Felicia have had access to David's cellphone?"

Clarkson exhaled a mixture of grief and fatigue. "I don't know. But after looking over David's notes and drafts last night and comparing them to Felicia's draft I reviewed a few days ago, I'm certain she has stolen David's doctoral dissertation to submit as her own."

Miranda gasped. "She plagiarized the whole thing?"

Shep said, "She must've been pretty sure you wouldn't be reading David's work, if she was brave enough to give you her draft to review."

"She would've been right, too," said Win, "if your hacker hadn't broken into David's Cloud storage. With David's laptop missing, it was likely nobody would ever read his work, nor ever compare it with hers."

Miranda said, "But, if all she wanted was to win the fellowship, would she have to get rid of both David *and* his computer? Why not just steal his computer? There would be no need to harm David."

"Yeah, there would, Bean," said Shep. "If the laptop went missing, David would do just what we did: he'd pull his saved document down from the Cloud. Or, with some hard work, he'd *recreate* his dissertation."

Miranda grasped his reasoning instantly. "Even if it wasn't exactly the same as the stolen document," she mused, "it would be close enough."

"That's right," Shep said. "Then, if Felicia had copied his paper from his laptop, everyone would know what she'd done as soon as they saw both papers side by side."

Clarkson said, "And she couldn't submit her *own* work against David's, because her skills as writer and researcher were noticeably inferior. Anyone looking at both of them would choose David every time."

"Yep. From Felicia's point of view, only *one* paper must be submitted," Shep concluded. "And the one paper must be submitted by Felicia. Ergo, both David and his computer had to disappear."

Silence blanketed the room once more. No one even took a sip of their coffee.

Miranda was first to speak. "Is this real? Are we really accusing someone we know of a murder – the murder of someone else we know? This sort of thing happens to strangers."

"It might be worse than we think," Shep said. "Win, do you still believe Felicia had no reason to go visit Tom at the farm?"

"No. There would be no reason for her to see Tom. I haven't even asked her to telephone him in quite a while."

"Well, she was out there. We have photographs to prove it."

"But where is she *now*?" Miranda asked.

Clarkson said, "I still don't know. I've kept trying to phone her since I heard she'd visited Tom, but every call goes straight to voicemail. And, naturally, nobody calls me back."

Shepard produced his cellphone and, using voice commands, sent a text message to Rocket Man. Moments later, the phone vibrated, and Shep activated the audible response.

"Female subject apartment is wrecked like she left in a hurry," the electronic phone voice told them. "Judging from what's gone and what's left, she ain't comin' back. Male subject has left his place, also. They got past me during the night, Chief. Sorry. I'll keep lookin'. Rocket out."

Nobody spoke for a minute, as they processed this new information.

Then, Win said, "Why now? Why choose last night to make a run for it? And what 'male subject'? Is she with David, after all?"

"The male Rocket was following is Maynard, David's former roommate," Shepard told them. "Remember when Carlo told you on Satuday, Felicia had been seen visiting Maynard secretly? Since then, Rocket has been tailing her. She might've realized she was being watched, so she and Maynard ditched Rocket and took off."

Win took this in and added his own conclusion. "If she discovered your man right after she gave me her draft to review, she probably thought – with her guilty conscience working overtime – that I recognized her plagiarism somehow and told the University. In her panic, she may have assumed the University's investigators were stalking her."

"If they're really gone," Miranda said, "Felicia won't be submitting her doctoral dissertation. Apparently, David won't either."

Shep said, "So, no Ph.D. in paleontology this semester, and no fellowship awarded to jump-start a career. Also, if Felicia is running, she's undoubtedly running with little or no money — students are always broke."

"Plus, she has a junkie partner," Miranda added, "and probably a boatload of student loan debt."

Clarkson added, "They won't get far with no money."

"You're right," Shepard murmured. "They desperately need money. And I know where they can get a three-hundred-thousand-dollar mammoth fossil."

## Chapter 27 - the Woods

*Friday afternoon*

Only two hours had elapsed since Shep and Miranda's early morning meeting with Professor Clarkson in Gainesville.

For the second time in her life, Miranda stood on the bank of the Pig River and watched Shepard's handmade, work-of-art canoe being shoved gently onto the water. She was not boarding the vessel herself this time, and she did not think anybody else should get in it, either.

Grabbing Shep's bicep and stepping between him and the river, she said, "Tell me again why you think this is a good idea?"

"Bean, we've already discussed this."

"We're not finished discussing it until you listen to reason."

"And by 'listen to reason,' you mean 'do it my way,' – 'my way' meaning *your* way, in this instance." He moved to sidestep her, but she moved with him and still blocked the way.

"How about this," Miranda urged. "We call nine one one and tell the police to get over to Rigby's farm on the double. Then we go home and wait to hear how everything turned out."

Carlo brushed past them to place two backpacks in the canoe. "And what will we say when they ask why they should race to *Signor* Rigby's farm, sirens blaring and helicopters circling?" He continued in a girlish falsetto, "Um, I'm pretty sure there are murderers out there, digging up a prehistoric elephant."

Miranda turned on Carlo. "Well, of course it sounds silly

when you say it like that."

She stood with her back to Shep, while Carlo collected the heavy wooden oars from the grass and moved them into the boat.

Shep stepped closer and put his arms around her waist, drawing her back against his chest. "We talked about this. We have a lot of suspicion and informed guesswork on our side, Bean, but we don't have anything the authorities would consider real evidence. That could change if we catch Felicia and Maynard red-handed."

"That's the problem!" She leaned her head back against his pectoral muscles. "They might actually *be* red-handed – they could have David Zhang's blood on their hands. Or Tom Rigby's. Or both! And, they might not hesitate to shed the blood of anybody who tries to stop them from getting what they want."

Shep kissed her ear before he spoke soothingly into it, "Think about it, Castor Bean. What's the difference if the police go instead of us – assuming we could even convince the cops to stop laughing and investigate? Felicia and Maynard could shoot at a policeman just as easily as they could shoot at us, right?"

Carlo added, "Plus, sirens and helicopters are very loud. The police will not sneak up in a quiet canoe, like us."

"*You* think about it!" said Miranda. "Police officers have guns and, and, and bulletproof vests and stuff! Do you have guns?"

"No, but—" Shep began.

"Do you have bulletproof vests?"

Carlo said, "We got those orange flotation collars, but I was not planning to take them. They are bulky, and the color looks terrible on me. I am not an Autumn."

Miranda turned within the circle of Shep's arms and flattened her palms against his chest. "You have no guns and no vests. What do you think will happen if these two criminals – who have nothing to lose – decide to shoot at you?"

"I'm going to hide behind Carlo," Shep said. Then he kissed her on the top of her head and stepped away from her to board the canoe.

"See? Nothing to worry about. He has a plan," Carlo said, from his seat in the bow of the boat.

Zeus trotted past Miranda on his way to join the men in the canoe. When he leaped from the bank to the canoe, the boat's slight movement alerted Shep.

"Not this trip, buddy," Shep told him. "Your job is to stay here and protect the womenfolk."

Zeus vaulted back to the shore and trotted to sit beside Miranda's feet.

Shep used his oar to push away from the bank, while Carlo sliced the river water with strong oar strokes that sent them into the current and downstream as if they were in a race.

Miranda waited on the riverbank until the river's course and overhanging foliage made them invisible. Then she took out her cellphone and scrolled through her contacts. She found a number and tapped to initiate the call.

When her party answered, she said, "Good afternoon, Deputy. It's Miranda Ogilvy. I need to tell you about a crime – maybe two crimes. One has already happened and one, I believe, is happening right now. See, I owe you a favor, and I thought giving you credit for single-handedly capturing a murderer could be good for your career. Am I right?"

♦

Less than half an hour later, Miranda and Zeus approached the front porch of Martha Cleary's cottage on Magnolia Street.

From her rocking chair on the porch, Mrs. Cleary watched them come. "Well, ain't this a important-lookin' delegation. What you two got on yer minds this fine day?"

Miranda stepped onto the bottom step and wasted no time on trivialities. "Shepard and Carlo have gone downriver to Tom Rigby's farm because Tom Rigby was murdered, and maybe David Zhang was murdered, and probably the murderer is digging up a dead elephant from Tom's new sinkhole right this very minute."

The rocking chair's rhythm never faltered. Calmly, Mrs. Cleary said, "Ain't no elephant, sweetie. It's a mammoth."

"Mammoth, then," said Miranda. "Did you hear me about the murderer?"

"Sure. I'm old, I ain't deaf. Question is, what do expect me to do with this momentous piece of information? You didn't come over here to borrow no cup of sugar, I reckon."

"I want to drive to Tom Rigby's farm, but I really don't want to go alone."

*"Myrrt!"*

"I mean, without another human."

"You don't wanna drive out there," said Mrs. Cleary, still rocking.

"Believe me, I don't want to. I've driven that awful road before, and I nearly crashed a dozen times. But I have to go. Shep and Carlo could be confronting a murderer! We have to—"

"Now, jest hold on, hold on. I don't necessarily disagree that we need to go, I jest think you don't want to go in a *car*. Too noisy and smelly; impossible to sneak up on 'em in a big car like mine – or yours." She nodded to Miranda's car, which had been returned to Miranda's driveway.

"Right," said Miranda. "So, um, do you have a canoe?"

"Heck, no! And I don't have no muscle-bound oarsman to power a canoe downriver, neither. Somehow I don't see you and me getting very far trying to paddle ourselves."

"You don't?" Miranda sounded deflated.

"Buck up, gal! I got somethin' better'n a canoe." Mrs. Cleary stood up from her chair, lifted her rifle from the floor by her side, and looked at Miranda. "Foller me. It's out in the shed."

Minutes later, Miranda approved the old widow's solution: the late Mr. Cleary's flat-bottomed aluminum jonboat, complete with quiet, electric motor. It was dented, scuffed and scratched, and the paint was peeling, but it was seaworthy, lightweight, and quiet.

The women rolled the boat trailer out of its shed and attached it to the trailer hitch of Mrs. Cleary's red Cadillac. In no time at all, they were at the nearest Pig River boat ramp, lowering their ten-foot yacht into the water.

Miranda more-or-less stumbled into the boat, while Zeus skipped easily aboard.

The old lady waded into the water to push the boat away from the bank and clear of shoreline plants and entanglements. Then she climbed in, took the rudder, and started the electric motor.

The cavalry was on its way to rescue Shep and Carlo.

(It was actually the navy, and nobody could guarantee who would actually need rescuing.)

Nevertheless, the ladies were on a mission, armed with stout hearts and pure motives – and Martha Cleary's .22 caliber rifle.

♦

On arriving at the Rigby farm, Miranda and Mrs. Cleary shut off their electric motor and dragged their flat-bottomed boat onto the shore beside Shepard's distinctive canoe.

Zeus abandoned ship and sat down on dry land to wash his face.

Mrs. Cleary was considerably more graceful than Miranda when disembarking and beaching the boat, but this was only the second time Miranda had been boating on the Sho-ke-okee.

On shore, Miranda took the lead, with Mrs. Cleary and Zeus following. They marched bravely up the trail.

Something large pounced in front of them from the bushes and blocked their path.

Miranda screamed.

Miz Martha almost shot it before she identified it as Carlo.

Carlo said, "I knew it! Why can you not resist putting your lovely self in danger, *signorina?*"

"I wasn't in danger. I was with Mrs. Cleary," Miranda answered.

*"Mrryt!"*

"Mrs. Cleary and Zeus," she corrected. "And *you're* the one doing something dangerous. Where's Shepard?"

"Calm down," said Carlo. "Shep is fine. He is at the sinkhole, where the killer had been working but is gone now – probably back at the farmhouse, loading bones into her vehicle — or Tom's truck."

Miranda plunked her fists on her waistline, indignant. "Shep's all alone, watching for 'the killer' to return. And you don't think that's dangerous?"

"Somebody had to stay there, and somebody had to run back to the river to intercept the incorrigible Captain Castor Bean…" he sent an accusing look at Mrs. Cleary, "…and crew!"

He refocused on Miranda, saying, "We never thought for a minute that you would not come. You do not have a history of taking good advice, *signorina.*"

"That's true, sweetie," Mrs. Cleary agreed. "Remember that time—"

"That was different," Miranda insisted.

Carlo placed gentle hands on Miranda's shoulders and turned her around on the trail. "We will discuss more later. Right now, please, turn around, go back down the trail to the river, get in your little boat, and go home."

A new voice said, "Oh, don't go! You only just got here!"

Felicia Harper stepped onto the trail behind Martha Cleary, snatched Martha's rifle, and shoved the 75-year-old to the ground.

Miranda rushed to help Mrs. Cleary up.

Zeus disappeared into the forest.

"Big help *you* are," muttered Miranda.

Carlo moved, but Felicia pointed the rifle in his direction. "Stay where you are. If you have any weapons, take 'em out slow and easy and toss 'em into the bush."

Carlo shook his head.

"No, you won't do it? Or no, you don't have any weapons?"

"I have no weapons."

"And Blondie, up at the sinkhole, does he have a gun? Yours, maybe?"

"We do not own a gun."

"Excellent. Let's hike on up to the sinkhole and join your friend. I gotta tell ya, it made me laugh when you two decided the best plan was to leave the blind guy behind as lookout!"

"He has excellent hearing," Carlo said.

Felicia scoffed. "Dude. Really? Anyway, he's not a lookout now. He's a prisoner. And you three will join him in just a few minutes."

A moment later, the four people walked single file through the woods, with Felicia in the rear, pointing Mrs. Cleary's rifle at their backs.

Earlier, when Shep and Carlo had arrived at the sinkhole, they'd found signs the mammoth-thieves had indeed been digging recently.

Most likely, Felicia and Maynard were at that very moment loading their first haul of bones into Tom's truck.

The students might as well steal the vehicle; they were already stealing something worth much more – and they could be guilty of murder, as well.

The two Minokee men drew straws to see who would wait at the hole to catch the thieves, and who would return to the river to send Miranda back home.

Shep had learned not to flip a coin to make decisions, because Carlo would lie to him about whether the coin turned up heads or tails – depending on which outcome would best keep Shep out of trouble.

By drawing straws, Shep could not be fooled. One straw was long, and one was short. If Carlo drew the long straw, he could not simply break it to make it shorter, because Shep would hear the break every time.

Carlo did not like leaving Shep alone near the crime scene,

with the criminals expected to return any minute. He went into the woods toward the river, despite his misgivings, because he knew Shep would be insulted if Carlo did otherwise.

Shep listened to Carlo's progress through the twigs, leaves, and vines. Unfortunately, Carlo's noises masked the stealthy approach of someone else.

Returning to the sinkhole from the farmyard, the two thieves spotted Shepard acting as watchman. Since Felicia was the brains of their operation, without doubt, and Maynard was the more capable digger, he was told to take care of the lookout and get back to work.

Felicia sneaked around the clearing and through the woods. Her stealth rewarded her with sounds of people talking, on the trail near the river.

She crept closer, her steps easily hidden by their conversation, and assessed the situation. The weak link seemed to be the old lady at the end of the line of three people. Also, the old lady had a weapon, which Felicia could turn to her own advantage.

Without a second thought, Felicia Harper attacked. The old lady went down easily, and the rifle was easy to snatch and turn against her new hostages.

That is when Carlo, Miranda, and Mrs. Cleary began their forced-marched through the forest at gunpoint.

Maynard was no hero. In fact, he took pride in his cowardice. He was happy to creep up behind the big man with the pony tail and whack him across the back with a four-foot, fifteen-pound club of oak.

The tree limb smashed into Shepard's shoulder blades with a solid whack. Shep flew forward and face-planted into the rough ground. While he lay in the dirt, trying to breathe and mostly failing, Maynard fetched a rope from the nearby pile of supplies, sat on Shepard's glutes, and tied Shep's hands behind his back.

As soon as Shep was able to draw breath, Maynard managed, with his help, to raise Shep to a sitting position and back him up against the nearest tree.

"Who are you?" said Maynard, squatting to look into Shep's face.

Shep said nothing.

Maynard passed his hand back and forth eight inches from Shep's face. "Dang! Felly was telling the truth for a change. You really can't see, can you?"

Shep said nothing.

Maynard leaned to one side to retrieve Shep's sunglasses from where they had landed in the leaf litter. He pushed the glasses onto Shep's face. "And you're the lookout for your team? Ha! You guys must be dumber than a bucket of sand."

Shep said nothing. Blood and loose sand clung to one side of his face, and the cheek bone on that side was lacerated, swelling and turning purple. The rest of him – at least, the front side that had smacked the ground – did not look any better than his face.

His shirt was torn, and multiple cuts and bruises showed through gaps in the fabric. Spiky, fallen tree limbs and bits of razor-edged limestone on the ground had proved effective accomplices for Shep's attacker.

Maynard rose from his crouch and stepped away. "I'd love to stay and chat, but I still got digging to do, and we're burning daylight. That's in all the cowboy movies: 'burning daylight.' I always wanted to say it. Ha! That's good. 'We're burning daylight, boys!'"

Shep heard Maynard chuckling to himself as he scuffled back down into the hole. Soon the sound of shoveling drifted up from inside the crater.

Shep had almost worked one hand out of Maynard's sloppily-tied rope when a silent cannonball of fur shot out of the woods behind him and crash-landed on Shep's shoulder. Shep smothered a cry of pain when Zeus slid down Shep's back, claws digging into flesh as well as clothing all the way down.

"Well, I know you didn't come with *me* on this trip, so you must have come with Bean," Shep whispered.

*"Mnyatt."*

"And you're here, but she's not, so I'm guessing we've got trouble."

*"Mnyatt,"* agreed Zeus, and added *"K-k-k-k-k-k-k"* for emphasis.

"Then let's go," Shep said, easing himself quietly backward on his butt, past the tree he'd been leaning against, and onward until nearby cabbage palms closed around him. Once they were well back into the foliage, Shep finished freeing his hands. Then he and Zeus melted into the trees.

Felicia and her three captives were hiking single file along the narrow game trail toward the sinkhole, when the younger female hostage shouted back at Felicia.

"What happened to David Zhang?"

Felicia seemed amused. "Oh, yeah, good old David. I heard he went back to China."

"You know he didn't," said Miranda.

Felicia chuckled. "Nope. He didn't. … He could have. We offered to pay if he'd go home and forget the whole thing."

Carlo asked, "What 'whole thing'?"

"The dissertation and fellowship, of course," said Felicia. "He was smart enough, he could have started over and written another dissertation, if he wanted to. He could've been a success at any university. Just not mine. That fellowship was meant for me."

Miranda stumbled over a jutting strangler fig vine, and Carlo grabbed her arm to keep her upright. "Thanks," she said. To Felicia she said, "So, all that romantic story you told me about David being your intended, the love of your life, that was all crap?"

Carlo chuckled. "Language, *signorina*!"

Felicia responded, "You believed it, though, didn't you? It would've been fine if his stupid mother hadn't emailed Clarkson."

"Did you even *like* David?" said Miranda.

"Oh, sure. I mean, David was perfect. That's why we picked him. He was exactly what the doctor ordered."

Carlo said, "'We'? Who is 'we'?"

Felicia hesitated a split second before answering, "Me and Maynard. Who else?"

Carlo pressed on, "So, Maynard helped you get rid of David?"

Mrs. Cleary interjected, "Lawd, cain't tell one player from another'n without a program. How many crooks does it take to steal one elephant?"

"Mammoth," said Carlo, Miranda, and Felicia at once.

"It was just me and Maynard," Felicia said, "and we didn't start out to steal the fossil. Too much hard labor to dig it up and haul it off, for one thing."

Miranda deduced, "No, you wanted to steal David's laptop, with his dissertation on it."

"We offered to buy it," said Felicia. "But David was such a Goody Two-shoes – Do they even have that term in China? – All he had to do was take the money, act all homesick, and go back to mama. Then I would turn in the dissertation, win the fellowship, and my honey and me could work together happily ever after, on dig sites all over the world."

"Your boyfriend is an archaeologist?" Miranda said.

"So, it's not Maynard," Carlo said, with absolute conviction. "What will you do with him? You don't really want to share the mammoth money with him."

"We'll offer him a payoff, like we did with David. If he's smart, he'll take it."

"David didn't take it," said Miranda.

Felicia shifted the rifle to her opposite hand, and she watched the captives while she used her free hand to lift her water bottle from her belt and take a swig. She did not offer water to anyone else.

"He almost took the money," Felicia said. "When he thought it was only the fellowship that I wanted, and that my paper could win it if he dropped out. And, it might've, but there was no guarantee. David's paper, however, was a sure thing.

"He caught me downloading his dissertation and research notes from his computer, the Saturday night after the Audubon trip. David was taking a shower, and I figured I had plenty of time. But I guess they shower fast in China, because he walked into the room before I was finished.

"Anyway, David knew what I was doing the minute he saw me with my hands on his keyboard.

"I panicked. I bashed him with the laptop, and he went down. Out cold."

Miranda sounded hopeful when she said, "So, you didn't actually kill him! He isn't dead!"

Felicia shrugged, even though she was bringing up the rear, and no one could see her. "I don't know. I didn't think so, but he didn't wake up the whole time Maynard and I were driving him out here to dump him."

"In the sinkhole, you mean," Carlo said.

Mrs. Cleary said, "You wasn't sure he was dead, but you was gonna plop him into the water? How'd you know he wouldn't wake up and swim right on outta there?"

"We weighed him down pretty good," said Felicia.

"Lord have mercy!" Miranda whispered. "So, if he wasn't dead already, you drowned him!"

A thousand tree shadows seemed to coalesce into one forest-sized cloud of twilight. Three prey humans and one predator crushed twigs and leaves underfoot in a somber march toward doom.

The image of David Zhang awaking to ropes, weights, deep water and total darkness bloomed in the minds of the hostages.

No one spoke until minutes had passed, and the initial horror relinquished its stranglehold on their psyches.

At last, Miranda said, "So, you have David's laptop. That's why we couldn't find it. I guess you had his cellphone, too – until you arranged for the police to find it in that dumpster."

"Yeah, I had 'em," Felicia boasted. "His car, too, rattle trap that it was. I followed Maynard in my car, and we pushed David's car into a deep canal on an isolated stretch of road, later that same night. The laptop was in it. I kept the phone a while longer."

Miranda stopped and spun around to shake an accusing finger at Felicia. "You! You tried to frame Shepard for David's murder!"

"What!" Carlo spat, spinning to join Miranda. Mrs. Cleary was forced to stop walking, so as not to trample the other two.

"I didn't hear nothin' 'bout Shep committin' no murder!" said Miz Martha.

"He didn't, of course," Miranda said, "but he was arrested for it. They used David's cellphone as evidence, but it didn't work out."

"Hmpf. Sloppy," Miz Martha said, shaking her head. "Y'all ain't very skilled criminals. New at it, are ya?"

Carlo turned on Miranda. "Shep was arrested? He was in jail? Why nobody told me?"

"He wasn't there very long," said Miranda.

Felicia poked the rifle at them and snapped, "That's enough! Story time's over. Get movin'. I wanna get this done before full dark."

The reluctant hostages turned toward their destination and resumed walking. A hog grunted and snuffled in the middle distance, but nobody was afraid of a wild pig this afternoon. Something more fearsome than feral swine walked the trail close behind them, and it held a loaded weapon.

# Chapter 28 - The Cavalry

When the hostages emerged from the forest trail into the clearing beside the sinkhole, they saw a small heap of dirt-encrusted bones.

They saw scoops of dirt flying through the air, flung by a shovel they heard attacking the earth deep inside the hole.

They saw churned soil near a sturdy tree and a discarded length of rope near the edge of the bushes.

What they didn't see was Shepard Krausse.

Carlo grinned. "I do not see a prisoner, *signorina*," he said.

Miranda said, "He's gone!"

Mrs. Cleary said, "S'prise, s'prise," in a tone that said she was not surprised in the least.

Felicia stepped around the three friends so that her rifle pointed directly at Miranda. The barrel ended barely six inches from Miranda's spine.

"Can you see me, Mister Krausse?" Felicia shouted at the forest. "In case you can't, let me tell you I have a gun pointed at a young lady here, and I won't miss at this distance."

Felicia paused and listened. No response.

"Of course, if you don't care about this lady, maybe after I shoot her I'll shoot Euro-Boy here. I know he's a close friend of yours. I'll save the old lady for last."

Again, nobody answered.

Felicia turned and shouted into another part of the forest. "On second thought, I might not kill your friends outright. I might only wound them seriously and leave 'em here in the woods to suffer."

No answer.

"You step out where I can see you," the T.A. yelled. "Maybe you two big, strong men can help me get this job finished. Then I'll tie everybody up and hit the road."

She aimed her voice at yet another part of the surrounding woods. "You come on out, Mister Krausse, and everybody lives. But this offer expires soon. I think you better get out here!"

Miranda yelled, "Stay away, Shepard! You know they're going to kill all of us, no matter what. Save yourself, at least!"

"You're right," said their captor. With the rifle barrel she nudged Miranda closer to the crater's edge. "In fact, since you guys are so interested in finding David, I think you should join him right now."

She moved as if to force the hostages over the precipice, into the bottomless, water-filled sinkhole. Felicia knew Maynard, halfway down the hole's inner wall -- with his shovel -- would ensure no one who fell in would be able to climb out.

When Felicia began herding the trio toward the crater, she dropped back from Miranda, to cover all three at once.

Carlo stepped between the gun and his two friends. He was only two paces from Felicia's rifle.

In a single instant, Miranda and Mrs. Cleary broke and ran, a shot split the air, blood spurted, and something big fell into the black hole with a hollow splash.

Mrs. Cleary and Miranda froze mid-step.

Miranda screamed, "Carlo!"

Inside the hole, Maynard had set his shovel aside to pull a fossilized molar the size of a tennis shoe from the muddy wall of the crater.

When Carlo fell in, Maynard reached out and placed a hand atop the man's head. Carlo surfaced, but before he could take a breath, Maynard shoved him under the water.

"Got him!" called Maynard. Then he tossed the fossil molar

onto the rim of the sinkhole and skittered up after it. He added the tooth to the pile of muddy bones already on the ground.

Miranda hurried to the edge of the dark shaft and looked in. Carlo had not surfaced, and she screamed his name again.

Mrs. Cleary grabbed Miranda's arm and stopped her from leaning too far over the unstable edge of the sinkhole.

Felicia aimed at the two women beside the abyss.

Maynard shouted, "Wait!"

Miranda shrieked, "Carlo!"

Mrs. Cleary yelled for Miranda to "Git back!" from the brink.

The loudest screech of all, however, came from the smallest member of the congregation: Zeus.

Wailing like a chorus of banshees, with his feet spread to all four compass points as if he were a flying squirrel, the little cat blasted down from an overhead tree branch and hit Felicia square in the face.

Four sets of claws sank into the flesh of her scalp and jaws, turning the cat into a firmly affixed, hairy facemask.

Reeling backward from the kitten's impact, Felicia squeezed the trigger of Martha's rifle.

The gun's booming only added to the screaming, screeching, yelling cacophony.

The bullet went wild, hitting no one.

Zeus's momentum shoved Felicia backward. When she slammed butt-first into the ground, the rifle jarred from her grip.

The weapon landed a few yards away, and Mrs. Cleary scooped it up – half a second before Maynard could reach it.

She swung the barrel in his direction.

He wisely backed away.

Almost before Felicia's head struck the dirt, Shepard dropped from the trees overhead. He landed nearby in a crouch and pounced toward the sound of Zeus screeching like an air raid siren.

Locating Zeus's victim by sound and touch, Shep grabbed Felicia. He flipped the woman belly-down and slammed one knee into the center of her back. She was pinned under his considerable weight.

Zeus then retracted his claws, stepped off Felicia's lacerated face, and sauntered away.

From the direction of the farmhouse, Luz Sheriff Deputy Tyrell Krothers came thrashing through the palmetto bushes into the clearing. He double-handed his pistol. "I heard shots! Anybody hurt?"

Maynard spun as if to escape into the jungle, but he tripped over the pile of mammoth bones.

He regained his feet and bolted toward the trees, but Mrs. Cleary was having none of that nonsense. She shot him.

Maynard, though bleeding, kept running – until a lady librarian smashed him to the ground. Miranda hit the man with a flying tackle worthy of any 300-pound NFL linebacker.

"I reckon somebody's hurt now," Mrs. Cleary told the deputy.

## Chapter 29 - The Darkness

“Any other weapons? Anybody?” Deputy Krothers panned the group in the clearing as well as the woods on either side.

“Naw, this is the only one,” said Mrs. Cleary, raising her rifle over her head. “It’s been passed around a bit, but it’s back in the right hands now.” She lowered the weapon and cradled it across her chest.

Something splashed in the shadowed depths of the sinkhole.

"Bean! Get Carlo!" Shep yelled, sitting heavily on Felicia’s fanny, crunching her wrist bones in one massive fist, clamping her hands tightly together behind her back.

"I'm all right, Tarzan!" Carlo shouted from inside the sinkhole, though he sputtered and panted after spending thirty seconds under water.

Deputy Krothers cuffed Maynard and left him lying on the ground. Maynard whined and complained that “the old lady” shot him.

Krothers was unimpressed. “Yeah, yeah. She only winged ya. I already called for paramedics and backup officers. Quit yer whinin’, ya big baby.”

Miranda and Mrs. Cleary carefully approached the edge to look down into the roughly bowl-shaped cavity, water-filled to within twelve feet of the rim. They saw Carlo clinging to a jutting fossil bone on the wall of the sinkhole.

He looked up at them. "I’m sorry to say it, but I believe I have found David Zhang."

Carlo was dripping, muddy water streaming from his black hair into his eyes. Clumps of damp dirt tumbled from his hair when he moved. He appeared unhurt, but the women saw a new rip in his shirt sleeve, and a streak of blood beginning to clot.

Deputy Krothers cuffed Felicia, allowing Shepard to rise from pinning her to the ground.

Mrs. Cleary and Miranda watched Carlo begin scaling the rugged wall of the hole. He soon joined them on the rim of the watery shaft.

"Bean!" Shepard yelled, fidgeting in the center of the clearing, with no idea which way to go.

"Coming!" In a blink she was beside him, offering her elbow. As she walked with him toward the crater's edge, she told him, "I wish you could've seen me take down the bad guy! Okay, Mrs. Cleary shot him, but he didn't *fall down* until I tackled him! It was just like Monday Night Football. I wish we had instant replay."

"I'm sorry I missed that," he growled. His grip tightened on her elbow. "But you are not even supposed to be here. Aren't you the one who said it was dangerous?"

"It *was* dangerous! That's why I called Deputy Krothers. And *you* were here. So, I *had* to come—"

"We'll discuss the concept of personal safety later," he said. "Where's Carlo?"

"Here," said Carlo from an arm's length away. "Don't get too close to the edge."

Carlo had been peering into the water at the lowest point of the crater. He directed their attention to a brightly-colored neon orange basketball shoe barely visible three feet beneath the dark water.

They remembered the distinctive shoe very well, from their canoe trip with David Zhang.

The shoe still encased a foot, attached to an ankle and a leg, which were all connected, underwater, to the rest of a person. "David is right down there," Carlo said. "I untied some of the concrete blocks that were keeping him on the bottom."

Deputy Krothers had joined the group looking into the hole. “Poor soul,” Tyrell said. “Fire department will be here directly. They’ll get him out of there.”

The friends drifted away from the hole. Each one found a place to sit on the ground and wait for police and paramedics.

"Well, Romeo," drawled Mrs. Cleary to Carlo, "you was shore lucky it were that college gal a-shootin' atcha with my gun, insteada me. I wouldn't 'a' missed!"

"No, *signora*, I know you would not," Carlo answered with a smile. “I believe, in another life, you were the commander of the *carabiniere*.”

"It wasn't only luck, Miz Cleary," Shepard said. "I expect there was a lot of praying going on in these woods. I know I was doing plenty of it, myself."

"Amen," said Miranda.

Police officers, firemen and paramedics, responding to calls from Deputy Krothers, soon filled the farmyard.

For about ninety minutes, the four witnesses from Minokee answered questions and gave detailed statements to officers of the Alachua County Sheriff.

At the same time, paramedics checked the injuries of Carlo, Shep, and the two ladies. Cuts and bruises – and one bullet graze – were cleaned and dressed.

Only Maynard required a trip to the hospital. Mrs. Cleary never missed, so Maynard’s wound, while not life-threatening, was no mere graze.

Zeus accepted adulation and ear rubs from numerous first responders, and he seemed to be having a great time.

When police dismissed the witnesses from the scene, Shep and Miranda walked away from the hullabaloo at the sinkhole. They followed the trail leading to the river and the waiting boats.

Carlo would have followed, but Mrs. Cleary held him back with a wink and a nod toward the silent couple ahead. "Let's give 'em a minute," she said.

Carlo winked back at her. "Let us give them five."

It took longer than five minutes, and twilight was visibly dimming toward night, but Shep and Miranda reached the riverside without incident. When they arrived at his canoe, he took her hand and helped her into it. She sat on the forward seat, facing aft, and he took his place on the aft seat, facing her.

"What do you think will happen to the mammoth bones now?" Miranda asked.

"I imagine, after they serve their purpose as evidence in the trials, the bones will be donated to the university, just as Tom wanted to do."

"Oh, I think he had changed his mind about that," a man's voice said. The speaker pushed past tangled bushes to step onto the shoreline.

Miranda whipped around to face him. "Doctor Clarkson!" She glanced at the shoreline all around them and saw no boats except Shep's and Martha's. "How did you get here?"

"Hiking trail," said Clarkson. "My car's parked at the trailhead about an hour's walk south from here. I've been birdwatching up and down that trail a hundred times."

Suspiciously, Shep asked, "What did you mean Tom 'changed his mind'? Was he not going to give the bones to the university, after all?"

"Tom and I had a buyer all lined up," Clarkson continued. "Planned to split the money. But I already had Felicia to think of, so I really couldn't afford to give half the money to Tom."

Miranda gasped, and her hand went to her throat. "Are you saying *you* killed Tom Rigby? Your oldest and dearest friend!"

Clarkson smiled. "He was old, but all things considered, he wasn't really so dear."

Shep said, "What do you mean, you 'had Felicia to think of?"

"You really messed up a good thing, there, Mister Sheep Counter. But you're famous for upsetting people's secret plans, aren't you. Sad to say, even if you survive this fiasco, I'm afraid we can no longer be friends."

"Let me guess," Shep drawled. "Felicia wasn't interested in

David Zhang, or even in her accomplice, Maynard – although Maynard probably doesn't realize that … yet. Felicia had something going with you!"

Miranda inhaled sharply. "When Felicia said 'we,' she meant her and *you*!"

"We don't have time to discuss details at the moment." Clarkson produced a pistol from inside his jacket. He pointed it at the couple. "I need you to come with me, before your friends show up. That could get messy."

"Shepard, he has a gun."

"Stay still, Bean. It'll be all right."

Clarkson said, "Hand me your cellphones, please."

Shep withdrew his phone from a pocket and passed it to Miranda. She gave it to the professor and gestured toward the jonboat. "I left my backpack in Mrs. Cleary's boat. My phone is in it."

Clarkson craned his neck and confirmed the backpack he could see tied to the front seat of the jonboat. He nodded to Miranda. "Please move to the center of the canoe, Miss Ogilvy," he said. "I will occupy the front seat, where I can keep an eye on both of you."

Shepard reached a hand toward her. "Here, Bean. Be careful."

She took his hand and carefully balanced herself while the canoe dipped and leaned with her movements. Soon she was settled cross-legged in the bottom of the boat, with Shepard at her back.

While Miranda was moving to her new seat in the canoe, Clarkson skipped Shep's cellphone like a flat stone across the surface of the river. Far from shore, the water swallowed the phone, sucking the electronic morsel down to its muddy belly.

"Is this where you shoot us?" Shep said. He put a soothing hand on Miranda's shoulder when she inhaled and stiffened.

"No. Your friends might hear it at this distance. This is where I push us off the bank, and you propel us downriver. I only shoot one of you if you make noise or cause trouble."

Miranda reached across her chest to her shoulder, covering Shep's hand with her own. "Which one of us?" she rasped.

"The one who isn't doing the rowing," Shep guessed.

"Absolutely." Clarkson held the pistol pointed at the couple while he bent to shove the boat off the sand and into the river. With ease born of many years' experience, the professor smoothly stepped into the canoe and settled himself on the forward thwart, facing his captives.

Shep placed both hands on his oar and, with Miranda directing him, steered the canoe toward the middle of the river and pointed it downstream.

Miranda tried to discourage Clarkson with, "It would be safer to walk through the woods. It'll be pitch black out here in a few minutes, and the river is extremely dangerous at night, without lights."

Clarkson chuckled. "Oh, it would take less time to take the trail through the woods, but I'll take my chances with the alligators rather than stroll among the wild hogs on shore, thanks. Besides, we have an experienced captain. Mister Krausse, how many times have you canoed this very river in total darkness?"

"Every time," the oarsman answered.

"There. You see, Miss Ogilvy? We couldn't be in better hands."

Shep's canoe was gone from the riverbank and nowhere in sight when Carlo and Mrs. Cleary stepped off the trail onto the sand.

"They coulda took the boat with the motor," the old lady quipped. "Then he coulda had at least one hand free fer cuddlin' in the dark."

"*Si, signora.* I have not trained him as well as I thought. Of course, if he were Italian, such ideas would occur to him naturally."

Night had chased the last deep blue streaks of twilight over the western edge of the planet. Through breaks in the tree canopy, the moon and stars sent their faint glow to reflect on the surface of the Sho-ke-okee.

Carlo helped Mrs. Cleary into her silvery jonboat.

While she retrieved two propane lanterns from beneath the thwarts, Carlo pushed the boat into the river and stepped into it behind his partner.

Mrs. Cleary, a seasoned night fisherman, lit the lanterns and set one in the bow. She passed another to Carlo for placement in the stern. Handy aluminum brackets, installed for the purpose, held the lights upright and in place.

Carlo started the electric motor and pointed the boat upstream. "I will go not so fast, I think."

"Right-o," agreed Mrs. Cleary. "We don't wanna accidentally sneak up on them two in the dark. Never can tell what folks in love might get up to, out in the night, unchaperoned."

Thus, the only people who knew Shep and Miranda were on the river, unwittingly sailed off in the wrong direction. They did not realize the couple was chaperoned after all; they were hostages of a murderer.

# Chapter 30 - The Detective

Shep steadily propelled his canoe downstream, with Clarkson still holding a gun on his companions.

At intervals, Clarkson produced his cellphone flashlight and shone it along both riverbanks and across the inky water.

Sometimes the eyes of alligators gleamed red in the light. They did not approach, but they watched the canoe in ominous readiness.

"You were dating a student." Miranda asked the professor, "Is that even allowed at the university?"

Clarkson's smile was barely visible in the moonlight. "Irrelevant. The university wasn't ever going to know about us. I would've made sure Felicia got her doctorate and her fellowship. She would have begun an illustrious career as my colleague, and she would've been my future ex-wife."

"You two lured David Zhang to your university, so you and your secret girlfriend could use his work to get her credentials," Shep said. "You must've been working on this plan for a long time. Even before Tom found the mammoth!"

"See there," said Clarkson. "I knew you would figure it out, given enough time to think. It's a shame you're going to run out of time very soon, now."

Carlo had kept his speed low, just barely making headway against the river's current. A half-hour had passed, but the jonboat had not covered a vast distance.

Mrs. Cleary suddenly broke a long silence with, "I cain't stop thinkin' we done missed somethin' important back there."

"Me, too," said Carlo. "But that is crazy, no?"

The old lady thought a moment. "Where's that kung fu cat that come with me and Miss Ogilvy?"

"I thought Zeus went home with Shep."

"Naw, he wuz in the woods with us after they left. I saw him."

Carlo reflected. "You are right, *signora*," he said.

Without another word, Carlo turned the boat around and headed back toward the Rigby farm. He went a lot faster than before.

In the canoe, Miranda spoke to their captor. "I hope you will pardon me if I say, for somebody who supposedly just lost the love of his life, you don't seem too upset that Felicia will be going to prison."

A faint dusting of starlight on his shoulders let her see Clarkson shrug. "Regrettable for her, but not really a problem for me. I won't have to share my profits with anyone, as it turns out. I think I'll retire to live like a king in a third world country with no extradition treaty."

Shep said, "How can you think you'll get away with all this? You murdered Tom Rigby. Felicia and Maynard will tell the police how you conspired to put David into the situation that got him killed, so you're probably an accessory to his murder. You'll be arrested before you can buy a plane ticket out of the country."

"No, I won't, actually. Felicia and Maynard may suspect I killed Tom, but nobody *knows* for sure."

The professor continued, "When they find David Zhang's

submerged car, it will have Felicia and Maynard's fingerprints all over it, not mine. Nobody is going to believe the claims of those two losers – and if someone did happen to believe their crazy story, there is absolutely *no evidence* connecting me to any of it."

Only twenty minutes after deciding to return to the farm, Carlo stopped the jonboat's electric motor and tilted it up, out of the river. He allowed the boat to glide toward the riverbank -- where Zeus sat waiting.

"There you are!" he said to the cat. "Any other time you would be the first one on board! How come you missed the boat this time? It is ten o'clock at night, we are tired, and we want to go home. Get in!"

"*Mwwrrrat!*"

Instead of coming toward the jonboat, Zeus turned and sauntered a few feet farther along the riverbank to where Shep's canoe had been beached. The cat then turned to face Carlo and sat.

Mrs. Cleary said, "Is he doing what I think he's doin'? I know I'm a mite eccentric in my old age, but I didn't believe I wuz gettin' plum loony until I met this dang cat."

Carlo was already stepping out of the boat, into thigh-deep water, carrying one of the Coleman lanterns. "Looks like Zeus also thinks we missed something."

As he slogged to shore and approached the cat, Carlo murmured, "I have a very, very bad feeling about this."

Win Clarkson had just completed one of his occasional flashlight-scans of the shores and the river. He turned off the cellphone and replaced it in his pocket.

Miranda asked, "Won't people suspect you, when you suddenly disappear to your 'third world country'?"

"Of course, they would, if I vanished immediately," said the professor. "That is why I will be returning to my teaching duties – after a day or two to recover from the shock of poor David's death and dear Felicia's horrendous crime, naturally."

"Naturally," she said.

Clarkson gave her a wry smile that she heard rather than saw. "I knew you'd understand."

Shep added, "And while you're bravely carrying on at the university, you'll be aiding the police in recovering, conserving, and carefully packing up Tom Rigby's mammoth, in memory of your old, not dear, friend."

"Exactly."

"Why do I think what gets 'carefully packed up' on Tom's farm will not be shipped to the university?" Shep asked.

Carlo stood on the riverbank and bent over the roiled gray sand. He shone his lantern on the bank, where Shep's canoe had left the shape of its keel clearly molded.

In the soft dirt of the riverbank, he could trace the center line of the canoe as it had angled toward the bank from the upstream direction, when it arrived. There should be a line angled in the opposite direction if Shep slid the craft away from the shore to point it back the way it had come.

There was a second keel impression in the sand, but the angle showed the boat turned downstream, not up.

"They did not go back to Minokee, *signora*," he told Martha.

"What! Why the heck not? Ain't nothin' but pigs, snakes and 'gators for miles in that direction!" She pointed unnecessarily downstream.

Carlo continued studying the ground near the keel marks. "I

see the small footprints of *Signorina* Ogilvy and the tread marks of the hiking boots I put out this morning for *Signor* Shepard to wear."

Zeus chose that moment to step away from his sitting spot. He stood looking at Carlo, at the spot on the dirt, and at Carlo again.

Carlo swung his lantern toward the cat and studied the tracks imprinted on the sand where Zeus had been sitting. "This cannot be good."

Miz Martha leaned forward from her seat in the jonboat. "Whose foot is that? Too big fer the gal, and too little fer Shep."

Carlo backtracked the new set of footprints with his lantern. "Whoever it is, they did not come down the trail from the sinkhole. They came out of those bushes."

"Ambush!" said Miz Martha.

"*Si, signora.* Give me one minute, please." Carlo raised his lantern and stalked up and down the bank several yards in each direction.

He returned to the jonboat and waded into the river far enough to climb into the stern.

Zeus hopped daintily from the shore to the prow and then to the forward thwart, where he took a seat beside Mrs. Cleary.

As Carlo lowered the silent engine and backed the boat into the center of the river, he said, "Three people went into the canoe. I do not find any prints leaving the canoe. The person from the bushes has taken them downriver."

"Well, git after 'em, then! No use lollygaggin' 'round here!" While Mrs. Cleary spoke, she produced her cellphone from a pocket. "I'm callin' the law."

"*Grazie, signora.*"

The electric engine shifted to forward gear, and – less than twelve hours after the first one – a *second* extraordinary rescue party motored downstream.

## Chapter 31 - The Attack!

Shep had been paddling for ninety minutes, but to Miranda it felt like ninety years.

After nearly a quarter-hour of silence, Clarkson turned on his cellphone-flashlight to scan the river and shore. More than one pair of red reptilian eyes watched the canoe from deeper water.

"Stop here!" Clarkson said, pointing toward the bank on their left. "This is where I leave you. The trailhead where I'm parked is a short walk from here. Take us to the left bank, Mister Krausse."

Shep angled the canoe in that direction, backpaddling to resist the current that stubbornly pushed them straight ahead.

The canoe was closer to shore, but still in water at least waist deep, when Clarkson lifted his gun, aimed it at Miranda, and cocked it.

The small sound of the gun cocking warned Shepard.

He lunged forward.

His left elbow shoved Miranda overboard.

She screamed.

With both of his strong arms Shep swung the heavy wooden oar, as if it were a huge baseball bat, toward where he last heard Clarkson.

Miranda disappeared under the water on the left side of the boat.

Shep's actions capsized the canoe and submerged him on the boat's righthand side.

As he met the water's surface, going down, the last sound he heard was Clarkson's cry of pain. While underwater, Shep heard the splash as Clarkson fell.

When Shep stood up in chest deep water, he heard Clarkson groaning and splashing, crawling from shallow water onto the shore.

Shep turned toward a splash from behind him. "Miranda! Where are you?" he shouted.

The splashing came closer. "I'm about ten feet from shore, I think," came her answer. "I can't see a thing! It's just as black above the water as it was underneath! Where are the alligators?"

He smiled. "It's okay, Bean. With all this screaming and splashing, they're probably a mile away by now. Of course, the snakes might still be around. *They*'re deaf."

"You're not funny," she said, splashing a little faster.

"Where's the gun?" Shep said, turning cautiously toward shore.

"I don't think he still has it," she said.

Shep walked out of the water and followed sounds to find Clarkson. "Where is the gun, professor?"

The professor was clutching his side and rolling on the ground, moaning and bleating, "My ribs! You broke my ribs! I think my lung is punctured! Get me a doctor!"

When he was near enough, Shepard aimed a kick toward Clarkson's voice and got a satisfying grunt of pain from the man.

Clarkson still breathed, but the complaining stopped. He snarled through clenched teeth, "It flew out of my hand. I heard it hit the dirt. When I find it, you'll be the first to know!"

Eyes adjusting to the moon- and starlight, Miranda recognized the outline of Shep scouring the ground on hands and knees. In a moment, he found the pistol that had been thrown from Clarkson's hand by the oar's crushing blow.

Providence was smiling on Shep and Miranda: the gun was the only thing from their canoe that had not gone underwater.

Miranda was slogging her way onto dry land when she saw Shepard lift Clarkson's gun and cock it.

"No! Shepard don't!" she cried, running to grab his left arm. "He's not worth you going to prison!"

"Don't move!" Shep said.

"What-- ?"

"Shhh!" He tilted his head as if listening. The jungle had gone silent.

Even Clarkson stopped moving and listened.

The moon slipped behind a cloud, burying them in utter blackness.

"We need Win's flashlight," whispered Miranda, and she tried to step toward the prone Clarkson.

"Be still!" Shep hissed,. He eased her behind him with his left hand, gripping the gun with his right.

Something agitated the plants at the jungle's edge, only a few paces away. Shep focused on the sound, tensed for action.

A twig snapped.

A bear-sized creature charged from the bushes, grunting its war cry. Heavy feet shook the ground as it pounded forward.

Shep fired the pistol at the animal's sounds, three times in rapid succession.

With each muzzle flash, Miranda glimpsed the attacker, closing fast.

She braced for impact.

The beast sideswiped the couple. Miranda inhaled sharply and staggered to her right.

With her safe on his right, Shep swung left, still following the noise of the animal.

Carlo was making good time down the river, his hand firmly on the throttle of Mrs. Cleary's jonboat motor.

While he watched the black water ahead, Mrs. Cleary's eyes strained in the lantern light to see any signs of life on the forested riverbanks on their left and right.

Three loud pops echoed from the south. The two friends recognized the sound. Gunshots coming from the direction in which Shep's canoe had gone were worrisome, to say the least.

Carlo gripped the throttle and increased their speed to the limits of their little electric motor. Mrs. Cleary concentrated her search toward the left bank, where the sounds seemed to originate.

A fourth shot reached their ears, and the two people in the jonboat began to pray in earnest.Shep's gun flashed a fourth shot.

The bestial war cry ceased.

With a thud, the attacker fell. It slid forward across several feet of sandy soil, plowing the mud of the water's edge with its snout and tusks.

There it stopped.

Dead.

Shep heard Miranda fall.

"Clarkson!" he said. "If you're still alive, turn on your flashlight! Now!"

The professor groused, "You mean the one on my phone? The phone you sent to the bottom of the river a minute ago? Ha! That phone is deader than the behemoth you shot! And what earthly good would a flashlight be to you anyway!"

Shep's snarl was scarier than the beast he had just killed. "The light's not for me, you jackass, it's for Miss Ogilvy! If you paid attention to anything but your own petty concerns, you'd realize she's injured!"

Shoving the gun into his waistband, he carefully felt around to find Miranda, and he sat on the ground beside her.

"Shepard?" she said softly. " I'm not very good around boats, so ... I zipped my phone in a plastic bag before I left home ..."

"I knew you didn't leave it in Martha's boat! Where's the phone now?" He lifted her head to pillow it on his forearm.

"It's in the back pocket of my jeans," she smiled weakly, "but don't get fresh, mister."

He smiled. "I'll behave."

He lifted her enough to slide a hand behind her back and pull the bagged phone from her wet jeans pocket. It didn't come easily, and she yelped when he was forced to tug on the wet denim.

When he had retrieved the phone, he let her rest a moment. Soon her breathing slowed and some tension left her neck and shoulders.

“Bean,” he whispered, “are you with me?”

She whispered, "Right here."

"Give me your hand.”

She lifted one hand and touched his face.

He folded the unbagged cellphone into her hand. “You have to turn on the light and take a look. Describe the injury for me. I’ll only hurt you more if I start manhandling you to find out for myself.”

“Okay,” she said, and tried to sit up.

“I got you.” Shep gently raised her until she sat in front of him on the ground at a 90-degree angle. He bent his knee toward the sky and pulled his heel in close to his thigh, so she could rest her back against his leg.

Soon the initial shock would wear off and the serious pain would begin. For the moment, however, Miranda already had enough pain to know exactly where to focus the light to examine her wound.

When she found the gash in her left thigh, she kept the light trained on it with one hand. With the other hand, she guided Shep's hand to her leg, near the bloody laceration.

She spread his fingers so he could feel the approximate size of the cut, without actually touching the wound. “That’s it,” she said.

He kept his voice strictly neutral while in his mind he was yelling and running in panicked circles. “Okay,” he told her. “What do I do first?”

She waited, letting her breaths lengthen and her heartbeat wane. Then she said, “Could you tear the jeans away, please? So I can see what we’re dealing with exactly?”

He let out a strong puff of air. “Whhh! ... Okay ... Why don’t you see if you can get a phone signal. Maybe you can call nine one one, while you pay absolutely no attention to what I'm doin'."

A soft laugh escaped her.

"What's funny?" he said.

"For a second I was thinking I should hold the light for you!"

He could hear the smile in her voice. The corners of his mouth turned up briefly. "No, thanks. But I appreciate the thought."

When he demanded Clarkson's belt, in order to fashion it into a tourniquet, the professor threw it to him immediately. No discussion. Smart man.

Shepard worked carefully to lengthen the tear in Miranda's jeans without touching or jarring the eight-inch-long gash in her leg. Some moving and hurting was inevitable, and he cringed inwardly with every gasp she tried to suppress.

Shep did not cringe when Win Clarkson moaned every few seconds.

Miranda was able to get a cellphone signal and call the emergency number. She asked the dispatcher to contact Deputy Krothers specifically, in addition to the nearest emergency services.

Eventually, Shep had the fabric split all the way around the leg. Then he slid the lower cylinder of blue denim away from the upper portion, drawing the remnant down Miranda's shin, over her foot, and away.

Using a phone app, with a minimum of whimpering every time Shep moved her leg, Miranda gave GPS coordinates to the dispatcher so that rescuers could find them.

She disconnected her call just as Shepard was lifting away half of her pants leg. She could not totally squelch a small cry, but she tried. She knew her pain rocked the big man and tore at his heart.

Miranda let out a long breath when the jeans went away, leaving her leg in relative peace for the moment. "They said they'll be here soon," she told Shepard. "Carlo and Mrs. Cleary already called it in. The dispatcher will call them back with the GPS numbers. They're headed this way."

"Excellent," he praised her. "Well done, Bean. You just stay still and rest now. Everything's under control. My lord that feels like a lot of blood! Are you sure you're not hurt anywhere else? There's no damage to an artery or something, right? Geez we gotta clean this! You don't want an infection! Heaven knows what was on those filthy tusks! I've got bottled water in the canoe. I'd kill that animal two or three more times, if I c--!"

Miranda stroked his cheek and spoke soothingly. "Shepard, calm down. You're babbling."

"Babbling? Yeah, okay, I'm babbling. *You*'re bleeding! You stop bleeding! Then maybe I'll stop babbling!"

Shep shook the jettisoned denim cloth cylinder to dislodge any dirt and debris. He turned it inside out, so that the cleanest side was topmost. He began folding the remnant from her jeans into a thick pad.

"Clarkson! You awake!" Shep bellowed.

"What now!"

"I need my backpack. It's tied to the rear seat of the canoe. My water bottle's in there. Get it."

Clarkson, of course, was not in a particularly helpful mood. "I can barely breathe!" He coughed for effect. "You think I'm going to slog to the boat, turn it right-side up, wrestle out a heavy bag, and struggle all the way back here just so you can have a drink of water? Not friggin' likely!"

"I need to clean this wound!" Shep's booming baritone shook seed pods from the nearest trees. "Frankly, I don't *care* if you come back! Just *get* to the canoe! *Untie* the backpack! And *toss it* over here, where I can *reach it!"*

Shep completed the denim pad he was making and, with Miranda guiding, placed it over the wound. He put pressure on it with one big hand and tried hard to ignore Miranda's squeak of pain.

In a voice low and deadly, Shep told the malingering professor, "If you don't find that pack and get it to me in the next two minutes, I will feed you to those 'gators out there, one torn-off body part at a time! Now, get me that *water*! *Do it!*"

The professor whined, "Even if I could move, there's a big, dead animal in the way."

"Yep. And I still have the gun that put him there. So, go *around* him, go *over* him or *join* him! Your choice!"

He heard Clarkson moving clumsily, with many theatrical groans. It was quite gratifying.

Miranda whispered, "What is it? Is it dead?"

"It's a Pig River wild hog. A big boar. And it's extremely dead. You're safe. Try to relax."

## Chapter 32 - The Date, Part 1

Win Clarkson surprised even himself with how he was able to get to his feet and wade twenty feet to Shepard's canoe, with minimal stumbling. He was even able to right the capsized craft and float it the few feet to shore.

Once there, the professor fell to his knees and leaned into the boat -- with considerable groaning -- to untie Shep's backpack from the rear thwart.

Moments later, the backpack whumped to the ground near where Shep was sitting. A half-second after that, Clarkson whumped to the ground to lie full length beside the canoe.

Working together, Shep and Miranda poured half his water bottle's contents over the pig-tusk gash in her left thigh. In the flashlight's beam, she could see a slash was still bleeding. Maybe it was beginning to flow more slowly.

She turned the light off.

Then Shep insisted she drink as much water as she was able, while he re-seated the denim pad over the laceration.

He wrestled his shirt off over his head and ripped it into four long strips. He wrapped those strips of cloth carefully around Miranda's leg to hold the pad in place and apply pressure to stop the bleeding.

Clarkson saw the glow of propane lanterns even before Mrs. Cleary's jonboat came into sight rounding a curve in the river.

"Help!" the professor shouted, raising his torso on one elbow and waving the other arm in the air. "Over here! Help!"

Although they could only make out a mass of lumpy shadows cast by the Martha's bow lantern, Carlo and Mrs. Cleary motored toward the riverbank.

A new engine roared from the south, growing louder fast. A white motorboat, with blue lights flashing, rooster-tailed a hard right turn toward Martha's lanterns. It beached its bow beside Carlo's boat even before the jonboat came to a full stop.

Deputy Tyrell Krothers switched on his boat's two large floodlights, turning the night around them into welcome twilight.

Krothers, Carlo, and Mrs. Cleary took in the tableau between the river and the forest verge.

Clarkson lay on the ground, blinking into the lights and waving weakly.

One large boar's corpse loomed like a boulder, its snout buried in the muddy bank. Blood stained its hide from two visible bullet holes.

Shep sat on the ground, shirtless, covered in blood, holding a gun in his left hand and an unconscious Miranda with his right. All three people looked as it they had towed downriver behind a submarine.

Carlo leaped from the jonboat and rushed to kneel beside Shep. From this new vantage point, he could see Miranda's left thigh encased in a thick, bloody bandage that used to be Shepard's shirt.

"You okay, *kemo sabe*?" Carlo asked Shep.

"Bean needs help fast," Shep told him. "She's sleeping now, I think, but she's lost a lot of blood."

"Help is almost here," Carlo said.

"The professor's been asking for a medic, but there's no hurry. Just leave him where he is. *Don't turn your back on him*! He admits he killed Tom Rigby, and that's only the beginning." Shep reversed the pistol in his hand and lifted it butt-first toward Carlo's voice. "Take this, will you, please?"

Carlo took the pistol and checked to be sure there was no shell in the chamber. He looked around to see Deputy Krothers talking to Clarkson.

"Don't worry," said Carlo, "if he does not confess to *Signor* Krothers, I will rat him out, myself. *Il profesore* is go nowhere but to jail."

A minute later, Deputy Krothers joined them. He accepted the pistol from Carlo. "Who shot who?" he asked.

Shep sounded unsteady. He had been awake nearly twenty-four hours straight, and some of those hours had been ... unpleasant.

"The *good doctor* over there was about to kill us," Shep told the deputy, "but we got the gun away from him. I thought it was all over. Then that *thing* exploded out of the bushes and attacked us."

He stopped and took several deep breaths. "I shot at it over and over, but I couldn't … it just kept coming! I could only guess where it was, and it was coming so fast! It wouldn't stop! It kept coming and coming!"

He seemed unaware of the tears crawling down his cheeks and into his muddy, bloody beard. "By the time I finally killed it, it had already gored Miranda! *Where are the EMT's*?"

Krothers put a hand on Shep's shoulder.

"Easy! Easy, they're right behind me," Tyrell assured him. "Are you injured, Mister Krausse? Or is it just your lawyer?"

"My *fiancée*," Shep said. "I'm fine, but she needs a helicopter to the hospital. If your department doesn't have one available, Carlo will get one, but somebody do it *now*!"

"I've got it," Carlo told Tyrell. "You better see to your prisoner."

Tyrell turned away and moved toward Clarkson.

While Carlo slapped his cellphone to life and called for air support, Mrs. Cleary knelt on the other side of Miranda. She reached across the sleeping woman to poke an open water bottle against Shep's chest.

He took the bottle in one hand, whispered his thanks, and drank.

Mrs. Cleary examined Miranda's makeshift bandage and then the dozens of scrapes and bruises the couple had both accumulated during the night's events.

*"Fiancèe,"* Martha Cleary murmured at Shep. "Sounds good. Didn't think y'all was even speakin'."

Shep handed the nearly empty water bottle back to Martha. "He meant to kill her, Miz Cleary. I heard him cock the pistol!"

"Well, the fool shoulda known you wasn't gonna jest stand by and let him do it," Martha commented.

Shep's bass voice resonated behind his pectoral muscles like an echo in a mausoleum. "He was going to have to kill me first."

"Durn tootin,' he was!" Mrs. Cleary agreed. "My only question is, since he tried to kill Miss Ogilvy, why ain't he dead?"

"She didn't want that," Shep murmured.

From a few feet away, the deputy said, "I'm glad that didn't happen."

Carlo pocketed his phone and knelt by Mrs. Cleary. She gave him a nod and left to study the dead feral pig.

Carlo said, "I spoke to Hansen. The pilot will call me as soon as the chopper is in the air. We will find the closest landing spot -- probably Rigby's farm. Do not worry. Madam's personal physician will meet you at Shands."

"Shands!" Shep erupted. "That's in Gainesville! We need something closer!"

"Do you want the *nearest* hospital, or the *best* hospital? It is only a few minutes' difference by air."

Shep seemed to hold Miranda even closer, if that were possible. His voice was barely audible, though it vibrated like a high-tension wire. "I'm scared, Carlo. I don't think I've ever been so scared."

"I know," Carlo whispered. "But you have never allowed fear to make your decisions before, and I do not think you will start now."

"*Merrauo!*" agreed the kitten, stepping from behind Carlo.

"And you!" Carlo told Zeus. "Get back to the boat before you get stepped on in all this confusion! Everyone will adore you and call you a hero when we all get home again. There's no time for that now."

Zeus sauntered back to the jonboat with exaggerated insouciance. He did not take orders well.

Carlo waited for Shep to answer the hospital question. While he waited, he composed additional arguments -- ones he hoped he would not have to make.

Shepard relented wearily. "Shands is okay. Just tell 'em to hurry."

Miranda stirred and opened her eyes, squinting against the floodlights. "I'm cold," she said, without lifting her head from Shepard's pecs.

Carlo offered, "That is because both of you are soaking wet, *signorina.* You should come over here and hug *me*, a man who is warm and dry."

"You can't be dry," Shep chided. "I distinctly heard you fall into the sinkhole."

"A fair statement," said Carlo. "But I am quite warm. It is the hot blood of the Italian male."

Miranda smiled and huddled close to Shepard. "I'm happy where I am, Carlo. But thanks for the kind offer."

"Any time, *signorina.* I am nothing if not kind."

"Oh, please," Shep muttered, keeping a firm arm around Miranda's shoulders. "If you were really kind — or dry — you would have given the lady the shirt off your back by now. Y'know, a warm Italian *blanket* would be more help than hot Italian blood right now, *Signor* Fratelli."

No more than a minute passed before a fire department boat from downriver joined the little flotilla of beached craft. The firefighters added two more highly effective floodlights to the scene.

A pair of emergency medical technicians debarked swiftly, carrying equipment bags. One went to the groaning Clarkson, and the other joined Shep with Miranda.

Despite the professor's vociferous claims that his ribs were rattling around loose in his chest and his lungs were pulverized, the EMT disagreed. After performing a thorough examination of the man's injuries, the paramedic taped Win Clarkson's two cracked ribs and released him to the deputy sheriff.

Deputy Krothers cuffed Clarkson and arrested him for the murder of Tom Rigby and attempted murder of Miranda Ogilvy. After reading the captive his legal rights, the deputy hauled him aboard the white boat with blue lights.

After promising to visit each witness personally in the next day or two, to take their statements, Tyrell Krothers took his leave of each person still on the shore. When everyone had assured him they no longer needed his help, he doused his boat's floodlights, started its engines, and cruised downstream, from whence he had come.

At Mrs. Cleary's direction, a pair of burly firefighters helped Carlo wrangle the dead boar into her jonboat. When Carlo and Mrs. Cleary joined their heavy, porcine cargo, their boat rode precariously low in the water.

Nevertheless, even though only an inch or two of gunwale showed above the waterline, the two friends backed into the river and motored upstream toward Minokee, with Zeus posing at the prow like a schooner's figurehead.

The last thing Shepard said to his friends was, "Do not call anybody's mother! I'll do it myself sometime tomorrow."

The EMT's soon had installed Miranda and Shep in the fire department's boat, with thermal blankets to warm them both, and intravenous fluids for Miranda. The powerful boat sped upriver toward Rigby's farm — the closest place they could meet the incoming helicopter.

Once on the helicopter, Shepard took one of the paramedics aside (as far aside as Shep could go without actually releasing Miranda's hand).

"I need you to tell me the absolute truth," Shep whispered.

"Are you the next of kin, sir?" said the medic.

"I am for the purposes of this discussion," Shep declared with generations of Montgomery-Krausse authority in his voice.

He could have told them he had donated the helicopter that carried them at that very moment. It would have been the truth. But he did not have to mention the donation. The voice was enough.

The paramedic said, "Works for me. What do you want to know, sir?"

"How bad is it?"

"Not life threatening," the EMT replied. "After some cleaning and stitching and some strong antibiotics, they'll send her home with some painkillers in twenty-four to forty-eight hours. It's a long line of stitches, but the wound isn't deep and won't require surgery.

"I expect she'll want to keep her full weight off it for a week or ten days, but she can get around on crutches. A visiting nurse will probably come to the house twice a week to change the dressing and watch for infection until the wound heals completely.

"It could've been a lot worse if you hadn't stopped the bleeding. She was lucky. The young lady should make a full recovery."

Shep sagged with relief. "Thank God. ... And thank you guys, as well. When you showed up out there, I had never been so glad to see anyone in my life!

"Just doing the job, sir. Glad we were able to help."

"How long before she'll be able to walk?" asked Shep.

"I'd bet she'll be walking short distances on crutches in a couple of days. She will probably limp for six or eight weeks, but that'll gradually go away."

"That's wonderful news!" Shep said. "Thanks very much."

Shep scooted close to Miranda and kissed her on the

forehead. She opened her eyes and saw the grandest smile she could remember, shining from his face.

"Hi," she said, just to make a noise so he would hear the answering smile in her voice.

"I've got exciting news, Bean. We'll be out of the hospital, and you'll be walking a little, in just two days."

"That's good."

Apparently, "we" would be staying together in the hospital. Carlo would probably be at the hospital with Shepard's clothes and toiletries by the time the helicopter landed.

Shep said, "So, we're getting married on day three!"

Miranda needed a moment to process the information.

He did not hear an immediate response.

He leaned close enough for his lips to brush her ear, and whispered, "We nearly died tonight!"

After two seconds of deliberation, Miranda said, "Okay. Day three."

She barely drew breath before Shep's lips closed on hers and stayed there for one kiss after another, until he backed off to let her rest.

## Chapter 33 - The Date, Part 2

*Two days later.*

In a sitting room of the Krausse mansion, Miranda's father answered his cellphone.

"Good morning, Muffin! What's new? Don't answer that if you think I'm better off not knowing." Although Carlo had briefly told Zeke that his professor friend had been arrested for murder, none of the parents knew the details. Zeke, for one, did not want to know.

"Hi, Dad," came Miranda's voice through the phone. "Shepard and I are getting married tomorrow—"

Zeke did not hear the rest of the sentence because he held his phone out toward his wife, with a grin, saying, "It's for you."

♦

In another room in the Krausse mansion, Rebecca answered her desk phone with, "Good morning. You have reached the line of Hermione Montgomery-Krausse. This is Rebecca. May I know who is calling, please?"

Rebecca's eyes widened and her jaw dropped when the caller stated the purpose of his call. She put the caller on hold and left her chair to walk briskly down the hall to Hermione's Baroque-style office.

"Madam, there is a call from Mister Shepard on the public

line," Rebecca said from the open doorway.

Hermione did not look up from the envelope she was addressing. "Ask him to wait—" She broke off, stopped writing, and looked at Rebecca. "Why didn't you simply buzz me on the intercom, instead of walking all the way over here? Is something wrong?"

Rebecca wrung her hands and inhaled deeply before saying, "I believe Mister Shepard prefers to tell Madam personally."

"Oh, for heaven's sake," grumbled Hermione, reaching for the phone's button. "If it's so 'personal,' why in the world is he calling on the public line?"

She punched the speaker button. "Shepard, what is the matter? And be brief, I have literally hundreds of envelopes to address – by hand, as proper etiquette requires."

"Good morning, Mother. I'm getting married tomorrow. You said you wanted to know as soon as we'd set a date, and we have."

Hermione stared at the phone as if it had become a coiled cobra.

In the doorway, Rebecca's knees wobbled, and she leaned against the doorframe. The color in her face paled from dark chocolate to milk chocolate.

"That is absurd," Hermione pronounced. "I haven't even had the final invitations printed."

"That's fine," Shepard's voice poured like hot fudge from the speakerphone and gently filled the room. "We went door-to-door and invited all the neighbors. Miranda called her parents, and I'm calling you. Invitations complete."

"Don't be silly. I have gowns ordered for seven bridesmaids and a flower girl. The most beautiful church in the state capital is booked, the flowers and food have to be prepared and delivered, the ringbearer's tuxedo is being specially made, and the white horse and carriage are being groomed and reupholstered. I think the photographer is in Europe on assignment for National Geographic until next week. You cannot expect me to pull all this together for a wedding only twenty-four hours from now!"

"Frankly, Mother, it would be a shame if you did pull all of that together for a wedding, because Bean and I wouldn't show up for a production like that one. We're getting married here in Minokee. And it's twenty-*six* hours from now, by the way."

In the doorway, Rebecca slid down the frame until her derriere thumped onto the floor. Hermione looked up from the phone and turned panic-filled eyes toward Rebecca. Both women wagged their heads side-to-side in silent denial.

"Wh— … *ahem* … why did you not tell me this sooner, dear?" his mother said.

"Well, two nights ago we had an … adventure … that convinced us life is short and unpredictable, so we're not going to procrastinate about the important things any longer."

"But, … does she even have a dress?"

"I expect she has a closet full of them, but it won't matter. Dress code will be casual," he told her.

Hermione watched Rebecca drop her face into her hands.

Hermione's eyes searched the corners of the room as if an answer would appear suddenly on a wall. She inhaled and stated, "Shepard, this is ridiculous. You cannot wear casual clothing to your wedding, and you cannot get married in the middle of the woods, with no caterers, no orchestra, no attendants, no bridal gown, no *press coverage*!"

"Actually, it turns out, we can," Shep said.

"Have you forgotten that you are the scion of the *Montgomery* family!"

"Irrelevant, since we're discussing the marriage of Mr. and Mrs. Krausse, of the Minokee Krausses. We'd love to see you there, Mother, but we'll understand if you can't make it on short notice. Talk to you soon, 'bye."

After a click, the line was silent.

Hermione tapped the button on her phone to disengage the line. "Rebecca, please get me a cup of very strong tea with far too much sugar in it. Give me a few minutes to organize myself, and then get Mrs-Doctor Ogilvy for me. No doubt, she needs consolation after receiving the 'happy news'."

"Yes, Madam," Rebecca said, using the doorknob to pull herself from the floor to her feet. "Shall I notify the staff, Madam?"

"Call a meeting at one this afternoon, please. I will make the announcement myself."

## Chapter 34 - The Date, Part 3

*Day Three -- Minokee*

On only two days' notice, Miz Martha and the Coffee Ritual Ladies of Magnolia Street (Miz Bernice, Miz Wyneen, and Miz Charlotte) had arranged a simple wedding in Martha's back garden, in Minokee.

Bishop Ebenezer Lincoln, retired A.M.E. church pastor and Orchid Street resident, presided over the ceremony. The entire neighborhood attended, as well as the parents of the happy couple.

Carlo Fratelli brought a date to the wedding. No one was surprised that his date looked like a European fashion model – with more curves.

What surprised and amazed everyone was that, like the bride, Carlo's date was a librarian. Her name was Annabelle ... um … Something-or-other.

Neighbors filled Magnolia Street with tables and chairs borrowed from a dozen dining rooms, and after the couple's vows were exchanged, they all enjoyed a covered-dish lunch.

Everyone agreed the wild hog barbecue was delicious

The End

## Thanks for Reading

Thank you for giving your time and attention to reading *The Mammoth Murders.*

A million activities vie for your attention daily. You have honored me by choosing to read my book today, and I appreciate that more than you know.

If you haven't had the pleasure of reading/hearing Shep and Miranda's previous adventure, the first book, *Finding Miranda,* is available in ebook, paperback, and audiobook.

Authors thrive or starve based on the reviews of readers like you. Won't you take a second to give *The Mammoth Murders* a five-star rating on Goodreads, BookBub, or your favorite book seller's website?

(Okay, technically, you could give it less than five stars, but why would you? Right?)

Your ratings or reviews tell me whether *you had fun* reading the book. If you did, my goal is achieved and I'm very happy.

## Become an Honorary Minokeean

If you have
read (or heard) both *Finding Miranda* (book 1) and *The Mammoth Murders* (book 2) — in any order —
you are eligible
to become an

*Honorary Citizen of Minokee.*

Visit my webpage, AuthorIrisChacon.com, and find out how to receive your Minokee Certificate of Citizenship

*What is the greatest benefit of being a Minokeean?*

No local taxes, because the town is invisible!

## Iris Chacon Novels

Minokee Mysteries
**Finding Miranda*, Book 1
*The Mammoth Murders*, Book 2

*Sylvie's Cowboy*

**Schifflebein's Folly, A Funny Way to Build a Family*

*Mudsills & Mooncussers, A Novel of Civil War Key West*

**Duby's Doctor, An Unlikely Bodyguard for a Killer*

**Lou's Tattoos, A Comedy of Errors*

All Iris Chacon novels are available in ebook or paperback.
*Indicates books are also available in audiobook form.

# Keep in Touch

Here's where to find me, so we can connect when I have a new novel coming or when you have questions, comments, or suggestions for me.

Follow my webpage, https://www.authoririschacon.com.

Follow author Iris Chacon on
GOODREADS, BOOKBUB,
FACEBOOK, TWITTER, and INSTAGRAM.

Join the IRIS CHACON IN CROWD
(https://www.instafreebie.com/free/zFcM1)
and receive news about giveaways, reviews, and new releases. (I won't write you every month,
I don't send spam, and
your email address will be kept confidential.)

When you join the IN CROWD, you'll also get a free ebook download of the award-winning humorous family novel, *Schifflebein's Folly*.

You can unsubscribe from the IN CROWD any time you wish. Every email from me will have an unsubscribe link for your convenience.

# About the Author

Novelist Iris Chacon has written for film, television, documentaries, and radio. She has worked in radio, law, and education (where she was a librarian and English teacher). Iris is a wife, mother, animal lover, and native Floridian, with a degree in mass communications from Trinity International University. *The Mammoth Murders* is Iris's seventh novel.

Coming Next from Iris Chacon

Enjoy this sneak preview of the upcoming novel:

## Emerald's Secret

### *by Iris Chacon*

*Four wildly mis-matched police officers reluctantly team up to pose as a family of vacationers at a Florida resort called "Emerald C's." The officers hope to bust a hidden casino — without dying, like other cops have. Finding the casino is perilous enough, but the owner's wife, Emerald, is keeping a dangerous secret from her jealous mobster husband: One of the cops is Emerald's former boyfriend.*

## CHAPTER 1 — BOOTS

In downtown Miami, Officer Louise Harper, in her police uniform, waited at the wheel of a Metro-Dade Police car, wondering if she had time to make another trip to the bathroom before her partner returned from his errand inside the Tropical Western Wear store.

Officer Greg Hallstead browsed a row of soft leather moccasins on a shelf inside Tropical Western Wear. He passed a mirror that reflected both himself and, over his shoulder, the chubby, peroxide-blonde salesgirl, who was making moon eyes at Greg's tight-fitting uniform.

Greg browsed onward, to a row of work boots. He passed another mirror, in which the salesgirl cast a hopeful smile at him. A man with Greg's physique got used to hopeful smiles from females. He smiled back, without showing teeth, and moved on.

When Greg came to a row of elaborately decorated cowboy boots, his eyes lit up. He pulled a flashy eel-skin boot from the shelf and held it high, with a toothy smile for the salesgirl.

"Got this in a 10-D, honey?"

"If I have to go to the *factory* for it!" the girl vowed, hurrying toward the stock room in the back.

Greg stood admiring the boot display. He could take his feet out of Montana — and he had — but he always liked to have a little piece of Montana on his feet.

Outside the store, Louise reacted to a radio call, grabbed the mic and snapped a response. Then she leaped from the car and raced toward the store.

By the time Louise arrived inside Tropical Western Wear, Greg was standing in front of a full-length mirror admiring the outrageously colorful cowboy boots on his feet. He handed the salesgirl his credit card without taking his loving gaze from the boots' reflection.

Louise entered the store on a run.

Greg saw her in the mirror and sent her a John Wayne drawl, "Whattaya think, Partner?"

"I think we've got a call, so you better get your cayuse in gear, cowboy." Louise ducked out the front door.

Greg ran after her, shouting and blowing a kiss to the salesgirl as he went, "I'll be back for my credit card, honey, and don't lose my shoes!"

Outside, the patrol car's engine roared. Louise had the door open and the car already moving when Greg jumped into the passenger seat. A beat-up red Camaro passed them at high speed a moment later.

"That's him!" shouted Louise, slamming the accelerator to the floor. "Call it in!"

Greg dutifully and tersely reported to Dispatch that he and Louise were in pursuit of the subject vehicle. He gave their position, speed, and direction, and he requested back-up units.

The red Camaro raced southward on U.S. Highway 1 alongside the elevated train tracks, under the elevated Plexiglas pedestrian tunnel, up the I-95 expressway on-ramp, and past the balconies of rainbow-colored high-rise condos.

Louise's patrol car screeched in pursuit as both vehicles wove through traffic, barely missing concrete sound barriers 20 feet tall, and sending a yellow cab spinning across the wide asphalt. The cab sideswiped a rickety-looking landscapers' truck that tilted crazily and spilled a dozen potted palms across eight lanes of Interstate.

The Camaro zipped down an exit ramp, made a U-turn on only two wheels, and swooped up the northbound entrance ramp. Now it raced northward on I-95.

Inside the patrol car, Louise concentrated on maneuvering the vehicle while Greg stroked his boots as if they were a new pony. "So, whattaya think?"

Louise was too busy careening onto the northbound expressway to spare him even a look. "Okay. What I think is, you blew a week's pay, and you'll be hysterical the first time you step in a cow pie in those things."

Greg gaped at her, open-mouthed. "You don't think I look like Clint Eastwood?"

The engine roared, the car swerved to miss a dump truck.

"Roy Rogers?"

Brakes squealed.

"Howdy Doody?"

Louise had to smile at this. "Okay," she said, "maybe Howdy Doody."

Greg grinned and touched her shoulder.

The red Camaro swooped from the far left lane to the right exit ramp, flew down the ramp, under a hotel skywalk, across a divided avenue, under the elevated train tracks, and nearly left the ground as it turned 90 degrees onto the boulevard skirting Biscayne Bay.

Pedestrians took cover when the pursuing patrol car careered, howling, around the corner.

The Camaro swerved to miss a MetroBus, skidded over the curb and across the wide sidewalk, over the grass toward the bay, and ended up — *smash* — *in* the Bayfront Park fountain.

In the park, pedestrians and picnickers ran screaming. The Camaro's drive jerked his door open, scrambled out, and ran toward the Bayfront Amphitheater.

Behind him, the patrol car bounced to a halt on the grass, and Greg jumped out to chase the man on foot. Louise backed the patrol car onto the boulevard and raced northward again.

The perp led Greg up, down and around the concrete amphitheater, and finally into the northside alley. The patrol car cut him off. He locked eyes with Louise through the windshield.

Greg slowed up behind the man, thinking maybe the chase was over, but the guy reversed course, trampled right over Greg, and ran up the alley — ducking into the Bayside shopping mall.

Louise shouted out the driver's side window, "I'll head him off at the other end!"

Greg scrambled to his feet, dusted off the new boots, and shouted back, "I'll get him, Louise! You stay in the car!"

She slammed into reverse and whipped the car out of there, taking off toward the other end of the mall. "The cowboy creed," she muttered. "Never take help from a female."

The suspect had a head start, but Greg was gaining on him as they wove through the open-air corridors of the waterfront mall, scattering tourists, shoppers, and kiosk merchants as they passed.

The prey took a desperate leap from the top of a fountain to the top of a flower cart, to the roof of a shop, and he raced along the roof toward the boulevard and freedom.

Greg's inappropriate boots slipped on wet tiles, plunging him into the fountain. He submerged totally and came up *really* disgusted.

"I'm not even supposed to be working today!"

Clambering out of the fountain, Greg ran again, knocked over a flower cart, and jumped like a kangaroo along the sidewalk beneath the roof, trying to keep his prey in sight. The man had a huge lead now.

The suspect reached the end of the mall roof, shinnied down a tall palm tree, and scampered between cars on the boulevard, apparently getting away.

Behind him, a bus screeched to a halt, so close it knocked Greg down. He rolled, came up and ran around the bus in time to see Louise's car zip onto the median strip of the boulevard.

Louise leaped out and pursued the fugitive.

Still running, but a long way from his partner, Greg shouted into his shoulder mic, "Where's that back-up?"

"E.T.A. thirty seconds," a dispatcher answered.

Greg's eyes widened as Louise took a flying leap and tackled the suspect. "No!"

Apparently believing in equality for women, the fugitive fought back, whomping Louise with a right cross.

In return for his faith in the power of her gender group, Louise decked him with her billy club and straddled his prostrate body on the sidewalk. She was fastening the cuffs behind his back when her partner and a second patrol car arrived.

Greg pulled Louise away, and the second car's two officers took the captured man.

Greg told the back-up officers, "We'll meet you at the station. Thanks."

Then he dragged Louise back to the patrol car, shoved her

into the passenger seat, and ran around to the driver's side. Before closing the door, he emptied about a gallon of water from each of his new boots.

When Greg had buckled himself in, he held his hand out to Louise for the keys.

She slapped them hard into his palm.

"You should have stayed in the car!" he said.

"You should stop being my mother, okay!"

"No, you should stop being my partner while you're becoming somebody else's mother. It makes me crazy."

"Greg, tomorrow I will be on maternity leave, and you will still be crazy, okay? I could've done just fine without you, okay? You're not even supposed to be working today."

"Gee, thanks. I'd forgotten." Greg started the car, put it in gear, then looked at Louise again. "You and the rugrat all right?"

"Yes, thank you. If you ask me that one more time before the end of the day, I promise to shoot you, okay"

"Ah, emotional roller coaster. I read that's normal. I forgive you." He looked down at his waterlogged boots. "Think I can return these?"

Louise looked at his feet. "Eel-skin, right?"

"Yeah."

"So, the original owners wore 'em under water all the time, okay? What's the problem?"

Greg gave her a look that said, "oh, thank you very much," and drove away.

Louise rolled her eyes and dropped her forehead into her hand. Her partner was hopeless.

End of Sneak Peek

Look for ***Emerald's Secret,*** by Iris Chacon, at your favorite online book seller.

Made in the USA
Lexington, KY
20 December 2019